Dear Reader:

Pat Tucker has finally exposed the truth! While millions of men each year escape into their own little worlds during football season and leave their women to fend for themselves, the women often have a "game plan" of their own. Think about it! Women have always been better cheaters, simply because we have the ability to use both sides of our brains. To be given the space and opportunity without our men worrying about our whereabouts from September until February is priceless…if we want to get into some dirt.

In *Football Widows*, Tucker explores the "wild side" of the wives of coaches. If you think the players are busy, imagine how hectic the coaches' schedules are. They get paid millions to bring home the ring and the trophy at the end of the season. If they don't, they're always the first to go. No excuses and no second chances, so their wives have to keep themselves busy…by "getting busy."

But when one of them gets pissed off because of a betrayed friendship, all hell can literally break loose. Secrets can be revealed that were supposed to go with them to their graves, feelings can be hurt, and revenge can become the main pastime, instead of shopping for new Jimmy Choos together. Tucker does a great job of once again creating an entertaining, humorous look into the lives of unforgettable characters.

As always, thanks for the support shown to the Strebor Books family. We appreciate the love. For more information on our titles, please visit www.zanestore.com and you can find me on my personal website: www.eroticanoir.com. You can also join my online social network at www.planetzane.org.

Blessings,

Zane

Zane
Publisher
Strebor Books International
www.simonandschuster.com/streborbooks

Z ANE PRESENTS

FOOTBALL WIDOWS

A Novel

ALSO BY PAT TUCKER
Daddy by Default

ZANE PRESENTS

FOOTBALL WIDOWS

A Novel

PAT TUCKER

STREBOR BOOKS

NEW YORK LONDON TORONTO SYDNEY

Strebor Books
P.O. Box 6505
Largo, MD 20792
http://www.streborbooks.com

ISBN 978-1-59309-315-0
ISBN 978-1-4391-9877-3 (e-book)
LCCN 2011928047

First Strebor Books trade paperback edition October 2011

Cover design: www.mariondesigns.com
Cover photograph: © Keith Saunders/Marion Designs

10   9   8   7   6   5   4   3   2   1

Manufactured in the United States of America

For information regarding special discounts for bulk purchases,
please contact Simon & Schuster Special Sales at 1-866-506-1949
or business@simonandschuster.com

The Simon & Schuster Speakers Bureau can bring authors to your live event.
For more information or to book an event, contact the Simon & Schuster Speakers
Bureau at 1-866-248-3049 or visit our website at www.simonspeakers.com.

"For all of the Football Widows out there;
it takes one to know one."

ACKNOWLEDGMENTS

I'd like to Thank God almighty first and foremost. The greatest appreciation goes to my patient and wonderful mother, Deborah Tucker Bodden; my number one cheerleader and sister, Denise Braxton; my new brother-in-law, Tavares. Thanks to my step-father, Herbert, for keeping my mom happy, and Lydell R. Wilson, thanks for your patience, love, and support.

I'd like to thank my handsome younger brother, Irvin Kelvin Seguro, and his fiancée, Amber; the two best uncles in the world, Robert and Vaughn Belzonie…Aunts Regina and Shelia…my older brother, Carlton Anthony Tucker, my nephews, nieces, and the rest of my entire supportive family.

We don't share the same blood, but I love them like sisters: Monica Hodge, Marilyn Glazier, LaShawanda Moore, Lee Lee Baines, LaKeisha Madison, Tameka Brown, Kevina Brown. My love and thanks to Tiffany A. Flowers, Keywanne Hawkins, Desiree Clement, Yolanda Jones and the rest of the most exquisite ladies of Sigma Gamma Rho Sorority Inc. and especially all of my sisters of Gamma Phi Sigma here in Houston, TX.

I know I'm blessed because I am surrounded by friends who accept me just the way I am. ReShonda Tate Billingsley—Thanks for your constant support, listening ear, and faith in my work; Victoria Christopher Murray for being such a kind and giving person; Nikki Turner.

Many, many thanks to Alisha Yvonne, Markisha Sampson, Lt. Col. Logan, Robyn Cuffee, Ron Reynolds, Marlo Blue, John Brewer, Luke Jones—you all make my days easier so that I can focus on writing at night!

Special thanks to my super agent, Sara, and a world of gratitude to my Strebor family, Charmaine, and Zane for having faith in my work, as well as Yona and Adiya.

My deepest gratitude goes out to you, the reader, times are changing in the literary world and we value you now more than ever! I'm so honored to have your support—There were so many book clubs that picked up *Daddy by Default*, and for that I'm grateful. A special shout-out to some of them: Divas Read2, Happy Hour, Cush City, Girlfriends, Inc., Drama Queens, Mugna Suma, First Wives, Sisters are Reading Too, Brand Nu Day, Go On Girl, TX 1, As the Page Turns, APOO and so many more! Also Huge thanks to all of the media outlets that welcomed me to discuss *Daddy by Default*: *Huffington Post*, *Houston Chronicle*, Guest Blog Junebugg Blog, Onnix Blog Interview, KFDM-CBS Beaumont, TX, 3 Chicks on Lit, Clear Channel Radio News & Comm. Affairs, KIX 96 FM, KARK TV Little Rock, AR, KPRC NBC Houston Beyond Headlines, Artist First Radio show, The Mother Love Radio Show, It's Well Blog Talk Radio March 7th.

Please look out for my next novel, *Party Girl*.

If I forgot anyone, charge it to my head and not my heart. As always, please drop me a line at rekcutp@hotmail.com or sylkkep@yahoo.com. I'd love to hear from you.

Warmly,

Pat

ONE

"Ww-what was that?"

B.J.'s pretty features twisted into a frown, and a perfectly groomed eyebrow rose. She tilted her head ever so slightly, straining to hear. B.J. needed a visual to go along with the foreign sound. It was so faint; it could've been her mind playing tricks. She stepped into her home's foyer.

The cool, crisp air was a welcomed relief from the smoldering Los Angeles sun outside. Something wasn't right; she could sense it. *Maybe it's nothing*, she thought as she consciously stepped lightly on to the marble floor. In case someone was rummaging through her jewelry box, B.J. didn't want to announce her arrival. Stranger things had happened.

There it was again!

This time, her heart slammed into her ribcage and her eyes quickly darted around the room. This was no figment of her imagination. She was certain she had heard something. She searched for anything that might be out of place, but nothing appeared to be. Maybe she should've grabbed something she could use as a weapon. She quietly closed the door and reached for her cell phone, fully prepared to call for help if needed.

Where could the noises be coming from? The house was supposed to be empty. Her husband's car wasn't in the driveway; she assumed he was still at the Los Angeles Sea Lions training camp.

Their two young kids were still away with their grandmother so the nanny had been given some time off. B.J. herself was supposed to be relaxing at a resort in Palm Springs.

But it was like some evil force was trying to keep B.J. from her much needed mini-vacation. She and the other NFL coaches' wives usually took a break before the hectic season began. But this year, things had started off on the wrong foot from the very beginning.

First, Ella Blu, the wife of one of B.J.'s husband's assistant coaches, and the last person still willing to take the trip, had backed out at the last minute. Ella said her husband, Melvin, had begged her to stay home. Since they were having problems, B.J. figured she'd let Ella slide.

Determined to salvage the trip, however, she decided to head out alone. But then, as B.J. drove down I-10, her tire blew out. When her husband didn't answer his cell, she was forced to wait nearly two hours for the AAA tow truck driver to come and fix the flat. Once on the road again, it was nearly an hour before she realized she didn't have any of the paperwork needed to get into the exclusive resort. She reluctantly turned around and headed back home.

By the time she pulled up to her Brentwood home, she wasn't sure if she even had the energy to venture back out today.

There it was again, that sound. Something told B.J. not to call out as she had started to do when she first heard the faint noise. She placed her designer Hobo on the bottom stair and followed the noises around the cascading staircase and toward the back of the house where the master bedroom was located. The sounds, although still faint, were becoming clearer.

Her steps suddenly became heavy, each more challenging than the one before. By the time she made it toward the hallway that led to her bedroom, B.J. experienced a sudden surge of adrenaline. She could feel a lone trickle of sweat running down her back. Her heartbeat began to race, and her throat suddenly went dry, but still, she cautiously padded toward the bedroom.

"What the hell..." she murmured, struggling to believe her ears.

By the time B.J. reached the door and clutched the doorknob, there was no denying those were sounds of passion that filled the air.

B.J. felt her face burn, and the vein on the side of her neck begin to throb. She swallowed back tears that felt like broken glass gliding down her tightening throat, but she managed a rugged deep breath, then blew it out.

When she finally mustered up the strength to push the door open, her eyes instantly locked on those of a naked young woman who was riding her husband atop her king-sized bed. It felt as if the air had been sucked out of the room as she stood trying to process what she was looking at. B.J.'s mouth fell open, but she was too irate to utter a single word.

"OHMYGOD!" the woman cried and froze mid-stride.

At first B.J.'s own voice seemed trapped in her throat. Her eyes narrowed to slits and tears started to burn in their corners.

"I can't believe this shit!" she spat, finally finding her voice.

"Oh, Jesus!" She heard Taylor, her husband, before she could actually see him.

"Don't call on Jesus now, you bastard!" Sheer venom dripped from B.J.'s words. "And you!" she hissed toward the woman.

Suddenly, it was like a scene from a movie; everything seemed to be moving in slow motion. Taylor bolted upright and inadvertently shoved the woman to the floor. She tumbled down and quickly began to scramble for cover.

B.J. stood, still trying to comprehend the scene that played out before her eyes. As the wife of an NFL head coach, she'd been through quite a bit over the years, but nothing could've prepared her for the heart-wrenching situation she had stumbled onto. Her husband had brought another woman into their bed.

"I can, um, I can explain!" Taylor stammered as he also tried to find cover.

"In our home? In our bed? How could you?!" B.J. shrieked, utterly disgusted. "And of all people for you to stab me in the back with!"

Beside herself, B.J. grabbed the antique vase and flung it toward the headboard.

"You sick bastard!" she screamed. "And you, you backstabbing bitch!"

Taylor ducked and the vase smashed into the wall.

"Wait, B.J., hold on a sec," he managed to get out. "Ella, get dressed and get out!" he instructed the woman. "Hurry!" he added.

By now, Ella had found her clothes. But she was huddled in a corner crying and shaking as she tried to get dressed.

"I'm so sorry, B.J. I'm so sorry." She sobbed.

"You're sorry!" B.J. screamed and lunged toward her. But Ella was way on the other side of the room.

B.J. was frantically looking around the room as if trying to find something else to throw at her husband. But this gave Taylor time to scramble up from the bed and tackle his wife before she could find another weapon. He cradled her body as she struggled to break free.

Ella quickly got up, stepped over them, and hurried out of the room as B.J. and Taylor continued to wrestle on the floor.

TWO

"I don't know about the rest of you, but I, for one, am glad it's finally out in the open." Jewel sighed, as if news of Taylor's infidelity offered her some kind of relief. She turned to B.J. "Listen, lady, I'm so sorry Ella did this to you, but I'm glad the cat's out the bag."

Jewel Swanson's husband, Zeke, coached the defensive backs for the Sea Lions. He was too handsome for his own good, and that meant Jewel had spent many late nights crying on B.J.'s shoulder when she couldn't get in touch with him.

Jewel was the cutie of the group. She was small and petite, with the perfect smile, olive skin, dark curly hair, and dark features. She was one of the fittest people you'd ever want to know. She taught aerobics at a private spa and had a body that was out of this world. Jewel had a sweet disposition, and was a people pleaser. Her friends thought it was so unfair how Zeke treated her.

"This thing has been driving me mad," Jewel added, shaking her head full of fluffy curls.

B.J.'s neck snapped in Jewel's direction. B.J. surveyed her with a critical eye. A frown lingered at the corners of her lips.

"C'mon, guys, she knows now," Jewel encouraged, looking around at the others for help. But only stone-faced stares peered back at her.

Eyes grew wide and everyone else held a long, collective breath.

B.J.'s own bright brown eyes darted from one woman to the next. She was searching their faces for any sign of what she suspected, but hoped wasn't true. Had they known about this all along?

"Whoa," Lawna protested, holding up a muscular arm that could rival that of First Lady Michelle Obama. "Bobbi, before you go into a complete tailspin, at least let us explain!"

It was no surprise that Lawna immediately jumped into compromise mode; that was her specialty. She was a former beauty queen who had done print work before marrying the team's offensive coordinator, Davon Carter. She and B.J. had grown closer when she'd confided in B.J. about all of the things she was doing to save her marriage. And none of them had been pretty.

But B.J. listened without going off, even though she was hotter than an overheated radiator. Lawna knew B.J. had an explosive side that very few ever cared to encounter, but in her own time of need, she had found B.J. a supportive confidante.

"We wanted to tell you," Jewel offered.

"But, well, we weren't sure how to go about telling you. No one knew for certain. At first, it was just a rumor, so we agreed..." Mona Brown's voice trailed off after picking up where Lawna had left off.

As one of the leading marriage motivational speakers in the country, Mona probably thought better of the excuse she was about to give, realizing it went against everything she preached.

The truth was, just about everyone knew Bobbi's husband, Taylor, had been having an affair for the past eleven months with one of the his assistant coaches' wives. Or at least that's when they'd found out about it. But while everyone secretly suspected the other, none had any hard proof of which one it was, except Mona. She and Ella had been best friends and Ella had recently confided in her that she was, in fact, the one sleeping with Taylor.

That had put Mona in a compromising and awkward position. She couldn't betray her friendship with Ella, and there was no way she could discuss it with the others, so she'd played along with everyone else.

Hours earlier, B.J. had held the entire room captive as she told the story of how she'd crept up to her bedroom, slid the door open quietly to find her husband and his mistress, who happened to be their friend Ella, in her bed.

The women had hung on her every word and listened intently. As the self-designated leader of the coaches' wives club, B.J.'s presence alone commanded attention. But to hear her tell a story was like having a front row seat to the action itself.

As if her dramatic facial expressions weren't enough, she'd used detailed and descriptive words. Then with arms flailing all around, she'd emphasized those words to the fullest.

"So you bitches let me go on and on about walking in on the two of them and you knew about it all along?" B.J. gawked in sheer disbelief. If looks could kill, the room would've been turned into a makeshift morgue instantly. With her eyes, B.J. threw lethal daggers at each of them.

"Dang, girl, it's not what you think," Lawna defended. "You make it sound like we made some conscious effort to…I dunno."

B.J. frowned; she looked as if she had been struck dumb.

"We came together and talked about it. This mess, the whole situation, put all of us in a very uncomfortable position. Think about it. We knew what Ella was doing was wrong, and all we could hope was that she would stop. When she wouldn't or didn't, what were we supposed to do?" Lawna explained. "Besides, in the beginning, we thought it was a friggin' rumor! If we all reacted every time we heard a rumor, you know damn well our lives would be miserable! And then to learn it was one of us?"

But the more she talked, with her words stumbling out all at once, the more enraged B.J. became. All B.J. heard was what a fool she had been for months on end, walking around like the leader of the pack when everyone saw her as the silly, unsuspecting wife.

And the fact that she and Ella had grown so close, that she had even counseled the woman about the trouble in her own marriage, infuriated her all the more. B.J. cringed at the thought that Ella had been using her all along to get next to her own husband.

"So no one thought it necessary to send me an anonymous note?" She shrugged. "Maybe drop a hint some kinda way?"

"We didn't want to believe it was even true," Lawna admitted, her head now hanging low. "And we definitely couldn't believe it was Ella."

"We all need to come together and talk about this," Mona said.

B.J. turned to her. "You, of all people," she hissed. "You can't sit here and tell me you didn't know; the way two of you are hitched at the hip."

"Let's talk about this," Mona insisted.

B.J.'s eyes narrowed to slits. "You knew all along; don't even try to lie. So you had to choose between me and her," B.J. continued.

"B.J., you're getting all worked up, I think you should calm down. We've all been going through a lot, myself included."

"Oh, honey, you ain't experienced a damn thing yet," B.J. promised with a cold snicker.

"Well, c'mon now, B.J., what's that supposed to mean?" Jewel wanted to know.

B.J. rose from her seat and placed the oversized wineglass onto the coffee table.

"I can show you guys a whole hulleva lot better than I can tell you," she shot back harshly. B.J. looked around the room again.

"Everyone in here has a secret or two. But by the time I'm done, you'll wish like hell you had found a way to confide in me about the sleazy skank my husband was fucking!"

"You can't be serious!" Mona cocked her head to the side, and rolled her expressive eyes in the most dramatic way. "What are you planning to do? Air all of *our* dirty laundry because we didn't tell you about Taylor's suspected affair?" Mona shook her head. "What does that make you, B.J.?"

"It makes me hell bent on revenge; that's what! And as we all now know, it wasn't a *suspected* affair; it was all too real! First, I plan to take Taylor's ass to the cleaners, but I swear I will make each and every one of you sorry you ever decided to cross me! Especially you and that skank Ella Blu!" B.J.'s doe-shaped eyes narrowed as she locked them on Mona.

She kept her murderous glare focused on Mona, then she put up a *say nothing else* hand. Before anyone else could utter another word, B.J. grabbed her designer Hobo and stormed out of the room.

THREE

Days later, a well-dressed and confident B.J. sashayed into her lawyer's office located downtown in L.A.'s financial district. The impressive glass tower office building instantly made her feel like she was part of a winning team. On the twenty-seventh floor, she walked down the long, carpeted corridor and past a sleek, glass-enclosed conference room. B.J. liked everything about the swanky firm, but mostly she liked the bulldog in a skirt who had already told her over the phone that they had a great case.

B.J. was led into Samantha Sloan's office. Samantha Sloan was a world-renowned divorce attorney, known throughout the city as a ruthless champion for women's legal rights. She only represented women, and her client list read like a Who's Who in entertainment and old money worldwide.

Samantha had on a khaki pencil skirt that looked like it was sewn specifically for her thin frame. She wore an impeccably tailored, crisp, white, Anne Fontaine shirt and a wireless headset that allowed her to move around the office as she wrapped up a phone call. She did a silent, three-finger wave to B.J. and smiled.

"Listen, my eleven-thirty is here. Let's talk more later, and remember what I told you," Samantha said into the mouthpiece.

B.J. sat quietly and stared out of the massive floor-to-ceiling window. This high up, she was looking through a haze of smog, but the view was still breathtaking. She could see the downtown Los Angeles skyline as far as her eyes could see from the sofa in Samantha's office.

Soon, B.J. was watching as Samantha wore a path through the carpet.

"So you are absolutely sure you want to do this, correct?" Samantha asked. She was squeezing a pressure ball as she walked and talked.

"I've given lots of thought to everything we talked about on the phone and I believe this is the way to go. I'm ready, and I think they both should pay!"

B.J. said it with such conviction Samantha didn't question her intent anymore. But as she stood squeezing her pressure ball, she looked at her client like she was trying to size B.J. up.

"Okay, so you do realize that this lawsuit will bring you more media attention than you'll know what to do with, right?"

"I've considered that." B.J. actually knew simply being Samantha's client would bring its own amount of publicity.

"And you understand that people are going to be coming out the woodwork. I've seen things like this before," Samantha said. "You should expect people you've only met in passing to try to figure out a way to profit from this. It can get really crazy!"

"Sam, this is only the beginning. I realize everybody and their mamas will be talking about this, but since I've decided to do the tell-all book, I figure it'll get me ready for my multi-city tour."

Samantha stared at B.J., and suddenly B.J. wasn't sure if she had said something wrong. She didn't want to turn Samantha off; she needed a really strong and powerful ally in her corner. Everything she had learned about Samantha made B.J. confident that they would make a great team, and that Samantha would fight tooth and nail to get her everything she wanted.

B.J. released a huge sigh of relief when suddenly, Samantha's face broke into a huge grin.

"I like the way you think, and that's how you've got to approach this entire thing. It's only a step to get you to the next level. By the time we're finished, you'll be the poster child for why a woman should think twice before she screws a married man!" Samantha said.

"Now, you're talking." B.J. laughed.

Samantha quickly switched gears and jumped into battle mode. She picked up a small digital voice recorder and started talking into it. She noted the date and time, then said B.J.'s full name and the case.

"Bobbi Almond, versus Taylor Almond and Ella Blu."

"I love the sound of that," B.J. said. "I really do."

For the next two hours, B.J. and Samantha mapped out a plan that involved taking their decision viral, discussing when B.J. should start talking to the press and exactly what bullet points she should focus on from here on out.

As if she'd nearly forgotten, B.J. turned to the bag she brought with her. It was stuffed with papers and documents she had gathered specifically for this meeting.

"Oh, this is the stuff I told you about," B.J. said.

"Let's see what you have there," Samantha said. She clicked off her recorder and focused on the items B.J. started pulling from her bag.

"It's everything we talked about. I have copies of his cell phone records, credit card receipts, and tons of proof that establishes the fact that the bastard and his mistress, Ella Blu, have been at it for months!"

"Bobbi, I wish more women were like you," Samantha said.

"How so?"

"You're not merely suing that lousy husband of yours for divorce, but you're suing his mistress as well!" Samantha smiled and rubbed her hands together. "And you've done your homework. In many of these cases, women are so emotionally distraught they can't even think straight, much less compile information that establishes a pattern and helps to prove our case." Samantha glanced at some of the papers as B.J. passed them along. Occasionally, she'd nod or an eyebrow would go up.

"This is all really good," Samantha said.

"I'm glad to hear it."

"Well, all I have to say is, buckle up, honey; this is about to be one hell of a ride!"

A few days later, B.J. was back in her hotel room going over another stack of valuable materials. These emails, phone records, and tons of flight receipts were items B.J. thought might one day come in handy. Never in a million years would she have guessed she'd be using them to back up some of her friends' deepest and darkest secrets. But that's exactly what was going on. She was preparing to write.

News of B.J.'s lawsuit and the forthcoming juicy tell-all book, *Blowin' the Whistle*, had spread through their little circle like an out-of-control wildfire in the Malibu hills. Everyone was beyond nervous, and the phone calls had been nonstop ever since.

Her cell phone rang again, but it had been doing that quite a bit over the last few days.

This time it was Mona leaving a voicemail.

"B.J., come on now. I realize that you're upset; I would be, too. But let's think rationally; you can *not* be serious about writing this book, or even suing Ella! It's too damn much! All of it! How tacky would that be? Call me so we can talk. We all want to talk to you, and Ella. We need to work this thing out, but not like this. Besides, we're all so worried about you. Call me."

Then she had the nerve to chuckle a bit, like this was a mere misunderstanding that a good bottle of wine and a major bitchfest could fix. *Oh, no, not this time*, B.J. thought as she hit the delete button and erased the newest pathetic message.

She had listened to each and every one of them. The worst by far was from her scumbag of a husband, Taylor. He had called every ten minutes and left one tearful message after another.

"Please let me explain," he cried. "It was just something that happened; it meant nothing. A divorce? A divorce, Bobbi? This whole lawsuit thing, you gotta stop this!" He sounded desperate. But B.J. wasn't the least bit moved by the passion in his voice.

"We can work this out," he protested. "Please come home so we can talk and work this thing out," he insisted. "I don't want to lose my family."

"Bullshit! Bullshit!" B.J. had screamed as she listened to his series of sobbing excuses.

B.J. was still burning with anger, but she wasn't sure what to be mad about the most—the cheating, or her friends who had betrayed her.

It was a massive dose of sheer humiliation and betrayal that she couldn't get over. Ella had dined at her table; they'd shopped for lingerie together. As a matter of fact, Ella had discussed some of her dirtiest deeds with B.J., and all along, this woman had been fucking her husband right under her nose. The audacity!

She couldn't stop thinking about what everyone must've been saying behind her back all along. B.J. cringed at the thought of what Sasha Davenport and the other players' groupies, girlfriends, and wives, must've been thinking.

Sasha Davenport was a twice-divorced vixen who moved between players with no shame and seemingly no regrets. Rumor had it she was once again on the prowl and on the hunt for her next victim.

She also seemed to go up a bra cup after each breakup, and had to have had a plastic surgeon on speed dial. She had an hourglass figure that was voluptuous on the top and the bottom, which her tiny waistline accentuated.

If Sasha weren't such a lowlife, she would've been somewhat tolerable since deep down, Bobbi felt like she was simply trying to find someone to love her. She was pretty enough, but the way she aggressively went after men, made her come off looking cheap and desperate. Sasha looked like a darker version of the talk show host Wendy Williams. Except Sasha's high cheekbones, cinnamon skin, and dark, long hair made her stand out. B.J. sat thinking about how messy and ghetto Sasha was; her name was always caught up in the latest drama. Then there were Sasha's trashy clothes that did nothing to help her image. It seemed as if she thought she had to dress like a slut to remain in the spotlight.

The coaches' wives usually held themselves to a higher standard. This was the kind of behavior they expected from the young rich jocks and the gold diggers like Sasha who went after them.

And how the hell were they able to keep that secret for so long? B.J.'s husband wasn't the brightest bulb in the socket when it came to matters of the heart, but he was a genius on the gridiron.

Taylor had been a rarity in the NFL. A head coach at the age of thirty-seven meant he was the youngest head coach in the league's history. There was such fascination with him and his story, the press couldn't get enough of him. Everyone seemed to fall in love with him instantly. He had spent ten years in the league as a decorated player, until an injury had sidelined his playing career.

But in Kansas City, Taylor was immediately offered an offensive coordinator position, which he had held for two years. That was followed by a short stint on ESPN as a celebrated analyst and then they spent two years coaching in Oakland. But their lives changed dramatically when the Los Angeles Sea Lions owners shocked the world and named Taylor as their new head coach midseason the year before.

B.J. and Taylor were the toast of Tinseltown. They had celebrity friends, access to exclusive parties, and the best of everything. B.J. realized she was walking to the head of an already closely knit group with the assistant coaches' wives, and she knew she'd have to work extra-hard to gain their trust. But she didn't mind.

It didn't take long for B.J. to ease into her rightful spot atop the coveted pedestal afforded to the head coach's wife. But the title didn't come without its share of problems. Sure, NFL coaches' jobs pay millions, but the toll taken on families is often immeasurable.

Coaches live and operate under a win-now-or-you're-fired specter. They're driven to around-the-clock work hours while being judged by more than just their win-loss record.

The legendary late Coach George Allen who coached the Rams when they were in Los Angeles, the Redskins, and San Jose State University, once said, "I always called the opposing coach at ten o'clock Wednesday night. If nobody answered, I knew we'd win on Sunday."

But make no mistake about it, it is the coaches' wives who keep the households together. They're the ones who maintain the finances, move the family from city to city, then befriend the neighbors because their husbands are always gone.

This time, when her cell phone rang, B.J. quickly reached to answer. It was her literary agent, Darlene Douglass.

"B.J., how are you holding up?" she asked.

Darlene Douglass was a legend in the literary industry. She led a stable of celebrity authors whose stories quickly catapulted them to various bestseller lists. And the projection for B.J.'s book was similar. The buzz her forthcoming book had already generated was like nothing anyone had seen in quite some time. And the lawsuit meant people would be talking about what to expect between those pages.

The players' wives and girlfriends, gossip columns, entertainment shows, and even the sports shows were discussing some of the scandals that were sure to make the pages of *Blowin' the Whistle*.

B.J. had already been pressed for interviews. But her team had yet to decide when she should start talking about the suit. As far as the book was concerned, the publisher was planning to go all out, with strategic marketing and a tour to coincide with the upcoming football season.

The thinking was, while the guys were engrossed with the games, the women, and even some men, would have their noses buried in B.J. Almond's new tell-all book. The publishers would milk the lawsuit for as much and as long as they could to garner even more publicity for the book.

"Oh, I'm wonderful, Darlene. How are you?"

"I'm well. And the reason I'm calling is because I wanted to tell you, your editor and the publisher are so excited about this lawsuit. The press you've already received is so unprecedented; they of course are looking for a way to fast track this book. They're talking about bringing on a ghostwriter to speed things up a bit."

B.J. wasn't sure how she felt about a ghostwriter. She wanted to tell this story herself, but if they wanted to speed things up, she was at least willing to hear Darlene out.

"What exactly would that entail? Working with a ghostwriter?"

She had heard of some big-name authors using ghostwriters, but she never understood how the process worked. And more importantly, B.J. didn't want anyone turning her story into something it wasn't. She wanted to tell this story her way; the only she felt it should be told.

"It would be someone to help streamline this story. Since news of the book leaked, the NFL commissioners are already trying to figure out what, if any, recourse they have to block it, so we don't want to give them time to get their ducks lined up," Darlene offered.

"Well, I'm at the Four Seasons, and I'll be here for at least several weeks. I think I can get it done in, say about four weeks," B.J. offered.

"Are you sure about that?" Darlene asked, her voice sounding uncertain.

"Between me, you, and these walls, I had been keeping somewhat of a journal anyway, so I think it should be easy enough," B.J. said.

"A journal?" Darlene's voice jumped an octave.

B.J. hadn't shared that little morsel with a single soul. It wasn't that she was planning to turn on her friends all along, but there was so much going on. And when the other wives kept coming to her for advice, sometimes she felt that writing things out seemed to help her think straight. It helped her gather her thoughts to give them the best advice possible. B.J. really cared about the women she considered friends. She knew that when they looked to her for guidance, she couldn't take that lightly. She rarely told them what to do based solely on an emotional reaction to whatever was going on at the time. B.J. took notes, weighed the pros and cons of her own suggestions, then warned that this was just her advice and nothing more. She never expected to take those notes and turn them into an actual book.

"How about we have you team up with the ghostwriter at the end of those four weeks? Once he does a read-through, we talk with the editor and see where we are. How does that sound?"

"That sounds fantastic, Darlene," B.J. said.

"Okay, well, I'll let you get back to work. Call if you need anything."

When B.J. hung up the phone, a smile made its way to her face. Her head was so full of scandalous juicy stories, she could hardly decide where she should start first.

"Would the visit to the doctor's office in Bakersfield be a good start? I remember we thought a two-and-a-half-hour drive would be enough to help hide the treatment for an STD!"

B.J. shook the thoughts away with a hearty laugh.

"No, maybe I should start with the swingers weekend in Hedonism? It was so good, someone decided she needed to run back there again, but this time with a sexy rookie!"

She took a deep breath and fired up her laptop.

FOUR

Writing was therapeutic for B.J. She was still hurt by the double betrayal she had suffered, but writing helped take her mind off it and the drama that was sure to come. What wasn't helpful was being holed up inside a hotel room all alone.

B.J. was used to commanding a vast ship at home, which meant constantly being on the go. She rarely had a moment to spare, much less a moment alone. If she wasn't busy with the kids and making sure their routines ran smoothly, she was overseeing the staff that helped around the house. Then there was always whatever project she was working on.

If she wasn't heading up a charity event for one non-profit organization, she was organizing a literacy event to stay true to the mission of the foundation that carried her husband's name. Being alone would be a challenge, but B.J. told herself this was the life of a real writer. Writing was a lonely profession. In order to create the kind of juicy tell-all her publishers were hoping for, she needed to buckle down and get busy.

If only she could stop thinking about what Taylor and Ella had done. How could she not have known he was cheating? B.J. wondered if maybe she had overlooked some obvious signs. Sometimes she would get so wrapped up in the kids she felt guilty, thinking she was neglecting her husband, but she didn't think he'd cheat and then with her friend?

B.J. started thinking about the week before her world was turned upside down.

"Where's my tie? The blue one," Taylor asked as he rushed into their bedroom. He looked frantic, as if only that tie would do.

"Did you check the tie rack in the closet, near the left corner?" B.J. turned her attention back to what she was doing. She was reviewing a computer program that was designed to teach toddlers how to read.

"I already looked there; it's the blue and gold one. You haven't seen it?" He sounded irritated.

"I'm really trying to focus on something right now," B.J. said calmly.

Taylor stopped in the middle of the floor as if he was about to throw a tantrum. He huffed and said, "B.J., I could really use your help. I have this meeting with the new General Manager and I have no idea what he wants to talk about."

"And your blue and gold tie is going to help how?"

"For once, B.J., can I get a little support here?"

Only then did B.J. look up at her husband. He couldn't be serious. Did he just say 'for once'? She ran back and forth to the cleaners to make sure his khakis were perfectly starched; when he couldn't find a shoe, she dropped to all fours, crawled on the floor and dug for it beneath their bed. When he lost his documents without backing them up like she suggested, she recovered his work, no matter how many hours it took away from her or the kids. Sometimes B.J. felt like Taylor was kid number three.

In a dramatic fashion, B.J. set the laptop on the table, pulled herself up from the chair, and sashayed into their massive walk-in closet. A few seconds later, she walked out holding the tie between her thumb and index finger.

Taylor frowned. "I looked in there."

Without saying a word, B.J. rolled her eyes, walked back to the sitting area, sat and picked up the computer.

"I don't know where you found that, but I swear, I looked in there," Taylor said, pointing toward the closet. "You know, if you didn't use up the majority of the space in there with handbags and shoeboxes, I might be able to find my stuff when I need it."

B.J. glanced up to see him fixing the tie around his neck. She didn't say anything; she wondered why men behaved so helplessly at times.

"Let's go to dinner this evening," Taylor said as he twisted his neck and tightened the knot in his tie.

"No can do. I'm interviewing piano instructors this evening, remember? We agreed we'd get the kids started early," B.J. said, barely looking up from the computer.

Taylor grunted and walked out of their bedroom.

If she had to, B.J. could recall so many other incidents like that one. She was by no means tired of her husband, but sometimes, she wanted him to fend for himself. Was that her mistake? Was she wrong to feel like that? Is that what drove him into her friend's arms? Would Ella have dropped everything to hunt down his tie? Would she have cancelled instructor interviews to go out to dinner? At the time B.J. thought nothing of it, but now looking back, she wondered if a bunch of little things weren't so little when they all began to add up.

B.J. started thinking about her life and the lives of the other wives during the season. They affectionately referred to themselves as "football widows," and for good reason. During the season, the men were so focused on the game that their partners often felt widowed.

Football widows are usually, but not always, women and in most cases, the "widow" has little interest in the sport itself. So it didn't take long for B.J. and the other wives to understand that while they might be married to their men, for half the year, their men were married to the game. And it didn't help that there was a constant rift between the coaches' wives and the players' wives.

B.J. ordered some mimosas and put on her favorite CD. Before she could write, she needed to remember one of the many scandalous trips she and the girls had taken. It was like it had happened yesterday instead of nearly two years ago. She started typing.

Our lifestyles are lavish and afford us the ability to do things most can't begin to imagine. If we need a new outfit, we can fly off to Fashion Week in New York. If we want to throw a birthday party, restaurants, and clubs fall all over themselves to house us and our friends. In most cases, we don't travel to away games, so that makes it easier for us to do what we want during the season. Traveling to those away games are more of a hassle than anything else. It is more like a business trip where we aren't even allowed to travel with the team on the chartered plane.

There's this huge misconception that wives travel on the team plane, but that's a myth. Occasionally, the head coach's wife might get a seat on it, but that's only because her husband is in charge. But even if she caught a flight with the team, once they land, she's completely on her own. No one is securing ground transportation for her, or booking her room. She'd better get ready to suffer because tickets for the away games are the very worst.

My theory about that is, management discourages women from traveling with the team, and their logic makes sense; they need those players focused on the game and they're serious about curfew! Taylor has three coaches assigned to walk the halls for room checks at curfew and if a woman is caught in any room, that player faces a serious and hefty fine.

Since we aren't welcomed on the road, we take trips of our own. One of the most memorable is a trip to an infamous resort in Jamaica.

"Bobbi Jo Almond, come out here so we can see what you look like!" Ella had screamed.

The Sea Lions were playing the Packers at Lambeau Field, and B.J. and the other wives had no desire to visit the Frozen Tundra. So they decided to go get some sun.

They were all gathered in an exclusive boutique in legendary Negril; they'd flown into town early. The boutique, a part of Hedonism II, catered to an exclusive clientele. In addition to cocktails, hot stone massages, and mud baths, when they came to visit they received the star treatment. They had a young woman who waited on them exclusively. She even had the hookup for some of the hottest designer clothes, which were shipped in prior to their arrival. They had just about everything including the latest haute couture, and everything in various sizes and colors.

"I look like a damn fool," B.J. had said.

"No, come out. It's not like we're taking pictures," Lawna had joked. "Let's see!"

They were drinking Sangria now, but the day had started early with Lemon Drop Martinis.

"I would not be caught dead in public in these," B.J. had said as she peered out of the fitting room.

"You act like such a prude sometimes; they're shorts, for Christ's sake!" Ella had said after taking a huge swallow of her drink.

"Well, maybe for you or Lawna, but these are sequined hot pants. Shorts come down to my knees," B.J. had said as she slowly eased out of the fitting room.

"OHMYGOD!" Lawna had gasped.

Ella's eyes had grown wide.

B.J. had stood there feeling awkward as she waited for the verbal verdict from her girlfriends. Their immediate reactions were a bit confusing and hard to decipher.

"I can't believe how f'in' good you look in those. I mean, damn!" Mona finally had blurted out.

B.J.'s eyebrows had inched upward. She had twisted just so, then caught a glimpse of her shapely form in the mirror.

"They do look nice on you," Lawna had said. "You should live a little, spice things up. Imagine the look on Taylor's face if he came home and found you in a pair of those!"

B.J.'s bashful responses had sent the room into a heap of endless giggles.

"You know what I think you should do?" Ella had asked mischievously.

That's when the laughter had subsided. Mona and Lawna had sipped their drinks as B.J. had twisted and turned in the mirror.

"You should wear those tonight, when we go out," Ella had said.

Still turning in the mirror as she had examined her ass and thighs from every angle possible, B.J. didn't immediately reject the idea. But she didn't agree, either.

The shorts were a stark contrast to anything B.J. would ever wear. The tight and flashy fit was a complete opposite of B.J.'s normal loose-fitting clothes. She was known for her elegant but borderline conservative dress style. B.J. barely ever showed bare arms, and her shorts were always perfectly tapered at the knees. She looked good in her usual clothes, but the new sequined shorts hinted at a slick and sexy secret side.

"I think you should wear 'em too," Lawna had chimed in.

When the sales clerk eased into the room, she pulled everyone's attention away from B.J.'s shorts.

"Are you ladies okay back here?" she had asked.

Everyone had said yes, except B.J. She had turned in the mirror once again, then looked at the clerk.

"I like these. I think I'll take them," B.J. had said.

Another fit of giggles had broken out. This time they were followed by the sound of glasses clinking as high-fives went around the room.

"So, you have the information for tonight's party?" Mona had asked.

"Yup." Ella had pointed a finger toward her temple and tapped. "All up here." She had winked.

Mona and Lawna had bought little black dresses while B.J. had added a cute designer tank to her shorts.

"So where we're going, how far is it from the resort? You know it's not safe to leave the premises," B.J. had said.

"We're good; don't worry," Ella had said, then she turned to the clerk. "Can you call for our car?" Ella had asked the young woman who had been at their beck and call all evening.

Later that night, B.J. and the ladies were on their way to their own event. The car had pulled up outside the bar and the first thing B.J. noticed was the line of women snaked around the building.

"Are we in the right place?" she had turned and asked Ella.

Jewel, Lawna and Mona were too busy sipping their drinks to notice what was going on.

"Yeah. I told you, I've been looking forward to this since we agreed to come." Ella had looked at the line and wondered herself. But she didn't want to concern the rest of the group.

"Why are those women standing in line like that?"

"I don't do lines," Lawna had tossed in.

"A line. Who has to stand in line?"

The driver had slowed at the front door and brought the car to a stop.

"We're not going to have to stand in line, are we?" B.J. had asked again.

Ella had looked toward the door as the driver pulled it open.

"Ladies?" he had said as he offered his hand to B.J.

"We've got tickets, so walk up to the front," Ella had instructed from behind.

They had bypassed the line and entered the club. As they had walked in, B.J. turned to Ella and asked, "How were we able to get in and there are so many women outside, in line?"

The room was dark, with certain sections of the room lit by colored bulbs.

"Well, we bought our tickets well in advance. When we agreed we wanted to do something different, I went to work right away," Ella had said.

B.J.'s eyes had finally adjusted to the lighting when suddenly, a slender, dark-eyed, busty brunette, wearing only a tuxedo jacket, a bow-tie collar, and a thong with a white rabbit's tail, walked past.

They were still trying to make their way to their table. But as they had passed others, B.J. couldn't help but notice all that was going on around them. She didn't want to behave like the prude they always accused her of being, but things were getting a bit out of control by her standards.

"Really?" B.J. had asked Lawna, who was closest to her as they walked toward the back of the club.

When Lawna had turned to B.J. as if she wasn't sure what the problem was, B.J. motioned toward the multiple naked bodies and the various paces, techniques, and furniture preferences of the participants.

Lawna had giggled and seemed not to be bothered by what was going on. And there was lots going on.

People were spread in threesomes on the floor. Some were clustered in foursomes on desk chairs near a corner window. They were humping side by side on a raised platform bed that seemed centered on a stage off in a corner opposite the window. Some were groaning softly. Others were silent, as if they were concentrating intently on the job at hand.

"OHMYGOD!" B.J. had squealed as they arrived at their section of the club.

"Is he watching?" she had asked, not intending to ask her rhetorical question aloud.

That's when Ella leaned over and had said, "If you're asking about the man over there, I believe he is!"

Everyone had started laughing, except B.J. For a while, she had sat staring at the one man who sat fully clothed watching the others.

It took a while for B.J. to loosen up, but the others seemed right at home amid the action that was going on.

Now, as B.J. pecked away at the letters on her keyboard, she marveled at the thought that back then, she had no idea just how wild and crazy their outings would be.

FIVE

"So, what did that make you feel like?"

The woman shifted in her chair. She snatched a tissue from the nearby end table and pulled it to her nose. She wore a floral dress that looked like it was a size or two too big, and a shrunken sweater that matched one of the flowers on her dress. Her hair was pulled back into a braided bun that sat to the side of the back of her head.

"He makes me feel like he doesn't appreciate me, like he could live with or without me," she said.

"I see," Mona said. She jotted something down on the legal pad she was holding, then looked back up at the woman.

"Knowing that he wanted to be with her, that the only reason he agreed to come and talk to you was because he didn't want to embarrass his daddy, well, it all just hurts."

"And is he aware of how you feel?"

Her eyes were red, but she held her tears before looking up at Mona.

"It's like he's doing this for all the wrong reasons. He wouldn't come if his dad wasn't forcing him to come. I know him."

"Let's not linger on him; let's talk about you. Let's talk about you and what you hope to accomplish. We can't force him to do anything he doesn't want to do. For now, let's focus on you."

Mona tried to keep her mind on work, but as the woman went on and on about everything her husband wouldn't do, she found it difficult to remain focused. There was so much going on in her own life at times when she sat and listened to her clients, she often thought they really didn't know what a real problem was. She and the other wives—now they really had a problem—and they all knew they needed to find a solution quickly.

After wrapping up her last session for the evening, Mona decided to try calling Ella before leaving the office. It was one thing for B.J. to ignore calls and not reach out, but Ella knew better.

The next day, Mona took a deep breath and held it in her lungs for as long as she could. She exhaled as she sat crossed-legged on her bottom, on top of her yoga mat in front of the wide opened French doors. The early morning breeze felt good against her skin. Again, she inhaled deeply, released, then muttered today's motivational words under her breath.

Her eyes were tightly shut, and all was quiet in her home. This was how Mona started each and every day, regardless of whether she'd gotten much sleep the night before. Sure, her life was in turmoil, but she knew better than anyone else, this was no reason to panic. Sure, she needed to *talk* to B.J. She needed to bring her and Ella together so they could work this thing out. But in the meantime, she needed to be at peace with herself and all that she had done.

Besides, true to form, Mona had already formulated a plan and she was certain, once it was properly executed, things would work out fine. And she and her friends, including B.J. and Ella, would fall back into their proper and comfortable zone.

Mona was the first to hear the news. After her shower, she held a cup of green tea to her chest and turned on the TV. The ladies from *The View* were all up in arms over a heated topic. Mona loved the show; she liked the way the ladies' different personalities provided enough drama to hold her attention.

When Whoopi repeated the question, Mona nearly dropped her mug.

"So, the hot topic for today is whether you think a wife has the right to sue her husband's mistress. Of course everyone is talking about the real-life case involving NFL head coach Taylor Almond and his now estranged wife, Bobbi."

"OHMYGOD!" Mona didn't know what to do first. Should she listen to the ladies, call B.J., or better yet, get Lawna and Jewel on three-way? Ella still hadn't returned her calls, either.

As she listened to the women give the pros and cons of whether it's right for B.J. to sue Ella, she placed her mug on the counter, and snatched the phone from its cradle.

The ladies were already on speed dial. She called Jewel first.

"What are you doing?" Mona asked.

"Hey, lady, I was about to go to the gym. Why do you ask?"

"You still at home?"

"Yeah, why? You're scaring me," Jewel said.

"No, it's nothing like that. Turn your TV on *The View*."

"Oh Lord!"

"Yes, but let me try to get Lawna on the line."

Mona was multi-tasking to the fullest. As she listened to Elizabeth, Sherri, and Joy weigh in on Bobbi and Taylor's case, she dialed Lawna, sipped her tea and wondered what the hell was next in this real-life drama that she was unfortunately connected to.

"I'm already watching," was how Lawna answered the phone. "I can't believe this!"

"You think they'll talk about the book?" Jewel asked.

"Oh, God, I hope not. I mean the f'ing lawsuit is enough, don't you think?" Mona said. "I have a feeling this is about to become a huge media circus! And we all know that's not good for any of us."

"Let's not panic," Lawna said. "Who knows? This thing could

end right here. Maybe the national attention will cause B.J. to see how crazy this whole thing is."

"Ya' think?" Jewel said sarcastically.

"Anything's possible," Mona added.

The three of them sat holding the phone as the conversation seemed to go on forever on the show.

"What are we gonna do?" Jewel asked. "She can't write that book! We'll be the laughingstock of all Los Angeles!"

"Has anyone talked to Ella?" Mona asked.

"She's not answering calls, or returning messages, either," Lawna said. "I wish we could all come together and talk about what happened. How low was Ella's self-esteem to fall for her best friend's husband?"

"There has to be an explanation for her behavior," Mona said.

"Explanation?" Jewel blurted out.

When the ladies on *The View* finally changed topics, Mona spoke up. "Yes, she and Sterling, they're going through a rough patch."

"I don't care. I'm with Jewel. I don't know what kind of explanation would justify one of you sleeping with my husband. I can't think of anything and I can usually see several sides to most situations," Lawna said.

"No, you guys, I'm not saying she can justify it, but let's face it, we know all three of these people, and we know them well, and you can never really know what a person is going through," said Mona.

Mona hated keeping more secrets from Jewel and Lawna. Ever since she had found out what Ella had been doing, she had been working overtime to convince the girl to stop. But Ella had stars in her eyes. She wanted to take B.J.'s place and Taylor had convinced her it was possible. Or at least that's what Ella thought.

"Well, I wanna know what was going on in her head. Did he

approach her? What could he have said to make her betray her friendship with B.J.? Or maybe she came on to him. If we knew what had happened, it might help us to better understand their thought process," Lawna said.

"That's too much thought right there, Lawna. Just know that if either of you ever touched Zeke, the ladies on *The View* would be talking about me and the two life sentences I was serving for premeditated murder!" Jewel said.

"Violence is not the answer," Mona said.

"Neither is sleeping with your girl's husband! I don't give a damn what the question or dilemma was. *That* definitely is not the answer!" Jewel said.

"Touché!" Lawna added.

SIX

E lla had been holed up in a hotel room by herself. She was
hiding out at a waterfront five-star hotel in Riverside.
Although the city was only sixty miles east of Los Angeles,
it might as well have been in another country.

She hated returning to her hometown, which was known as the
citrus industry's birthplace. But at a time like this, she appreciated
that she was far enough away from the drama and close enough
to the Santa Ana River that she was able to walk along its shores
every morning.

This morning, in particular, her mind was dominated by thoughts
of being sued by her lover's wife. What kind of stupid stunt was
that? B.J. was so desperate Ella actually felt sorry for her.

After a long, hot shower, Ella sat on the edge of the bed and dialed
Mona's number. Mona had never approved of her relationship
with Taylor, but like everyone else, Ella felt she'd eventually learn
to accept them as a couple. Mona's phone rang two times before
she answered.

"You alone?" Ella asked.

"Um, yes, what's going on?"

"Girl, can you believe B.J. is suing me? I mean seriously!" Ella
said.

"I've been calling you for quite some time," Mona said.

"Girl, I'm trying to get my mind right."

Mona was uncharacteristically quiet and Ella didn't know what to make of it. She was close enough to Mona to understand how drastically her mood could swing. But while she was hiding out, she recognized Mona would be her only connection to the outside world.

"What are Jewel and Lawna saying? They know you knew?"

"I would never tell them I knew. I don't want anyone to know I knew," Mona replied.

"You sure you okay?" Ella asked.

"This whole thing is a big ol' mess. I keep trying to call B.J., but she won't answer. She's not talking to any of us."

"Bitch," Ella snarled.

Mona didn't say anything.

"She really needs to let this thing go. Taylor doesn't even want her anymore," Ella said.

"You really think he'll leave her for you?"

Ella didn't like the tone Mona was using. But she wasn't about to say anything. Mona and everyone else thought she was a fool, but they didn't know what she knew. She'd get the last laugh because she understood Taylor's heart. He was sick and tired of B.J.'s rigid, overbearing, controlling ass and when he came to *her*, he didn't have to worry about a thing. She knew how to make him feel like the powerful man he was.

Sure, what they had started out as a fling, but it had quickly blossomed into so much more. Ella couldn't wait until she and Taylor would step out together as a couple for the entire world to see.

"Listen, I'mma call you back, okay?" Ella said. She was tired of the lopsided conversation with Mona. She wasn't sure what her problem was, but she had enough on her mind, she didn't need to try and figure out Mona's issues, too.

"Okay," Mona said flatly.

After hanging up the phone, Ella flopped back onto the bed. When she did, her bath sheet fell open. As the ceiling fan's blades whipped around, the cool air settled on her body. She lay there naked, and closed her eyes. Soon she was back in the middle of bliss, back with her man right where she belonged.

Taylor was breathing hard as he entered their hotel room and quickly closed the door.

"What's wrong, Daddy?" Ella purred. Dressed in fine lingerie, she had been lying across the king-sized bed and atop the fluffy down comforter. She loved the fine linens and pillow-soft comforter that always made her feel like she was floating on a tender cloud when they were able to sneak away.

"Strangest thing," Taylor said as he moved closer to the bed. He reached for her thigh. "I dunno; all of a sudden I got the feeling someone was following me. You know how paranoid I get sometimes. I couldn't shake the feeling, so I got off the elevator on the wrong floor, then slipped into the stairwell and rushed up five flights of stairs to get here."

By now, he was sitting on the edge of the bed. Ella eased up behind him and began to rub his shoulders. At first, she rubbed softly. Then her strokes intensified.

"Oh, feels so good," he moaned.

Ella rubbed harder. She enjoyed making him feel good.

"I can feel the stress leaving your shoulders," she said.

"Yeah, babe."

Before long, she allowed him to lay back and she crawled around and straddled him. She kissed him gently at first. Then those kisses turned to licks, all targeting that spot on the side of his neck. When she hit that spot, it always seemed to trigger something raw in him. Ella enjoyed savoring the taste of him.

"So good," he managed.

He sounded at peace. Her hands traveled the length of his torso. She loved the feel of his body. Where her husband, Sterling, was soft and mushy, Taylor was firm and solid.

"I wanna make you feel good," she whispered sweetly.

When her hands arrived at his crotch, she tugged at his zipper until she freed him. As always, his excitement for her couldn't be denied. Ella's heart swelled with pride as she used a powerful grip to stroke his length. He felt warm and wonderful.

"Your hands. You feel so damn good." He spoke painstakingly, like he meant every word he said.

Ella eased back a bit.

"Let's take these off," she said, tugging at his pants.

Taylor wasted little time doing as she suggested. He stepped out of his pants, then quickly eased his body back into position. Ella's crotchless La Perla teddy was already nearly soaked. That was the effect he had on her. He could blow out a breath from across the room and she'd feel a shiver up and down her spine. Ella spread his legs apart and straddled his left thigh.

"Jesus, girl!"

When her moist slippery flesh kissed his hairy, muscled thigh, Taylor yelped. Ella beamed with pride. She loved the control she had over him when they were together. After a powerful but passionate hand job, Ella tried to swallow him whole. He palmed her ass and tightened his grip, but that did little to throw her off. Ella worked with such careful concentration she could feel his body squirming beneath her, and that made her feel even better.

"Enough. I need to feel you. Now," Taylor managed through gritted teeth.

In one swift movement, he eased her body from his thigh and positioned her onto his hardness.

Ella swore he reached her core as he filled her. Their eyes locked as she rode him intensely and unmercifully. At that moment, Ella knew her grip held Taylor so tightly that not even his wife could loosen it.

The ringing cell phone reluctantly pulled her away from the pleasure-filled memory. But the moisture between her thighs proved precisely how real her trip down memory lane had been. Weeks after the last time they made love, Taylor still had a lasting impact on her. A pang of sadness tugged at Ella's heart. Why hadn't she heard from him yet?

The familiar ring-tone told her without even a glance, that the caller was her mom. She sank back onto the bed and cried.

Ella was lonely. She was tired, and she wanted her man.

SEVEN

B.J. had returned from a short break and was back at her laptop again. This time she started dishing about how she was pulled into the sick and dysfunctional union that was Lawna's marriage to Davon Carter, the offensive coordinator.

She rolled her eyes, thinking about those two and the drama surrounding them. She started typing.

I often wondered what would've happened if I hadn't answered the phone. It was so late, morning was hours away. I nearly allowed the call to go to voicemail, but answered because Taylor and the team were staying in a hotel. The night before home games, coaches and players are secluded so they can focus on the next day's game. And although I knew they were at a hotel, I still feared he might venture out and I'd stay up worrying about his safety.

All those times, I thought my worst fear was him drinking and driving. Now I wondered if he might have been out screwing Ella all along.

It was nearly two years ago now, and at the time, B.J.'s mother was at the house for a visit. Before the phone could ring a second time, B.J. snatched it from its cradle. She didn't want to wake her mother or the kids.

"Hello?"

When no one said anything right away, B.J. wondered if it was a crank call. She almost hung up until she heard what sounded like a soft whimper.

"Hello?" she called out again, straining to hear who was on the other end.

"Beee Jay?"

The caller sniffled a few times, and that's when B.J. realized it was one of her friends. She couldn't tell who it was right away, but she couldn't miss the sobbing.

"Yes, this is B.J. Who is this? And what's wrong?"

"Oh God, B.J., I'm so glad you answered. I couldn't reach anyone else. I'm so sorry."

"Okay, that's fine, that's fine. But who is this?"

At first there was more sobbing, followed by a few sniffles.

"Dang, girl, I'm sorry. This is Lawna. It's like super late. I'm so sorry. I tried to call someone else, but I don't know where Jewel, Ella, or Mona are. I know it's—"

"Lawna, what's the matter?" B.J.'s no-nonsense tone had suddenly kicked in.

"I'm in a little trouble here," Lawna said.

That was obvious to B.J., with the crying and sobbing and the ungodly hour, but she wanted to know specifically what Lawna had gotten herself into.

"Lawna, what's the matter? I realize you're in a bind, but what's going on?"

"Well, I'm… is there any way you can come get me? I have no money; my purse is gone; and I really need some help right now."

Panic rushed through B.J.'s nervous system. The worst scenarios flooded her mind.

"Your purse is gone? Have you been robbed? You need to hang up and call nine-one-one. Where are you? What happened?"

"B.J., I um, I don't want the police involved in this. I need you to come get me. Can you do that?"

"Of course! I'm sorry. You don't need me preaching to you right now. It's just that this isn't making much sense. Where are you?"

"I'm on Western, in South Central," Lawna said.

"You're where? What are you doing in South Central this time of the morning? And where on Western? Lawna, what's going on here?"

"B.J., please. I'm at the Snooty Fox Motor Inn," Lawna admitted.

"Ooh," B.J. said.

She got up and walked quietly to her children's room. She eased the door opened, looked in on their sleeping faces, then gently closed the door. B.J. hoped they wouldn't wake while she was gone. Her mother handled the kids fine, but still she didn't like the idea of them waking while she was gone.

Less than thirty minutes after the phone call, B.J. was behind the wheel and on her way to the address Lawna had given her.

Now as she wrote about it, she thought about all of the wild thoughts that flashed through her mind while she was on the road. What in the world was Lawna doing in a sleazy South Central motel? And why in the world was she crying? And why was she calling for help?

B.J. pulled into the parking lot at 4120 S. Western Avenue and looked for the room number Lawna had given. She frowned as she looked around the two-story building that was shaped like an L.

Yes, the Snooty Fox was in the hood, but nothing could've prepared B.J. for what she found when she knocked on the door and Lawna pulled it open.

"Dang, girl!" Lawna exclaimed. "You don't know how glad I am that it's you."

B.J. was a little confused, but she didn't ask who else it would be. Lawna was wrapped in a bed sheet. It was obvious she'd spent quite a bit of time crying, but she put on a smile as she stepped away from the door.

"This is all so over the top, but I didn't know what else to do, and well, you said if I ever needed anything, that I should call you. I'm so sorry to have to drag you into this mess, but as you can see, I didn't have a choice."

Lawna used a hand to make a sweeping motion around the room. Her other hand clutched the sheet at her chest.

B.J. hadn't said anything after the meek greeting she gave Lawna. Her nose was instantly assaulted; her eyes took in the room. It was huge, but the carpet had massive black stains all over it.

"What in the world are you doing in here?" B.J. finally asked as she looked around the room.

Suddenly, Lawna's shoulders began convulsing, and she started dry heaving. B.J. didn't know what to do. She was confused. Lawna wasn't talking and she was running short on patience with all the crying and sobbing.

"Okay, calm down, calm down. Let's sit you over here."

When B.J. got closer to the bed, as she guided Lawna to it, she noticed the sheets weren't clean. She also noticed there were big chunks of food on the floor close to the bed, so she moved carefully trying to avoid stepping on any of it.

Near the head of the bed, she noticed trash was strewn all over. She wanted to be helpful, but she definitely wanted to know what was going on with Lawna. B.J. wasn't sure how much longer she could stand all of this.

"Look, where are your clothes? Let's get out of here," B.J. suggested. "We can talk on the way home."

But Lawna didn't move. Instead, she started crying louder.

"What's the matter? What happened? Why are you even in a place like this?"

"That's what I'm trying to tell you. All of my stuff, everything, is gone. B.J., I don't even have any clothes!"

B.J. was confused. She frowned as she looked down at Lawna.

"Help me here," B.J. said, throwing her arms up in mock defeat.

"He took everything," Lawna finally sobbed.

"*Who* took everything? *Who* is *he* and what are you talking about?"

"The man I met here. He basically lured me here and robbed me," Lawna said before sobbing again.

"Oh," was all B.J. said. Her eyes grew wide as she watched Lawna break down in front of her.

"Here, let me get a towel for you," B.J. said as she headed toward the bathroom.

What was she thinking? When she stepped into the small bathroom, she saw the toilet had urine stains all around the seat. B.J. nearly gagged. Suddenly, she heard noises coming from the bathtub area. When she pulled back the raggedy shower curtain, water was bubbling up from the drain and it smelled bad. It bubbled again, then went back down and left a stain.

B.J. covered her mouth and rushed out of the bathroom. Unfortunately, Lawna hadn't moved from her spot on the bed.

They both jumped when the knock sounded at the door. Lawna turned to it and her lips began to quiver. She looked petrified.

"Look, we need to get out of here. I don't want to be here when your friend comes back," B.J. said.

At the door, a child stood staring at B.J. She popped the gum she was smacking on and looked like she was ready to serve up much attitude.

"Umph, I must be at the wrong room," she said.

"Let's go," B.J. ordered over her shoulder to Lawna.

"But what about my clothes?"

"You don't have any, so keep the sheet and come on. Let's go!"

Lawna clutched the sheet tighter at her chest, then jumped up and followed B.J. out of the room like her life depended on it. The girl stood in the doorway and watched as B.J. and Lawna made it to the car.

The office was closed, but B.J. noticed there was a lot of activity going on outside the room. She simply wanted to be gone.

"Y'all coming back here or what?" the girl asked from her spot in the doorway.

"Nope!" B.J. yelled.

"It's paid for?"

"Yup, and it's all yours!" B.J. said as she helped Lawna into the passenger side of the car.

EIGHT

Lawna checked her false lashes in the rearview mirror. Her entire reflection was as she expected, flawless. She picked up her Apple iPhone and looked at the map again. She had no business doing this, considering the fact that B.J. had already threatened to blow the lid off all of their *extracurricular* activities, but how else was she supposed to relieve the enormous amount of stress she was experiencing?

Besides, ultimately, this was all her husband's fault. She never wanted to bring others into their bed in the first place! As she drove, she thought back to that night last year. As a matter of fact she remembered it each and every time she met a new *friend* on the internet. Davon had called and asked her to meet him at the Four Seasons; he said he had a surprise for her.

"A surprise at the Four Seasons? Sounds interesting," Lawna said into her cell phone. She was so excited.

"Are you gonna have an open mind?" he asked.

"Of course," Lawna said teasingly. She was glad he was trying to be spontaneous. Lately she felt as if their lovemaking had become so humdrum. His call put a naughty smile on her face. Maybe things were finally turning around.

"You remember that talk we had the other day?" Davon asked.

"What talk?" She knew very well what he was talking about, but she had hoped it was a conversation and nothing more. Now here he was bringing it up again.

"You know," he said.

Lawna paused for a second. Suddenly her heart started to race. He really was talking about what she thought he was talking about! When she didn't respond right away, he spoke up.

"Remember, I told you we should try to spice things up a bit. You know, get a little freaky," Davon said.

Oh, she remembered the so-called talk. How could she forget? What does a woman do when her husband comes home and tells her that he wants to bring another couple into their bed? Lawna had hoped it was merely a fantasy that would fade with time, but obviously it hadn't.

"Look, I need to run, but I'll see you later at the hotel," he said.

For the rest of the day Lawna was nervous. She couldn't concentrate on anything and her mind kept conjuring up thoughts of this mystery couple. Why did Davon need to bring anyone into their bedroom? Since when was she not enough? She hadn't gained weight; she'd kept herself up, working extra hard to be the epitome of a trophy wife. Why couldn't that be enough for him?

Later, Lawna walked into the posh hotel lobby and gave her name to the clerk at the front desk.

"Yes, Mrs. Carter, here is your key." The young woman smiled.

Lawna's legs felt like wet noodles as she wobbled to the elevator and waited for the doors to open. The excitement she had originally felt when Davon called was completely gone now. If she wasn't so afraid of what he might do without her, she wouldn't have shown up at all.

When she arrived at the room, she used the key to let herself inside. Much to her surprise, it was empty. Lawna released a huge sigh of relief. She figured she'd have time to get her mind right. She placed her purse on the coffee table near the door and stepped out of her stacked heeled pumps. The room was dimly lit, but her eyes quickly focused on a tall silver ice bucket that stood near the bed.

"Oh God, champagne, just what I need," she said. Lawna rushed over and grabbed a glass. When she finally worked the cork off the bottle, she had to slurp all of the overflowing liquid. She poured herself a glass.

Lawna was wearing one of the tight-fitting minidresses Davon had bought. She didn't understand why he wanted her to look slutty, but she decided it was best to do what would please her man.

She noticed the double-mirrored closet doors and chuckled to herself.

By the time the bottle was empty, Lawna was up dancing in front of the mirrored closet and having a good time all alone. But soon thereafter, she was sprawled out across the bed. She hadn't heard from Davon and because she was more than a little tipsy she didn't even care.

Maybe his plans fell through. She eased herself onto the soft bed and curled into a comfortable position. Lawna yawned.

Suddenly there was a knock at the door. Startled, Lawna jumped up from the bed. What should she do? Davon would have a key. Why would he need to knock; this was his surprise.

"Ah, just a minute," she said.

Lawna stumbled a bit as she got up from the bed. She didn't realize how much of an effect the champagne had had on her. She giggled a bit as she wiggled her hips to straighten the tight dress.

She finally made it to the door, but didn't bother to look out of the peephole. She swung it open, expecting her husband to be standing there. Instead of Davon a chiseled mass of chocolate perfection stood in front of her.

Lawna's mouth dropped literally.

His features were perfect, his eyes dreamy, his lips succulent; even his nose looked perfect. But none of his pretty features could compare to his perfect body.

"Ah…" Lawna was at a complete loss for words.

"You must be Lawna," he said.

Her mouth was frozen in a near perfect "o," as Lawna stood holding the door, and staring at the stranger with wide-eyed curiosity.

"I'll take that as a yes." He smiled. "Can I come in?"

"Uh," Lawna managed.

"Coach said you'd be here early," the stranger said.

Did his eyes just twinkle?

"Oh, yes, you can come in," Lawna finally said.

As the handsome stranger walked in, Lawna thought of how good he looked, both coming and going. Everything about him was perfect.

Once the door was closed, she leaned against it, unsure of what to say or what to do.

"You're even more beautiful than your husband said," he said.

Lawna smiled awkwardly.

"I'm not sure what's taking him so long, I um, I thought he'd be here before me," she said.

The stranger's eyebrows went up. "Why don't you come over here. I won't bite, unless you want me to."

"Shouldn't we wait for Davon, um, I mean, Coach?" Lawna asked nervously.

"C'mere." He beckoned her with a crooked index finger, and even that was sexy.

Lawna was torn. He was handsome; his body was perfect. Just looking at him turned her on, but where was Davon? Slowly, she walked toward the bed. He came and stood right next to it.

Before she could say anything, he pulled her close and kissed her so passionately she struggled to break free.

"W…what's…I mean, what are you doing; we need to wait."

He snapped.

"What the fuck is going on here? What's up with this?"

Lawna jumped back.

Suddenly the closet doors flew open and Davon stepped out. He was mad.

"Why are you trippin'?" he asked her.

Lawna was confused. She was drunk, but he had been in the closet all along?

"Dude, what the fuck?" the stranger asked.

Davon turned to him. "Just lemme talk to her," he said.

Lawna was disgusted.

Davon turned back to her. "What's wrong? We talked about this. Why didn't you go with the flow?"

"What flow? What are you talking about?"

"We talked about this. I fucked his wife, he watched, he was supposed to fuck you; now you trippin' we talked about this," Davon said.

Lawna couldn't believe her ears. But her eyes were not mistaken; not only was Davon mad, but so was the handsome stranger.

"Dude, you said this shit was all good," he said.

Davon turned to him. "It is, it is; lemme handle this."

That night, Davon took his place back in the closet watching through a two-way mirror as the handsome stranger fucked his wife.

The honking horn pulled her away from that dreadful night. Lawna threw up her hand in a friendly gesture and pressed the pedal. That night had forever changed her life. Things had started slow in the beginning. At first Lawna felt good about meeting these strangers on the internet. It was her personal way of getting back at her husband. She'd wait until Davon went to sleep; then she'd log on. But soon, typing what she and the strangers could do to each other was no longer enough.

Their words were enough to get her hot and they drove her imagination into overdrive, but after a while, she started wondering what it would *feel* like to meet these guys in person. A few weeks later, her opportunity came when one of her chat buddies discussed taking the party on the road.

U down or what?

Lawna sat staring at those words on her screen for what felt like hours. Would she be safe? How did she know she could trust him? They'd been chatting back and forth for a few weeks, and he'd told her all about himself, but she had no way of knowing whether what he said was the truth.

????

When she saw that pop up on the screen, she took a deep breath, then started typing. And that's how it started. Once that meeting went well, she escalated quickly and started targeting certain types of chat rooms. Now here she was doing what had suddenly become the norm for her.

Lawna followed the GPS voice and made a right turn on Avalon Boulevard. She was far away from her own Beverly Hills neighborhood, but this is how she preferred it. At first she told herself she'd only go 'out' during the season, when most of the wives sought adventure. But it didn't take long for her to carry the good times over to the off-season as well. The strategy hadn't failed her yet, and something told her deep down inside that B.J. would come to her senses. B.J. had to realize there was no point in ruining a good thing if it had been working well for so long.

And her good thing was definitely not in need of any fine-tuning.

Momentarily, she thought back to the argument with her husband, Davon. Ever since she'd reluctantly agreed to start swinging with him, their own sex life had all but vanished. Now he either needed to watch a porno flick or listen to a live sex-chat to get it up with her. How embarrassing!

"C'mon, Lawna, lighten up a bit," Davon had said.

But Lawna sucked her teeth. Here she thought he was in his media room watching old practice and game films, but instead, he was in there getting off on some slutty girl-on-girl flick.

"You know what," she had hissed. But instead of fighting with him, she threw up her hands, then stormed out of the room and out of the house. He wasn't coming after her. With the way he was palming his member, she'd have enough time to make a clean getaway.

After finding a parking spot on a residential side street, she checked her makeup again. Satisfied after applying more gloss to her shiny lips, she eased one stiletto-clad foot out the door and got out of her car. She glanced around the neighborhood, then finally made her way into the small storefront that served as a club.

Lawna walked up, paid the cash cover, and stepped inside. Her bright eyes scanned the room and took in the cheap-looking furnishings. But she didn't venture into these places for the ambiance.

"Why he wanted to meet here is beside me, but oh well." She sighed as she strolled to the back of the room. The instructions had been simple enough.

Arrive at the Boom Boom Room at 11:45; go all the way to the back near the mirrored walls; sit through two performances and I'll come and get you. She didn't believe there was actually a club by that name. She thought back to the Eddie Murphy movie *Life* in which it was referred to as a fictional place. But here she was at the Boom Boom Room.

"Would you like something to drink?" the waitress asked Lawna as she sat looking toward the stage. The place was full and smoky. Women occupied all of the booths and chairs, and some were even standing next to stairs that led to the makeshift stage. Lawna knew this place was ripe for the type of encounter that had lured her there.

"I'll take a glass of Nuvo," Lawna said. She raked her fingers through her thick shoulder-length black hair and looked around the room.

It didn't take long for the waitress to return with her drink. Lawna gave her a generous tip and smiled. Usually that drink was reserved for her time with her girls, but she was more than a little nervous. She didn't particularly like meeting in such a public place, but figured she had very little to lose, considering her time was running out anyway. And the fact that none of these people knew her gave her an extra sense of comfort, but still she was nervous.

"Thank you," the waitress said.

By the time the second dancer made it to the stage, Lawna was ready to see everything he was willing to show. His music mix included a few slow, sexy tracks from Trey Songz and Robin Thicke.

She wasn't one to shower men with money, but the way this dancer moved his hips and gyrated as he worked the entire room from his spot on the stage, Lawna was seriously considering making a sizable contribution. He had the women screaming and going wild in the small club. Lawna could see why. He looked delicious.

Her eyes stayed glued to the tassels that swung wildly from his crotch. His oil-drenched body was ripped in all the right places and made her realize how horny she was.

"You like what you see?" a deep voice suddenly asked. "I know I do," he added before Lawna could respond.

She smiled, but kept her eyes on the dancer who seemed to be eyeballing her just as hard. She didn't realize how much the dancer had mesmerized her. She never noticed the man who slid onto the seat next to her.

Her date had no way of knowing how perfect his timing had been. A moment longer and Lawna would've aborted the plan for a spontaneous encounter with the dancer. She realized he was feeling her and the feeling was mutual.

"Why'd you want to meet here?" she asked. Lawna still hadn't turned to look at him yet. The truth of the matter was that she really didn't care what he looked like. She didn't even want to know his name. Lawna had grown accustomed to hooking up, getting what she wanted, then going back to the mess that was her real life.

"I like to see a woman when she's being stimulated," he said.

That's when Lawna finally turned to face him. He was handsome. His features were rugged—chiseled jaw line, thick dark eyebrows with hooded bedroom eyes beneath. She could get into him.

"Who says I'm being stimulated?" she said. But what she really wanted to do was give the dancer her full and undivided attention.

His show was over far too soon for Lawna's taste. But when her date stood, she was suddenly glad to go with the original plan.

"You wanna follow me or what?"

Her eyes raced up his stallion-like legs, took in his thin, but visibly muscled midsection, and feasted on his broad and power-ful-looking chest. His shoulders were so wide, they reminded her of that of a linebacker. Just thinking about the possibilities gave her a shiver of arousal.

Yes, this, she told herself, would be well worth the uncertain ride she took coming to this part of town.

Once outside, they rounded the corner and made it to the small parking lot.

"Where'd you park?" he asked.

But instead of answering, Lawna cornered him into the first dark area that was secluded from the street.

"Whoa, a live one, huh?" the man joked.

Before he could say another word, their tongues had intertwined. Her tongue started to explore the depths of his mouth. Her hands were wildly searching his body and he seemed to be enjoying every minute of it.

"Damn, you ain't playin', are you?"

But her sexy stranger gave as good as he got. He grabbed her hair, pulled her head back, then rammed his face into hers. They tore at each other hungrily, like they were in a five-star hotel suite instead of an alley behind a club in South Central Los Angeles.

Lawna's heart was racing. Her blood was boiling as she struggled to regulate her breathing. Her entire body felt like it was on fire. In the midst of doing all the freaky things that had turned her husband on, she realized how much she enjoyed the rush of being with other men. She'd been hooked ever since.

Her lover slammed her up against the wall, switching positions with her. Once he pinned her arms above her head, he started sucking her neck, moved down to her breasts, and ravished every part of her body that was exposed.

"Take it; take it," Lawna huffed.

He worked like he understood her body well. This wasn't how it was supposed to go down. They were supposed to get a room near the Normandy Casino; fuck for a few hours. Then she'd make her way back home to soak in a hot lavender and vanilla bath.

But Lawna realized once lightning struck, you had to grab a hold and hang on for the ride.

When he lifted her up off the ground like she was a feather, then hiked up her skirt, she moaned.

"Shit!" He had her feeling fabulous.

In one swift movement, he ripped off her panties. Her heart was racing even faster. Her adrenaline was rushing like Niagara Falls. With her back up against the wall, and her legs wrapped around him, he balanced her body, then dug for a condom.

When they heard a few people shuffling in their direction, neither of them flinched. Lawna was glad the group of women, who simply giggled as they passed, knew how to mind their own business, because her lover didn't break stride. He brought her to a shuddering climax that was so intense, it left her lightheaded, with colorful stars dancing before her eyes.

The guilt washed over Lawna before they were even finished. She immediately started thinking about how she had turned into this person she could barely recognize at times.

It had all started with that request from her husband, Davon. But when she reluctantly agreed, she had no idea it would lead to the sorts of things she'd been doing. Hers had been a gradual progression. First she was chatting on the internet; then she'd meet for drinks. After the adrenaline rush from her first sexual encounter with a stranger, there was no turning back. And the sad part was, she didn't know how to make herself stop.

NINE

B.J.'s fingers were gliding across the keyboard, and she had a huge smile on her face. The book was going well as far as she was concerned. Her mother's voice was still nagging in the back of her head, but she tried her best to ignore it. What she was doing was right; there was no question about it, or was it? B.J. kept typing.

Chapter Four

Now Jewel Thompson Swanson is really a sweetheart. She's a little naive, being from Fresno, California, and all, but she brightens every room she enters. And why wouldn't she? With her golden blonde hair, light brown eyes and that cute beauty mark beneath her right eye. We call her Jewels. She's married to Zeke Swanson, the Sea Lions' Defensive Coordinator.

Most of the players' wives and girlfriends immediately hate Jewel sight unseen. That's because they don't know her. She's petite, with a perfect body and a bubbly personality to match. There are lots of differences between the coaches' wives and the players' wives. When we go to games, we're dressed in classy clothes. If we're in jeans, they're top-of-the-line, designer brands. The footwear is usually Manolo Blahniks or something comparable, and Birkin, Louis Vuitton, and Gucci are the bags of choice. We always say you can tell the level of importance by the way NFL women dress.

For instance, if you see a cute woman sitting in the players' section with a number on, that screams "newbie." Poor thing, she has no idea, but usually the legitimate girlfriend and wives are betting on how long the newbie will be around.

And more often than not, the cards are stacked against her. A girlfriend is going to be well made-up, and provocatively dressed. Her jewelry will be modest, not by choice, but just because she hasn't earned the all-elusive ring. Now the wives have levels, too. If her player is a star, she is going to dazzle—top-of-the-line labels, big flashy, but tasteful jewelry, and flawless hair and makeup. The veteran players' wives are just as nice looking, but they don't want to come off like they're trying too hard. Then there's us, the coaches' wives. Our attire is somewhere between the star players' and veteran players' wives.

And no one knew how to keep it cute quite like Jewel, which made her a target in more ways than one. But Jewel's cute face was hiding a nasty little secret.

Here's how it first began.

B.J. stopped typing as if she was trying to remember the details of her first encounter with Jewel's secret life. The coaching staff was due to return from the NFL Scouting Combine. It's a six-day circus that takes place every year in late February or early March in Indianapolis. The combine is where college football players perform physical and mental tests in front of NFL coaches, general managers, and scouts. Although the combine itself lasts six days, Taylor and his staff added a few extra days.

During the time the men were gone, most of the wives were busy with their own projects and schedules so there hadn't been much time to get together.

As usual, the drama started with a frantic phone call to B.J. and Taylor's home. But this time, to her surprise, it was Zeke on the other end.

"Hello?"

"B.J., where's Coach?" Zeke, Jewel's husband, asked. He never even bothered to say hello, something B.J. couldn't stand.

"I don't know. I didn't realize you guys were back. How long have you been home?"

B.J. knew her husband was probably moments from arriving because he liked to come home after his trips and stretch out on the sofa. She had missed him. Nearly two weeks was a long time to be away from each other. But since having kids, B.J. traveled with him far less than she used to when it was only the two of them.

"What's going on?" B.J. asked Zeke. She wanted to tell him he should try to solve his own problems; she had plans for her man and they didn't involve playing counselor or problem-solver to Taylor's coaching staff. But B.J. knew she couldn't say those words despite how tempted she was.

"It's Jewel. She's trippin' and I'm trying not to lay hands on her, but I dunno," he stammered.

That's when B.J. suddenly heard Jewel's voice in the background. If she hadn't been hearing it with her own two ears, she would've sworn it couldn't be Jewel. The usually mild-mannered Jewel was calling him every name in the book and none were good.

"Zeke, what the hell is going on over there?"

"She's trippin'; that's what's going on! Throwing shit into walls, screaming, and she won't listen to me!"

Zeke sounded helpless, not to mention a bit scared.

B.J. sucked in a deep breath. She was planning a romantic night for Taylor, but she didn't want anything to happen to Jewel, and the last thing she wanted was for the police to show up. That would make things bad for everyone. B.J. knew that old cliché "any press is good press" was nothing but a myth. She understood that in the NFL, bad publicity for the team wasn't good for anyone. Owners, fans, and league representatives want winners who can be leaders with private lives that can survive public scrutiny.

"You know what, let me make a quick call, and I'm on my way."

"Aw, man; thanks, B.J. I swear, maybe you can talk some sense into her. She done already went upside my head with one of them high-ass heels of hers. I dunno how much more I can take."

"Don't do a thing, Zeke. I'll be there as quickly as I can," B.J. said.

When she finally made it to Zeke and Jewel's home, it looked as if a tornado had blown through before she arrived.

Jewel looked like a madwoman who had barely survived the storm—tears mixed with snot, hair all over her head and wild-looking eyes. Her tank top was torn and the yoga pants she was wearing looked like they were on inside out.

"He's a fucking dirty-ass bastard and I'm sick and tired of his shit!"

"Jewel, calm down, honey," B.J. said softly as she approached Jewel.

"I don't need to calm down. I need a fucking gun! That's what I need! The bastard better be glad he's still alive!" Jewel turned to her husband. "You should be dead, you fucking punk! You should be dead!"

"I told you the bitch is lying! This is what she wanted. She wanted you to get all up in my ass over a bunch of bull and you're falling right into her trap!"

B.J. turned to Zeke.

"Can you leave us alone for a bit? Let me try to talk to her. Maybe you can go for a walk, calm yourself, get some air."

"B.J., I should kill his ass! Do you know what this tramp said when she came to my front door?"

Playing mediator was nothing new to B.J. Growing up, she always took on the role to settle disputes between her brother and sister, and even her mom and her siblings. But this was a side of Jewel she'd never seen. She was usually quiet, with a huge infectious smile on her face, even in the most stressful situations.

"Here I am planning to swing from the chandelier to welcome his sorry ass home and just as I strut out in my good La Perla outfit and heels, he's at the front door fighting with some dirty-looking trick! At my front door! My fucking house! You that damn bad that you gon' bring your tricks home?" she shouted at Zeke.

"That's not what happened," Zeke said.

B.J. whipped around to face him again.

"I really need you to go! You're not helping here!"

"Okay, okay. I'm gone. But, B.J., I was trying to tell her that chick's been jocking me for months now. She won't take no for an answer! Why would I be stupid enough to bring her to my house, or even tell her where we live? It don't make no damn sense!"

Little did B.J. know, asking Zeke to leave at that very moment wasn't the best idea. Jewel picked up what looked like a wooden cane and took off after him. Just as he made it outside, they both stopped cold in their tracks.

"What the fuck?!" was all B.J. heard before she also took off toward the front door. At the door, B.J. saw a young woman who had obviously pulled up in a flashy Mercedes SUV. The driver's side door was still wide open and the woman, who B.J. assumed was the driver, was pummeling Zeke's upper body with swift and continuous blows.

"You lying bastard!" the young woman screamed. "I fucking hate you! I hate you!"

Jewel attacked the woman.

"Nobody puts their hands on my husband but me!" Jewel yelled.

Before long, the three of them were rolling around on the ground, and all B.J. could do was hope and pray one of the neighbors didn't call the police.

Not knowing what else to do, B.J. rushed over to the open vehicle and leaned on the horn.

Everyone stopped what they were doing and looked in her direction.

"This madness needs to stop now!"

B.J. chuckled as she thought about how she had to take control of a situation that could have gotten completely out of hand that day. She continued typing.

Yes, Zeke was known for his many girlfriends. Rumor had it he was a groupie fav. He fit the complete stereotype of a coachcocky and was aggressive with a chip on his shoulders. He thought he was God's gift to women.

No one knew how true it was, but rumor had it that the most infamous groupie of them all (Sasha) was said to be a regular in his room while he and the team were on the road. Jewel had long prayed for a fine for the coaches similar to what was in place for the players. Her situation was so jacked up!

So it was no surprise when, during one of the many late-night cries, Jewel told me what she'd been doing to get even. I still can't believe she'd go to that extreme, but trust me when I say the bimbo in the Mercedes was one of many. It was like the Negro, Zeke, couldn't keep it zipped!

B.J. deleted the paragraph, then typed it again. If they didn't like it, she was sure her editor would suggest an alternative. So she decided to keep it and move the story forward.

TEN

Jewel was so sick and tired of dialing B.J.'s number she didn't know what to do. She was surprised her fingers weren't worn to the bone. Could she pay someone to find her? She wondered why *she* seemed to be the only one worried about the power this woman had over them all.

Ella was still M-I-A, but Mona seemed to think this was just another issue she could explain away. Lawna behaved as if this was a minor blip on the radar of everyday life. Jewel could picture her now, probably still bouncing around as if there wasn't a real threat looming over them all. From Jewel's perspective, they all had so much to lose they needed to put their heads together and do whatever was necessary to change B.J.'s mind, and they needed to do it fast.

Jewel sighed as she slammed her phone back into its cradle.

"Bitch!" Jewel spat.

Despite how angry she was, Jewel knew for certain she had no one to blame but herself. She realized from day one that she was playing with fire. But she was the epitome of a people-pleaser. It was hard for her to say no, and she often did or said whatever might make someone happy in order to keep the peace.

Tierney's reputation was well-known, but still Jewel strayed into that trap like a blind sheep. In the beginning, all Jewel could think about was exacting some sweet revenge against her own cheating husband.

But now, she felt like an even bigger fool, having spilled every scandalous detail to B.J. like she didn't know any better. Jewel knew better, but she loved the feeling she got from retelling their stories. It was almost like reliving the excitement, and the sheer bliss she seemed caught up in whenever she and Tierney were able to share a few stolen moments.

Although she couldn't justify her behavior, Jewel thought back to past relationships. But that pissed her off even more. She was so tired of being used as a damned doormat for men who wanted to dump on women. Why did men always take her considerate ways, soft heart, and kind demeanor for weakness? Most of her relationships ended because of a man's infidelity. They cheated on her constantly. At first she thought it was only the black men, so she dated outside of her race.

It took a little longer, but the Hispanic man, the white man and even the Jewish man she dated, all wound up in the arms of another woman while they were supposed to be committed to Jewel.

Despite her past experiences, Jewel knew what she was doing was wrong. She wasn't planning to leave her husband. There was that nagging part of her that was hell-bent on giving him a hefty dose of his own medicine.

That was the plan, but how could she have known she'd get all caught up the way she had? And even worse, who knew her so-called *confidante* would want some revenge of her own?

"Tierney, Tierney, Tierney." Just saying the name seemed to do something to Jewel's insides. It tingled, came alive, and rubbed her the right way. Jewel couldn't hide the effect this new relationship was having on her. And to think it all started when she first discovered what her skirt-chasing husband was up to. Jewel didn't know then that it would be the beginning of a long and bumpy road for her marriage. Thinking back now, it felt like it was just the other day. It had been one of the lowest points of her life.

She wanted to love her husband, but she couldn't keep giving her love to a man who blatantly disrespected her and their vows on a regular basis. Every time she revisited their past she got more upset than before. Thinking back, she wondered what she could've done differently.

Jewel looked down at her cell phone, noticed her husband Zeke's cell number, and wanted to puke.

"Fuck you, Zeke!"

Now the bastard wants to call. Jewel ignored it and him, then pressed down on the pedal. She had told his cheating ass if she checked his voicemail one more damn time and heard some bitch on there, thanking him and talking about what a good time she had, it was over for him. Obviously he didn't realize how much she meant what she said. Sure the calls didn't confirm anything, but it was enough to make her more than a little suspicious.

"These are business calls," Zeke had said when she confronted him.

Jewel decided she hated being married! But because of her husband's position, she wouldn't dare leave his ass. She had grown accustomed to their lavish lifestyle and was biding her time.

She needed to make it to ten years! She and Zeke had been married for four years, and not even a good year into their marriage she found out the snake was cheating. The first time she caught him, he had the nerve to cry, but he knew what he was doing because the tears made her instantly feel sorry for him . She took him back, convinced he'd change his nasty-ass ways.

Then there was the night Jewel had finally taken all that she could. She wasn't sure whether it was the phone call or the information the caller had anonymously delivered.

"Not this fucking time!"

ELEVEN

B.J. was beginning to get amused by the voicemails being left by her husband and her so-called friends. In his latest message, Taylor had the nerve to explain that with the NFL draft right around the corner, he needed to make peace at home.

"Hmm, shoulda' thought about that before you started screwing your girl," B.J. said as she listened to him begging on the message.

She had to roll her eyes several times because his plea was becoming more desperate by the second.

"Weren't thinking about stress when you were screwing Ella, were you?!" B.J. yelled into the phone as if Taylor himself was on the line versus his message.

B.J. wished her heart didn't ache the way it did. Was she that bad of a wife? Did he have to turn to her friend? Sure she had changed in the bedroom after their second child, but is that a reason to turn to someone else? B.J. remembered one of many painful times in their bedroom.

"Just do it," Taylor had said.

It was so obvious he was frustrated. B.J. had come in from shopping to find candles lit, soft music playing and a trail of rose petals leading into the master bedroom. When she walked into the room, Taylor was on the bed wearing nothing but a massive smile.

"What's going on?" B.J. asked, looking around at all the flickering candlelight.

"You've been stressed lately; thought a romantic night might help," he said.

B.J. dropped her bags at the door. She wasn't sure why her husband thought she was stressed, but she figured she'd go with the flow.

"I even fixed you a drink," Taylor said. He motioned toward the nightstand.

On it sat a tall fancy glass with a colorful drink. B.J. felt guilty. She couldn't explain it, but lately she wasn't the least bit interested in sex with her husband. She'd read about women on the internet who reported a drop in their libido after giving birth and suspected this was her problem, but she didn't appreciate her husband behaving as if he hadn't had sex in years.

"Yeah, you fixed me a drink, but what do I have to do for that drink?" she joked.

Taylor didn't respond.

"Sit," he said, patting the space next to him on the bed. "I wanna talk to you."

Reluctantly, B.J. eased herself onto the bed next to her husband. She still had her purse hanging from her shoulder and didn't even bother to remove her shoes.

"I don't know what's going on, but I miss you," he said.

"Nothing's going on. I've been gone all day, I'm a little tired, but other than that, I'm okay," said B.J.

"Have a drink; relax a bit."

"I'm not in the mood to drink," B.J. said.

"Babe, have a drink with your husband; it might loosen you up a bit."

B.J.'s head snapped in his direction. By the time her eyes met his, she could already see the regret settling in them.

"I didn't mean nothing by it," Taylor said.

"Oh you meant something by it, and I'm tired of it, Taylor," B.J. snarled.

"What do you expect me to do? You act like I can't touch you anymore; you act like having sex with me is the worst chore you have to struggle through. I tried to do something nice, but even that seems to piss you off!" Taylor threw his hands up and rose from their bed.

B.J. sucked her teeth and rolled her eyes at his back as he walked away. He was walking into the bathroom, and she didn't really care. So now she needed to loosen up? He should try working hard around the house all day with two small kids, being pulled in several directions with her other projects, then having to switch gears and turn into some sex goddess at the drop of a hat.

So what, she was no longer sexually attracted to her husband? Did that give him and her friend the right to betray her? And the others who helped them hide the affair? They were all pathetic as far as she was concerned—Taylor, Ella, Mona, and the entire group. How could those heifers not tell her what was going on? She'd been there for each and every single one of them. She'd done things for them that she didn't do for her very own blood and this was how they repaid her?

She realized Mona and Ella were close. As a matter of fact, B.J. was the newbie to the group, but she felt like she had earned her stripes and for that reason alone, she deserved their respect. But instead, they had played her for a fool, just like Taylor had.

Every time one of them called or left a message it infuriated her even more. Like this latest message from Mona.

"B.J., this f'ing thing has gotten completely out of control." One hundred percent Mona, straight to the point, forget the small talk. "I'd like to set up a meeting with you, Taylor, and Ella. What we have here is a failure to communicate; each of you needs to be heard. I want you to call me when you get this message so we can set this thing up. Enough is enough!"

This time, Mona's take-charge attitude was not going to work! Who the hell did she think she was talking to, one of her clients? B.J. was tempted to call back and say, "Go counsel someone else. You had your chance over here and you blew it!"

But she couldn't do that. What good would it do? Instead she listened and chuckled at their stupidity. If they had common sense, they'd leave her alone and pray that she decided to forgive. But no, not these heifers; they kept calling, one after the other. Not everyone called though.

Ella, the hooker, didn't dare pick up the phone, and B.J. thought that was the smartest thing for her to do. If B.J. wasn't suing the tramp and writing the book, she would've put her foot knee deep into Ella's behind. After all she had done for that girl, for all of them really! She couldn't wrap her mind around it.

And as if dealing with the problems surrounding her husband and the other coaches' wives weren't enough, as the self-designated leader of her family, B.J. shouldered her mother's problems as well.

Since B.J.'s father had died years ago, she had taken over as the leader of the family. It didn't matter that she had a brother. B.J. considered Jack, Jr. to be useless. He was up to his ears in baby mama drama and her younger sister was obsessed with finding a husband. So B.J. decided *she* was the only stable one in a position to lead.

After listening to most of the stupid messages, she called her mom.

"Mother," B.J. greeted.

"Hi, Bobbi," Vernice Jackson said.

"I'm calling to make sure you got the new insurance cards. And don't forget I have a mechanic coming this Saturday to work on your car. What about the air conditioner?"

"Oh, it's gon' be okay. Junior said he's—"

"Mother," B.J. used a tone better suited for a three-year-old than her own mother. "What did I tell you about Junior? I'm sending a service technician out there tomorrow! I cannot believe you're waiting for Junior to do anything, and remember what I told you about those crumb snatchers of his," B.J. said.

"Oh, Bobbi, those are my grandkids, too," Vernice said.

"Yeah, but I don't want them there while my kids are over. I mean it, Mother!"

"I got the cards, but, Bobbi, I'm glad you called. I wanted to talk to you about something," Vernice said.

"What is it, Mom?"

"Taylor's been calling—"

Vernice didn't even get to finish her sentence before B.J. started going off.

"Mother, do not talk to him! Do not tell him where I'm staying! Do you have the nanny pick up and drop the kids off?"

"Yes, yes. Now normally I do everything you tell me to do, but, Bobbi, this time, I'm speakin' my mind. You should go and talk to your husband, chile. You don't let no jezebel ruin your family without a fight!"

B.J. couldn't remember the last time she had heard her mother speak so passionately about anything. But this was none of *her* business. She did not need advice from her old, widowed, retired mother.

"Mom, let me handle Taylor."

"I know you don't think this is my place, but this is your *family* we're talking about, chile. Everybody's human. Ain't none of us above making mistakes. Don't throw your marriage away over…"

"Enough, Mom! I'll call Mona if I want counseling," B.J. said. B.J. had recently realized that cutting her mother off mid-sentence was the best way to prevent long and drawn-out emotional tantrums. B.J. had no appreciation or empathy for emotional rants. She needed people to get straight to the point and do it as quickly as possible.

"Mom, put T.J. on the phone," she said, referring to her son, Taylor, Jr.

"Mommy!" the child squealed.

"Hey, Mommy's big boy," B.J. said. She missed her children, but she needed to be away from them if she expected to finish the book.

After talking to her son, she said a few words to his sister. Then her mother got back on the phone.

"I want you to think about this whole thing," Vernice said once again. "This is your marriage we talkin' 'bout, chile. I don't know what you gon' do, but whatever you do, don't throw it away!"

Once she ended the call with her mother, B.J. got up from the bed, where she used a laptop to write, and walked out onto the hotel's balcony.

B.J. was still pissed about what had gone down. But she was sure the lawsuit would send a clear message about exactly what she would do about her marriage.

TWELVE

There was a constant battle brewing in B.J.'s head. Her mother's warning voice echoed in her mind, but she was determined to fight it.

You don't let no hussy take your husband...

It was a mistake; that man loves you and them kids...

What if the others she was writing about really hadn't known what was going on? Should they have to pay for Taylor and Ella's betrayal? Eventually their alliances would lie with Ella; regardless of how wrong Ella was. It only made sense. The other women had known Ella far longer; they had to have known what she was capable of.

B.J. shook the thoughts from her mind and started writing again. B.J. had arrived at the chapter in which she would discuss Mona and her borderline, obsessive-compulsive behavior. B.J. had to think back to some of the things her girlfriend had done that really spoke to the disorder.

B.J. and the other ladies were convinced it was a disorder because Mona didn't choose to behave the way she did; she simply couldn't help herself. The irony wasn't lost on B.J. Here Mona was, one of the best counselors in the country, and she was hiding issues of her own.

We would tease Mona, but it was all in good fun. No one really believed she was mentally ill, but what would you call it? On any given day, the girl went through so many mood swings it was hard to keep up. One minute she was in an overly good, euphoric mood. Then she'd crash like the market on Black Friday. It was crazy! Holding a conversation with her during one of her episodes was the worst! She'd talk very fast, then all of a sudden, jump from one idea to the next, leaving you good and lost!

When something bothered her, the girl would go on a cleaning binge. I don't mean vacuuming and washing dishes; I mean scrubbing the cracks in the driveway's sidewalks, or using a toothbrush to clean the grime from the fountain in her backyard. I always wondered, how someone so special could tell other people how to solve their problems! And going out to eat with her, well, that was a whole 'nother story!

"Am I the first one to arrive?" Mona asked as she breezed into the Ivy, one of their favorite meeting places.

The little cottage that served as one of the best celebrity hot spots in L.A. was always packed. But unlike the super-sleek lounge look of other power dining spots, the interior at Ivy was shabby chic and completely cluttered.

The furniture was plastered with peeling paint, and the once brightly colored fabric was now completely faded. Old paintings were spread throughout the restaurant. There were enormous bouquets of fresh flowers atop tables packed so closely together it was almost a requirement to weigh less than 100 pounds to maneuver the tight aisles.

"No, Ella's in the bathroom," B.J. said.

When Ella returned to the table, Lawna came in and the four ordered. But not before Mona adjusted and readjusted the items on the table.

Her friends ignored her little habits.

Later, after the waitress brought their entrees, Mona turned and asked, "Do you have plastic ware?"

No one at the table flinched. They were accustomed to Mona and her different ways. Everything had to be perfect at all times.

"Yes, ma'am, we do," the young redhead responded before dashing to the back.

Unfortunately when she returned with a single plastic fork and knife and extended it to Mona, she may have well insulted Mona's mother.

"It's unwrapped!" Mona shrieked.

Ella stepped in.

"It's okay," Ella said to the waitress. She dug into her own purse and pulled out a set of plastic ware. It was perfectly sealed in its plastic and hadn't been tampered with.

"Oh, thanks, girl," Mona said.

"So, did you all hear about the drama at the Green Door the other night?" Lawna asked.

"What drama?" Jewel asked.

"One name," Lawna said. "Sasha Davenport!"

"Uhmph, well, wherever Sasha shows up, there's bound to be some kind of drama," Mona said between bites. "Whose husband is she screwing this time?"

Rumors had paired Sasha with Zeke, but there was never any real proof, so the ladies did not mention her name too often around Jewel.

"Don't look now, but speak of the devil, two-o-clock," Ella muttered and motioned toward the door.

"I'm so over her," Jewel said, and rolled her eyes.

Sasha always traveled with an entourage. It was obvious that she was the leader of her pathetic little pack. The others followed behind her like they were part of a marching band's formation. Together they looked like they were walking off the set of the latest raunchy rap video.

"Hey, guurrrls," Sasha sing-songed as she glided toward, then past their table.

No one smiled. Their eyes took in Sasha's suggestive outfit, but no one actually said anything to her. Her denim miniskirt left nothing to the imagination. And the bright tube top looked like it might slip down if she stepped wrong in her platform sandals.

If their plates hadn't been full with their own drama, Sasha would've instantly become the center of their conversation. But not today; there was too much to talk about.

Lunch continued without any other interruption until Mona decided she needed to have exactly six cubes of ice in the iced tea she ordered.

B.J. often wondered how Mona ate off of public plates, drank from public glasses, with straws of course, and even sat on chairs that had been used. But she didn't dare suggest any other quirks for her friend to pick up.

Even B.J. had to laugh when she thought about how, while traveling, they would have to rush to eat breakfast before noon in Mona's presence for fear she'd gag if they didn't make her self-imposed deadline.

THIRTEEN

At the usual time, Mona ended her daily meditation session. Her eyes snapped open and she took a mental picture of the Hollywood sign that was visible from her bedroom balcony. She took a deep breath, rose, and prepared for another fabulous day.

Done with her regime, she was on the verge of losing it when she still couldn't reach B.J. Suddenly, she began to experience a surge of restlessness. Mona couldn't concentrate, and she started experiencing extreme irritability.

Hours later, the entire house had been cleaned from top to bottom. The wood floors sparkled with a fresh layer of wax; the cherrywood furnishings shown like they were spanking brand-new. All of the crown molding had been scrubbed, marble countertops buffed; and ceiling fans whipped around spewing a light lavender and vanilla fragrance. Still, Mona was in the midst of a cleaning frenzy.

She worked like someone would soon come to inspect the job she was doing and she didn't want to disappoint.

When the doorbell rang, she was wiping Windex from the massive picture frame on the formal living room wall. *Just a few more strokes*, she thought as her muscled arm swiped away the streaks.

"Coming," she called toward the door. But first, she stood back to inspect the frame and dabbed at a wayward speck of dust.

The doorbell chimed again. She snapped her head in its direction and noticed the couch's cushions could use a good fluffing.

Mona hurried to the foyer and pulled the large double oak doors open. It was Lawna and Jewel. They were wearing workout clothes.

"Hey, lady," Jewel said as she started looking around.

"Oh, come in. I was tidying up a bit," Mona said, stepping back to allow them inside.

Lawna and Jewel exchanged awkward glances as they followed Mona into the pristine house. Mona's house was always cleaner than the most sterile hospital room.

As they followed her toward the back, Mona pulled off the apron and purple cleaning gloves. She dropped them onto the side of the cleaning cart that housed all of her products. She wore a pair of yoga pants and a matching tank top. Her hair was tied down with a matching bandana.

"It smells so good in here," Jewel said as they assembled around the table in the breakfast nook. She glanced around. Everything was perfect.

"Is this the flyer for your upcoming event?" Lawna asked, picking up the flyer and inspecting it closely. The flyer had a massive picture of Mona's face, and information about the Staples Center event. It also showed smaller pictures of Mona on stage at previous speaking engagements. The pictures of her looked really polished and glossy.

"Yes, they sent it over for me to approve," Mona said.

"Well, it's nice. The place is really nice, too. Ah, did you do all of this?" Lawna asked, noticing the glistening floors and how wonderful everything looked. It wasn't that Mona's house was ever dirty, but it looked as if an army had made it their mission to make the place shine.

"You guys know how I get when something's on my mind. I

gotta do something with myself," Mona said. "Anybody want a drink?" she asked, and rushed toward the refrigerator.

"How long have you been cleaning?" Jewel asked.

With her head now buried between the refrigerator's double doors, Mona called out, "Well, I called B.J. a few times last night. When she still didn't answer, I had to take out my frustration on something, so I started cleaning."

"Last night?" Jewel mouthed to Lawna. Lawna shook her head.

Mona returned to the table carrying a tray with sliced fruit, and grabbed a bottle of Nuvo. She pulled a nearby cabinet door open.

"So, you woke up and finished cleaning?" Lawna asked as she reached for a plump strawberry.

"Woke up?" Mona chuckled, placing three long-stemmed wine-glasses on the table. "Who could sleep with all this mess looming?" She unscrewed the lid on the bottle and started pouring. "I didn't get much sleep, but I did get a chance to meditate this morning." She smiled.

"Uh, that's why we came over…to check on you," Jewel started slowly.

Mona frowned. She poured the pink liquid into her own glass last. "What are you guys checking on me for? We need to try and find B.J.'s behind. That's who y'all need to be checking on!"

"True, true," Lawna said as she sipped, then savored the drink. "But let's keep it all in perspective here. B.J.'s gonna do what she's gonna do. We can try to appeal to her, but in the end we can't control what she does. So I think we should start trying to prepare ourselves for some possible worst-case scenarios."

Mona looked at Lawna like she had suddenly developed a third eyeball in the center of her face.

"Listen, I don't know about you guys, but I have far too much to lose. I can't simply sit back and hope for the best. I've gotta find B.J.'s f'ing ass, slap some sense into her, then make sure my secrets stay right where they are—buried!"

It was March and Mona was gearing up for a major multi-city tour that was set to kick off in May. Her agent had lined up engagements with various women's organizations, church groups and a few youth programs. She was excited this time around, because although her husband, Melvin, was rarely able to join her because of the team, they had already coordinated a couple of events during the off season.

Together they were going to kick off her new couples' boot camp at the Staples Center. The event had already received lots of publicity; she was even featured in a two-page *People* magazine spread. They were at 80 percent capacity with only a couple of months to go.

"But what if we can't stop her from writing this book?" Lawna asked, sounding worried. "And since she's probably gonna write it, we should think about how we're gonna deal with it. You've gotta think about that possibility, too."

"No, I don't," Mona said confidently. "I need to find her, reason with her, lay everything out there, and make her see how foolish she's being. There's no need to ruin everyone over *Taylor's* indiscretion. Trust me, I counsel couples in their position all the time. I need to find her and talk some sense into her."

Jewel and Lawna exchanged knowing glances.

When Mona's phone rang, she sprang from her seat and grabbed the receiver.

"Mona, it's me; Ella. Girl, what's going on?"

"Uh."

"You not alone?"

"Hold on a sec," Mona said. She got up from her chair, covered the mouthpiece with her hand, and looked at her friends. "This is a private call. You guys don't mind if I step into my office for a few, do you?"

"Go on," Jewel said.

Lawna had a strawberry in her mouth, so she used her hands to shoo Mona away.

Behind her closed office door, Mona whispered into the phone.

"Where are you? When are you coming back so we can work this thing out?" she asked.

"B.J.'s still pretty hot, huh?"

"Yeah, but I think we can talk about this. Where are the kids? Where are you?"

"You know if she's been talking to Taylor?" Ella asked.

"We haven't talked to her since she set out to make us pay for what you did."

"Umph. Well, I need some time to myself. My mama's got the kids. I need to get my head together."

"You would be able to do that a lot faster if we could all sit and talk," Mona said.

"I don't think that's a good idea. B.J. don't wanna talk to me, and I can't say I wanna talk to her right now either. So what she say, about you knowing all along?"

"I told you, I didn't really get a chance to tell her that. She assumed we all knew, and that's why she's taking revenge against us all."

"I can't believe she is writing a tell-all! Between the book and this stupid lawsuit of hers..." Ella sighed. "Mona, you gotta talk some sense into her. If anybody can do it, it's you. Make her see how stupid and embarrassing it would be for her to go through with this."

"She won't take my calls! Uuggh, this is a mess! I'm not trying to make you feel bad, but, Ella, how did you think this was going to end? I kept telling you to leave him alone," Mona said.

"You know what? I'd better go." Ella sulked.

"This whole thing has torn us all apart. That's all I'm saying. Why don't you come back home. We'll catch up with B.J. and work this thing out."

"Yeah, okay, Mona," Ella said unenthusiastically.

But Mona realized that wasn't about to happen anytime soon. Besides, if it was that easy, reconciliation would've happened by now.

FOURTEEN

B.J.'s manuscript was coming along fine. The more she thought about the times with her former friends, the more juicy stories she remembered.

"Did Lawna cause that girl to lose her baby or—" B.J. sat, trying to remember the facts the way they had happened. She shook her head at thoughts of all she and those women had experienced together. It was the strangest feeling; while she was mad at all of them, she didn't want to think of her life without them. She couldn't believe that Ella had stabbed her in the back the way she had, but B.J. decided dwelling on that would only slow her down.

B.J. thought again about all they had done together and wondered what would happen when their husbands found out what was really going on while they were focused on the game during the season. She hoped they'd all die miserable and painful deaths. She wanted Ella to get stuck with some incurable disease and she wanted Taylor to lose his job. For a man who often slept in his office during the season, *that* to him would be the equivalent of dying a slow and painful death.

Suddenly a thought struck her. Was he really sleeping in his office during the season, all those times when he called late to say he'd be even later? B.J. began to rake her memory; she must've missed out on a clue in one of those many phone calls.

"Babe," Taylor's voice sounded tired.

"Hi, what's wrong?"

"I'm so sorry; time got away from me. After I sent the other coaches home, I started watching the game again, and I lost track of time. I was thinking, I should crash here. What sense would it make to come home, lay my head on the pillow for a minute, then have to be right back up here before the crack of dawn?"

"Oooh, not again, Taylor."

"B.J., you know the drill, you're not new at this," he said.

"I know. It's just the kids were bouncing off the walls earlier, and I had to force them to go to bed, but I told them I'd wake them when you got home."

"I'm really tired, B.J." He yawned. "It's best if I call it a night, right here on this sofa."

"Well, you do sound really sleepy, so it's best you stay there. But call first thing in the morning!"

"Will do baby, I love you. Kiss the kids for me." He yawned again.

For all she knew, Ella could've been curled up on that sofa right along with her husband. B.J. ended her daydream and got back to writing.

When the Sea Lions played Pittsburgh last year, we hadn't planned a trip, but we did have a watch party. It wasn't anything too fancy. It was at my place. One of my favorite caterers took care of the food and we invited some neighbors and friends.

As usual, most of the drama in the wives' lives started with a late-night phone call, and this time was no different. I was fortunate enough that this time, I had received the call after most of the drama had gone down, or so I thought. The only reason I was spared the brainstorming session was because I had hosted the watch party and people weren't in any hurry to go home.

So by the time I got the call, even though I was completely worn out, I still jumped in my car and hit the road.

When B.J. walked into Lawna's house, she was not surprised to see the whole gang there. She hated when they got together without her. It reminded her that no matter what position she held, she would always be seen differently since she was new to the group. But B.J. wasn't about to make a fuss over it; especially when she saw somber expressions on every face.

"What happened?" B.J. asked, poised to take control of the situation, as usual.

Lawna's head was buried in the palm of her hands.

"We've got a real situation here," Ella said.

That was obvious to B.J. from the moment her phone rang. She looked around the room again.

"What kind of situation?"

"Well," Mona began after she took a deep breath. "Lawna found out that Davon knocked up some groupie."

B.J.'s eyebrows shot up. This was the kind of shit you heard about among the athletes and the groupies who followed them; not the coaches' wives. They were supposed to be above this kind of drama and scandal.

"Could this be a mistake?" B.J. asked.

"No. We didn't want to tell you before; we were waiting for confirmation. Well, it's been confirmed. You know Gail Tremor who works in administration? Well, her sister works at the chick's doctor's office. We got all the information we need and there's no doubt about this one," Jewel said.

B.J. stood, thinking. She couldn't say how she really felt; the others were looking to her for some kind of leadership.

B.J. walked over to the table and grabbed the bottle of Nuvo. She poured herself a drink and swallowed it in nearly one quick swallow. Afterward, she turned her attention back to the ladies.

"Okay, tell me everything. What happened? How did Lawna find out? And what's going on now?"

Lawna finally lifted her head. She had been crying. She looked at B.J. "I don't know how much more of this shit I can take. I don't understand why he got married if he still wanted to screw everything out there."

"It's what they do," Ella tossed in.

"Enough of *them*. Let's try to figure out what you're going to do," B.J. said.

"Yeah, are you leaving him?" Ella asked.

The room fell silent for a while. Lawna was breathing hard and staring off into space, but she didn't answer. The truth of the matter was, everyone pretty much understood that she wasn't leaving. But the others didn't know how long she would be able to endure such blatant disrespect.

Before B.J.'s arrival, the ladies had come up with a plan. By now, it was eight the next morning.

"Get the burner," Mona suggested, reaching for a prepaid cell phone Ella was handing her.

"A burner? Who are you people?" B.J. asked, confirming they really had brought her in on the tail end. It was obvious there had been careful planning prior to her even knowing what was going on. Someone had even bought a prepaid cell phone that couldn't be traced?

"I told you, we came up with a plan," Mona said in B.J.'s direction.

B.J. felt out of the loop, but she didn't complain. She sat back and watched as the ladies put their plan into action.

Mona used the phone to dial Lawna's house line so the others could listen. They'd make the call on three-way. Jewel, B.J., Ella, and Lawna listened by muted speakerphone on the house extension.

The phone rang for a few minutes but voicemail didn't pick up.

Suddenly, a woman answered. She sounded as if she had been pulled from a deep sleep.

"Good morning. May I speak to Penny Jones?" Mona said, sounding every bit the professional.

"Um, who is this?" the groggy voice asked.

"This is Sally Garrett with Doctor Lafore's office," Mona said.

"Oh, is everything okay? This is Penny," the woman said.

"Well, Penny, there's a bit of a problem, but nothing serious. Your blood work shows some abnormalities and to be on the safe side, Doctor Lafore wanted me to call in a prescription for you."

"OHMYGOD! Is my baby gonna be okay? I can't lose this baby!" she shrieked.

"Calm down; calm down. It's nothing like that. The doctor's only a little worried about possible infection. Once you take this medicine, you and the baby will be fine. But we don't want to take any chances."

"Look, miss, I mean, nurse, I can't lose this baby. Please tell me what I need to do," Penny said.

She sounded scared, but Mona played her part to the hilt.

"Okay, well, first I need your pharmacy's number. I'll call the prescription in; I need you to go and pick it up immediately. When you get home, take two of the pills and get lots of rest."

"Okay, lemme get the number. Oh, God! Ohmygod!"

Jewel was shaking her head as she listened on the other line. B.J. was amused by how calm and confident Mona was playing the role, and Ella seemed stunned into silence.

They listened to a few muffled sounds; then a few seconds later, Penny was back on the line.

"Okay, I got a pen," she said, sounding desperate.

"We're calling in a prescription for the medicine Cytotec. Please take it as prescribed. Next week, we want to see you back here in the office."

"Okay. Should I make my appointment now?" Penny asked.

"No, not yet. Please get over to the pharmacy and get that filled as soon as possible."

B.J. couldn't believe it. By the time the call had ended, she wasn't sure what she should do. Jewel, Ella, Lawna, and Mona were all cracking up laughing.

"Did you hear her? You hear how scared and desperate she sounded?"

"That's what the hell she gets," Lawna said.

B.J. started thinking about the drama that followed after that girl miscarried.

It was not my idea to be involved in something like this, B.J. typed. *I was just glad to know that Mona had enough sense to use the burner to make the call. What they were doing with one of those untraceable, disposable phones was beyond me until I realized this could lead to serious jail time.*

As B.J. sat back and looked over what she had typed, she wondered if she was setting herself up for a possible lawsuit from the woman Davon had impregnated. Up to now, no one realized that the coaches' wives were behind what had happened to Penny. She'd have to rethink that and decide later if she should keep the story in the manuscript. She wanted the manuscript to deliver on the dirt, but not if it would mean possibly going to jail.

FIFTEEN

Lawna was hot. She needed to talk to someone, but none of the girls were available. She wanted to tell them the best way to combat B.J.'s book. B.J. was still ignoring everyone's calls. Lawna didn't know what to do; she was nervous, scared and frustrated at the same time. Here she had an idea and couldn't find a soul to share it with. Lawna picked up the phone and decided to try Mona again. But when Mona didn't answer the phone, Lawna thought she'd die for sure. Instead of waiting around, she snatched her keys and headed out of the house.

"She's got to listen to someone! This is crazy and it's gone far enough."

The others could sit back and act like the information B.J. had on them all didn't really pose a threat if they wanted, but Lawna didn't want to take that chance. As she was heading toward B.J. and Taylor's house in Brentwood, Lawna started thinking of all the things she would say to try and convince B.J. that this book was not a good idea. Sure, she wanted to show a united front, thinking her chances of getting through to B.J. would've been better if the others were with her, but she was running out of time. She needed to reason with the woman face to face.

What if they simply threatened to make up stuff about B.J.? Lawna thought for sure it might work. What was the likelihood that people would believe that the other wives were up to no good and B.J. was an angel?

Of course it wouldn't go that far. Lawna thought the threat alone would be enough for B.J. to see how foolish she was being. As she drove, she thought that her idea might work.

To Lawna's surprise, Taylor's Hummer was parked in the driveway when she arrived at the house. She thought he'd be out getting ready for the upcoming draft, but instead he was at home?

Lawna took the winding road that led to the Almonds' front door, parked and slid out of the car. She always admired the lush greenery and exotic-looking landscaping that seemed so inviting. They had massive palm trees in the front yard and flower beds with birds-of-paradise and other exotic flowers. Somehow it didn't look too over the top; just enough to give you the impression you may have traveled to another location outside of L.A.

When Lawna knocked on the massive double doors, she wondered if she'd luck out and find B.J. here. It would be so simple if they could simply sit and talk. But that hope quickly faded when the doors swung open and Taylor stood in front of her looking like a desperate and broken man.

"Aeey, Lawna," he said. His hooded eyes looked red and dreary. Even the bags beneath his eyes were sporting bags.

She almost didn't want to ask; the deranged look on his face told her B.J. was still gone.

"I was hoping to catch your wife at home," Lawna said.

"And I was hoping you could tell me where she is," Taylor said.

Now Lawna was mad at herself for even considering popping in on them.

"You gotta talk some sense into her," Taylor said.

"Coach, I don't know what to say." Taylor looked as if he was about to start crying again. His red, puffy eyes already indicated he must've spent a good amount of time shedding tears. She didn't know what to say to him. And now she feared showing up might've made things worse.

"When was the last time you talked to her?" Taylor asked. He was so fidgety, it was making Lawna nervous.

Lawna didn't even remember. She didn't want to tell him that none of them had seen or heard from B.J. since she dropped the bomb and stormed out. She wondered if he knew that his wife was planning a tell-all book. She'd be damned if she'd be the one to break the news to him. With the divorce and that lawsuit looming, she didn't think he could handle much more.

"Oh, I'm sorry. Come in; come in." Taylor stepped aside a bit.

"No, I was on my way somewhere and I stopped by 'cause this was on the way," she lied.

"Maybe if you tried to call her, you know, before you leave?" Taylor sounded frantic and Lawna felt bad for him. "I can't handle this shit right now. We got the draft coming up. I need to get this shit straight; we have too much riding on this season," he said.

Before Lawna could turn to leave, he was rushing back into the house.

"Here, let me try her again," he said.

In an instant, he was gone and back. When he reappeared this time, he had the phone to his ear. Before Lawna could say anything, Taylor was rambling into the phone. He sounded like he had gotten used to holding conversations with B.J.'s voicemail.

"Hey, B.J., your friend is here and she's worried about you, too, baby. I really need you to call home or something. Here's Lawna." Without any warning, he shoved the phone to Lawna's ear.

Lawna avoided eye contact; she couldn't take the hopefulness his eyes showed. She realized that B.J. wouldn't answer and she wondered why he didn't also realize it.

"Uh, yeah, B.J., it's me, and like Taylor said, we're all worried about you, so when you get this message, please call and let somebody know you're okay."

Lawna felt like a fool. She wanted to tell Taylor to forget it, to give B.J. her space, but he looked like he hadn't showered; he definitely hadn't shaved; and she could smell him, so she thought better of it.

He snatched the phone back and started rambling again. But the voicemail must've ended; he hung up and feverishly started dialing again.

"You know, Taylor, I'm gonna head out now," Lawna said. He was too wrapped up in the second message he was leaving for B.J. to even acknowledge her.

Instead of hanging around, Lawna eased off the front stairs and back to her car. By the time she took off and glanced into her rearview mirror, she saw Taylor standing in the doorway looking at the phone as if he was wondering why it had malfunctioned yet again.

"Now, if I was B.J. and I wanted to write a book, where would I go?" Lawna asked aloud as she pressed her stiletto slipper and mashed the pedal.

SIXTEEN

B.J. had to do some soul searching when she thought about writing about Ella Blu. She still didn't want to believe that the woman had grinned all up in her face, sat at her table and eaten her food, and all along she was yearning to take her place.

There was a tiny part of her that wished she could've been in the room when the lawsuit hit Ella's hands. She knew for a fact that the girl would crumble. Ella was weak. She needed to be led, and B.J. couldn't figure out how in the world Taylor was even attracted to her. He wasn't the type who looked for women who needed to be rescued. And Ella was the epitome of a damsel in distress at all times. None of it made sense to B.J.

"How could I not have seen this coming?" B.J. had cried so much she was tired. Her tears were a mixture of pain and disappointment. She was disappointed with her friends, but more so with herself. She should've known better than to allow someone into her inner circle. She was usually a superb judge of character. Some of her earliest memories involved her being strong. She recognized early on that she was destined to be a leader; her strong personality always catapulted her into that role among her friends. Whether it was high school, college, or at a job, followers seemed to gravitate to B.J. and she gladly took on the leadership role.

B.J. was a newcomer to their group, but still, she had done so much for the other wives. It was B.J. who had gotten up in the wee hours of the mornings when their husbands didn't come home. B.J. who babysat so wives could go chase down groupies or follow up on some lead they had gotten wind of, and this was how they repaid her? She couldn't fathom that she, of all people, was in this situation, and that her pain was caused by a woman she thought was a close friend.

"What is happening to my judgment?"

B.J. had long prided herself on being able to spot the sleaziest, most conniving skanks from a mile away. Was she losing her touch? And shouldn't she have known that Ella Blu was bad news from day one?

"Come on, Bobbi, shake it off and get back to writing," she told herself.

That's where she decided to start.

Ella Blu and I first met when Taylor was brought in mid-season to coach the Sea Lions. Ella was the first wife I met. She was at the press conference at administration where Taylor and I were introduced to the press as the new leadership for the team.

Now looking back, I must say, I had a bad feeling about her from the moment our eyes locked. Where the other reporters were all focused on Taylor and the team owner, Ella's eyes were focused on me. At first I thought maybe she was admiring my hairstyle or my outfit, but she kept staring. After a while, she was making me uncomfortable.

But I sat there with my smile intact. The reporters threw questions at Taylor like they were at a firing range.

"How do you feel about the change in mid-season?"

"What are you planning to do differently?"

"Coach Tomlin was known for relying on the passing game. Is that what you're sticking with?"

B.J. stopped writing and suddenly, she was back in that room, with bulbs flashing like crazy, and cameras fixated on her and Taylor.

Soon B.J. started wondering if she might have owed Ella money or something. Ella stared at B.J. like she needed to study her face because one day she might be asked to pick B.J. out of a line-up.

When the press conference was finally over and Taylor stood posing for pictures, B.J. tried to work her way farther into the background. Or so she thought.

A couple of female reporters approached and asked her a few questions, but when they moved on, Ella stepped up.

"I've seen you somewhere before." Ella smiled. She was cute enough, but B.J. was leery of people who tried to befriend her too eagerly.

"I can't imagine where," B.J. said as she eased onto the seat near the young woman who looked like she was trying way too hard. In addition to the extra-long, bone-straight hair weave that swung beneath her waist, Ella's makeup looked like she was headed to a porno set. It was too over the top and all the wrong colors for her complexion.

"Junior League?"

"Not a member." B.J. smiled.

"Jack and Jill?"

"Nope."

"It'll come to me," Ella said.

B.J. took in Ella's three-inch nails and the body that had to have been paid for, and she figured she had Ella Blu's number. Her fake boobs were at instant attention and even when Ella smiled, her features hardly ever moved.

"Where do you work?" Ella asked.

B.J. chuckled. "I don't."

That caused Ella's eyebrows to rise ever so slightly.

B.J. tried to ease back and look away, hoping that would be a signal to Ella that she didn't want to talk. But then Ella started talking again.

"I got it!" she screamed excitedly.

This woman was relentless.

B.J. could only thank God the room had thinned out a bit.

"Were you ever an NFL cheerleader?" Ella asked.

Unable to help herself, B.J. laughed aloud and that seemed to be all Ella needed. Even her body language changed a bit. B.J. noticed Ella had eased in closer.

"I've never been a cheerleader. Are you a reporter?" B.J. asked.

"Oh no, but I wanted to scope out the new head coach, and I was so shocked to see you. Honestly, when I picture a head coach's wife, someone like you doesn't come to mind; all young and sexy looking. I don't know. Instead, I pictured some wrinkled-up old lady who's sporting a bouffant and thinks she's fly!"

That made B.J. laugh, too.

"Well, I'm not old enough for wrinkles just yet," B.J. said.

"That's what I'm saying. You're all young and hot," Ella insisted.

B.J. shrugged her shoulders.

"So you're what it's like to be the head coach's wife?"

The way Ella asked it was almost as if she hadn't given thought to that possibility.

B.J. knew she was like most people who had a stereotypical image of a coach's wife, but for some reason, she could see herself with Ella. So against her better judgment, she decided to go out on a limb and open herself up to Ella.

Suddenly, Ella's eyes lit up and she smiled. "The girls are gonna love you," she said.

"The girls?" B.J. asked.

"Oh, yeah, some of us coaches' wives; we spend quality time together. Don't worry; you'll fit right in."

Since then, the early days, I thought I had witnessed a great transformation; I saw Ella blossom from a hootchie who was rough around the edges into a refined young lady. But little did I know, you can dress a hootchie up, but under all the designer labels, quality, toned-down makeup, and flashy, but tasteful jewelry, she's still a hootchie.

B.J. kept typing, and thinking about how easily Ella had pulled the wool over her eyes.

SEVENTEEN

After Ella's walk along the beach, she returned to her room and began pacing the plush carpeted floor. She'd been doing it for so long, she thought her legs would surely give out, but she had to do something with the nervous energy that was driving her crazy.

Her business was all over the news and she was scared to show her face. She still couldn't believe that Taylor hadn't reached out. Even with B.J. suing her! WTF? And what must Sterling be thinking? She still hadn't mustered up enough courage to call him.

"What to do? What to do?"

She'd been asking that question for the past few days, but the answer never seemed to surface. Thanks to B.J.'s lawsuit, Ella was certain everyone knew about her betrayal. Ella felt bad about the way B.J. had found out, but truth be told, Ella was glad the truth had finally slapped that one in the face.

She wanted to reach out to B.J. and tell her that Taylor's choice should be respected. She was sure they could all come to some sort of arrangement that would work out for everyone involved. But B.J. would never settle down enough for a civilized conversation like that.

It wasn't that Ella was jealous of B.J. or anything like that. She actually admired B.J. From the day they had met, B.J. was the epitome of the woman she wanted to one day become. But despite how she felt, she'd never set out to steal the woman's husband!

Taylor had simply caught her in a moment of weakness and by the time things spilled over into a full-fledged affair, well, she was hooked. Initially, there were so many times she wanted to break things off, but as time passed, she felt doing so would be detrimental to her husband's career, not to mention that she had broken one of the cardinal rules in Affairs 101: Never catch feelings. And that's exactly what she had done. She had fallen for Taylor something terrible.

Now everything was a mess. This wasn't how it was supposed to go down. She kept telling herself to forget it all. She hadn't planned to fall into bed with Taylor; she hadn't expected him to be as good as he was; and she definitely hadn't planned on getting hooked the way she had. Now all she wanted was for Taylor to come and fix everything. She knew he would. They meant too much to each other for him to do otherwise.

Besides, it was Taylor who complained about his life with B.J. as much as he could. He constantly talked about how bossy she was; he talked about how he had so much riding on his shoulders at work every day, that he'd love to come home to a woman who wasn't so tightly wound. Ella realized that B.J. was intense, but she really thought the woman was only like that with them. Never did she believe she wouldn't tone it down a bit for her husband. Didn't she understand that men needed to feel like they were in charge and running things at home? Every time Taylor complained about B.J., Ella would instantly compare herself to his wife. And in most cases she always came out on top, so why wouldn't she think she and Taylor were about to be together now?

Ella got up from the bed when the cell phone rang again. She looked in its direction, toward the credenza where she'd placed it. But she didn't move toward it.

"Damn!" She didn't even have to check caller ID to know who was calling. His ringtone was a dead giveaway. Her husband, Sterling, had been relentless with the calls. He was still trying to convince her to come back home so they could talk.

Ella didn't feel like talking to him, or anyone else. She needed to hear from Taylor; no one else would do. Lately she'd only been talking to herself, wondering what she could say to make her heart stop feeling the way it did. How come she couldn't remember any of Mona's motivational tips when she needed them most? Truth be told, she was doing everything she could to stop herself from dialing Taylor's number, and each day, her resolve was getting weaker and weaker.

She flopped down onto the wing chair and positioned herself to stare out of the window. But unfortunately for her, the glare from the window caused her reflection to bounce right back and she was face to face with herself. She was nothing without Taylor.

Then the images started again. Taylor had her head so messed up, she didn't know whether she was coming or going. Early on, Ella needed Taylor to end it; she didn't have the strength to do it on her own. He was drawn to her like a moth to a flame.

"Why isn't he calling?" Ella asked aloud. She gnawed on her bottom lip, bit at her fingertips, then inspected her nail bed. All the while, her mind traveled back to that night, the night that forever changed her life.

"Your first time here?" the thin man with a slick comb-over asked as Ella walked into the back room of the exclusive club. When she first stumbled onto the website that bragged about sugar daddies looking for younger women, she thought it was a joke.

Being new to L.A. at the time, she wasn't sure if she should trust it. But after weeks of logging on and reading some of the profile messages, she soon found herself in the chat rooms.

Nearly two months later, she had finally built up the courage to attend one of their private events, and that's where she had met Sterling. She was a twenty-three-year-old, bouncing from one temp office job to another, struggling to make ends meet, and hoping to find herself a rich and generous professional athlete. But Sterling had changed all of that.

He wasn't her type. He was much older, too full around the middle, and nothing like the hard-bodied studs she had grown accustomed to when she chased athletes. But after talking to him for three hours that night, she was intrigued. And daydreaming about being with him reminded her of the other women she wanted so desperately to emulate. They had secured their futures with a rich ball player, and Ella wanted to do the same.

"So you actually coach, like a real football team?" Ella had asked. At the time, she knew very little about the NFL, except that the players were paid very well, so she assumed a coach had to be paid just as well, if not better.

"Been coaching for more than twenty-five years," Sterling said.

Damn, that was longer than she'd been alive.

Ella noticed how he stuck his chest out a little more as he bragged about his job, and she thought it was cute.

"So, um…" Ella started. She allowed the straw to dangle between her lips, then lapped her tongue around it and sipped hard. Sterling was taking in her every move. "What's it like, being an NFL coach?"

It took a moment before Sterling answered. He sighed, then started, "Well, it's a stressful job. We're worked up all week about winning the next game, and when we wake up the morning after that next game, we're faced with the challenge of winning again and again. The pressure is incredible, and in all honesty, sometimes, it makes it kinda hard to enjoy what should be a fun job."

"Wow," Ella said, hanging on to his every word. She realized nervousness caused him to ramble on, and she thought that was kind of cute, too.

"Yeah, for most of us, the fun is in game preparation, the on-field stuff with players during the week and execution of the game plan on Sunday. That's what got most of us into the business in the first place—the love of football. It's all the other stuff—the endless scrutiny and heightened expectations—that eventually wears us down. But honestly, a lot of us coaches, especially by mid-point in the season, wake up each day feeling miserable."

She wasn't really *that* interested in what he had to say about coaching, but she figured if she appeared to be intrigued, he'd feel even more important, and that was something all men liked.

Two weeks after they'd met, Ella was moving into the exclusive Wilshire Towers apartment homes where Sterling lived lavishly and all alone. Six months later, they were married in a Vegas ceremony and, eleven months after that, Ella had given birth to one of their two daughters. That had been four years ago. She'd quickly fallen into a comfortable life with luxury at her fingertips and at her feet. She had a live-in nanny, a maid, and a part-time chef.

But Ella's life was far from the fairytale she had envisioned. She often thought about their first night together. She knew then, the only way she'd make it with Sterling, was if she kept something trustworthy and hard on the side. She hated thinking about sex with her husband, and that first time was enough to make her cringe each time it invaded her thoughts thereafter.

Ella squeezed her eyes shut and tried with all her might to swallow Sterling's little member between her walls, but it wasn't an easy task. Ella shook off the sweat that was running down the sides of her face, and clutched the headboard with all the strength she could muster up. She was overwhelmed with emotions, but not the kind that one would expect during a time like this. Ella was sweating. *She* was working overtime, not because Sterling was handling his business. She needed this to be over.

"Oh God, yes, baby, yes! Right there!" Ella screamed like a banshee, hoping he would cum soon.

"You like this cock, don't you?" Sterling asked through clenched teeth, like he was really delivering. Ella rocked her hips to match his strokes, but it was hard; his massive belly was in the way, making this far more difficult than Ella needed.

"Oh, Sterling, oh yes, baby. Ella loves it!" she screamed excitedly.

But the truth was, the only thing Ella really loved about fucking Sterling was the glue that seemed to seal her fate and future with him.

"I love this pussy," he proudly proclaimed, smacking her ass for good measure. His skin was covered in hair and pimples, but Ella told herself no man was perfect.

"Eeemmm-hmmm, Ella can tell! Is that why it's been so hard for so long?" she asked.

Their lovemaking never got better, but Ella told herself bad sex was a very small price to pay, considering Sterling Blu made sure she had everything she could possibly want.

When the phone rang again, she pushed those thoughts from her mind. It was Sterling again, but still she needed to think, and talking to him now would only make thinking even harder to do.

Ella thought about how she had wound up in such a fine mess. But she knew. It had started where all her problems had begun. She had always struggled with the ability to say no. It was no mystery why and how she had wound up married to a man twenty years her senior. Their friendship had blossomed into something she wasn't quite ready for, but she couldn't say no out of fear of hurting Sterling's feelings. Sure, she had grown to love him, but if she had a choice, he wouldn't have been her number one, and most definitely not her husband.

She realized that there was no way to go back in time. Her cell phone rang again. She rolled her eyes at it. Outside of Mona, Ella hadn't talked to anyone—not her husband, not her friends, and certainly not her lover.

"I wonder what Sterling did when he heard about the lawsuit?"

Ella had to chuckle to try and stop herself from crying. What in the world was she going to do?

EIGHTEEN

B.J. had been on a roll. She couldn't believe all the drama that surrounded her and her so-called friends' lives. Their lives didn't read like anyone's real life. She could hardly wait to finish the book. But just as she was about to get back to writing, she caught a glimpse of an old picture of herself, Taylor and Ella on the TV screen.

"Jesus!"

Since she was writing, she kept the TV on, but the volume down low. It helped her to not feel so alone. When she saw herself on TV, she quickly grabbed the remote and turned the volume up.

"Yes, this real-life soap opera is spiraling out of control. In addition to a lawsuit, word is that Bobbi Almond is also supposed to be writing a tell-all book!"

There were two of them. Male and female anchors sitting at a desk and they were having fun with the story. B.J. hated the sports' shows; they were always kind of loose with the facts.

"Have you seen any details of the lawsuit?" the woman asked the man sitting next to her.

"Oh, like you don't know!" B.J. yelled at the TV.

"I'm glad you asked," the man said through a phony-looking smile. "There are accusations of drug use, borderline abuse, payments for prostitution, a gambling problem, and we haven't even seen the pages of this forthcoming tell-all yet! Rumor has it, the title is *Blowin' the Whistle*!"

The female anchor turned to the camera and smiled, with wide eyes.

"Well, if that's any indication of what we can expect in the new book, *Blowin' the Whistle*, I don't know what to say about Coach Almond and his staff. With all this going on *off* the field, we'll be lucky if they can concentrate and win a few games."

"Who cares about him winning games? Let the bastard lose!" B.J. yelled at the TV screen again.

She poured herself a glass of ice water and tried to calm down. She needed to get back to the manuscript.

"Focus; focus," she said as she started typing where she had left off before.

Chapter Thirteen

The night Jewel was nearly arrested, I thought all of our husbands' careers would surely take a complete nose dive. But we were able to work it out. Don't get me wrong. Zeke was a lowlife of a dog, but at times Jewel let her anger get the best of her.

And the night that she decided to fix what was wrong with her marriage, there was no stopping her. But as much as her husband ran around, the groupies made it their business to fuck with her. The weekend the Giants were coming for a home game, Jewel got an anonymous call telling her exactly where she could find her husband's car, when it should've been at home.

Jewel cursed as she slowed to stop at the light. In addition to the phone call, she had also received a voicemail message, and an anonymous letter telling her where she would be able to find Zeke's car. The information was accurate; there it was, parked in front of the east L.A. apartment of some woman named Tameka Washington. Unfortunately for Zeke, his truck was exactly where the letter, message, and caller said it would be.

Jewel sat behind the wheel of her own car for a very long time. She didn't know what to do. She was so far beyond the "why is he doing this" stage, or the "why aren't I enough," but she couldn't leave him; no matter what. She didn't want to wind up like her mother. Jewel wanted to age gracefully, not working some dead-end nine-to-five to make ends meet. She saw how it had aged her mom and following in those footsteps was one of her biggest fears.

The first thing she was accomplishing was taking very good care of her body. Jewel worked out religiously and had started a business to help women look and feel their very best. Unlike her mother, who didn't care about her appearance, Jewel wanted people to have to guess her age in her golden years.

If she could hang in there with Zeke for ten years, she would be guaranteed half of his NFL pension, and *that* money would allow her to live the lifestyle she'd quickly grown accustomed to. No, she couldn't leave Zeke, but she needed to let him know that she meant business.

Jewel took a deep breath.

Instead of banging on Tameka's front door, or screaming and carrying on like some woman scorned, Jewel stepped out of the car and pulled out her box cutter. Drastic situations called for drastic measures, as far as she was concerned.

She went to work on his beloved, royal blue Yukon Denali. She worked quickly and efficiently. By the time she was done, all four tires were slashed, and a few choice words were carved deep into the paint on every side.

When she was satisfied, Jewel wiped sweat from her forehead and stood back to admire her work.

"That'll teach his ass!" She spat on his car and climbed back into hers.

She'd been on the road about twenty minutes when he started

blowing up her phone. Jewel figured he must've realized she knew he was lying up with Tameka.

By the time she pulled up in front of their place, Jewel was no longer in the mood to be home alone. This time when her cell phone rang, she snatched it up real fast.

"B.J.!" she screamed.

"Hey, what's going on?" B.J. asked. "You don't sound so good."

"Hey, lady, that bastard Zeke has done it again." Jewel sighed.

"Umph, what has he done this time?"

That was one of many late-night talks she'd have with B.J.

"Okay, let me see. I guess I should've asked who's Zeke screwin' this time?" B.J. said sarcastically.

"I'm so tired of his shit," said Jewel.

"Why don't you swing by so we can talk? Taylor's gone and the kids are at my mom's," B.J. said.

"Okay, I'm on my way."

As she drove, Jewel kept a nervous eye on the rearview mirror. She was certain either Zeke or the police would soon be on her trail. A little while later, Jewel pulled up at the Almonds' house. She parked, hopped out, then rushed up to the large double doors. She was still as nervous as she had been when she had finished redesigning Zeke's beloved vehicle.

The door swung open before she could knock or ring the bell.

"Hey, lady," B.J. greeted.

B.J. smiled and stepped aside to allow Jewel inside.

The moment Jewel entered the house, she was about to unload a heap of misery. But B.J. had made it clear she was always there for the other coaches' wives. She understood that being married to such high-profile husbands came with its own set of problems.

B.J. had popcorn and cold wine waiting. Jewel figured B.J. already knew the earful she was about to receive. By the time

Jewel was on her third refill of wine, she had told B.J. every detail of the sinful story, including her role in vandalizing Zeke's truck.

"That's what he gets," B.J. said, rising from the sofa.

"Umph, umph, umph!" Jewel took another sip of wine. Her mind was racing with thoughts of what else she should've done.

The entire time she was with B.J., Zeke kept calling.

When Jewel finally got tired of him calling like he had no sense, she turned the cell phone off. Jewel considered crashing at B.J.'s, but decided that probably wasn't the best thing to do. She didn't know when Taylor would come back and she didn't need him all in her business.

"So what you going to do about that husband of yours?" B.J. asked.

Jewel used her palms to dry rub her face, and looked at B.J. Jewel shook her head, then sighed.

"I have no idea," she said.

"It is a tough one," B.J. said.

B.J. knew how Jewel felt about Zeke.

"You know what? It's time for me to start fighting fire with a little fire of my own," Jewel suddenly said.

B.J. raised an eyebrow, but she didn't say a word.

Then there was a knock at the door.

"Who the hell could that be at this hour?" B.J. got up to go answer the door.

The two officers stood at the door and they looked like they'd rather be anywhere but there.

"Is the owner of this vehicle here?" one officer asked as he pointed at Jewel's car.

"Yes. Is there a problem, officers?"

"We're investigating a vandalism case," one of the officers said. "Mister Swanson said we could find his wife here."

Luckily, Taylor arrived home at that moment and, between him and B.J., they had convinced the officers not to haul Jewel off to jail. When all was said and done, she had gotten off with a warning and the officers had left with game tickets.

NINETEEN

Jewel had no business walking into this scene as if she didn't have a care in the world. But she couldn't help herself, or she didn't want to; not yet. She'd try to get in touch with B.J. later, but for now, she needed this.

Usher was crooning softy in the background. Jewel noticed that Tierrany had replaced the regular bulbs with red ones, softening the room, in anticipation of the evening ahead. And candlelight flickered all around the room, giving off a kind of surreal ambiance. Couple that with the aroma from the rose petals strewn all around, and the mood was just right, prime for what was about to go down.

Jewel had pushed all thoughts of her skirt-chasing husband and B.J.'s vindictive behind from her head. She wanted Tierrany to fix everything that ailed her, make it all okay, if only for a few hours. That was the kind of power Tierrany had over her and Jewel willingly succumbed to it every chance she got.

"Come here; stretch out on the chaise; let me make you feel good," Tierrany said.

Jewel did as she was told and spread her legs wide. Tierrany sat between them and passed Jewel a chilled champagne flute. They touched their glasses and sipped as Tierrany used her free hand to massage Jewel's inner thigh, her weak spot.

Jewel watched Tierrany intently; then they kissed. Jewel enjoyed the way Tierrany sucked her face and neck hungrily before moving down to her full breasts. She released a moan.

When Jewel pulled her head back and watched Tierrany at work, she could hardly contain her excitement.

"Oh, Teeearny," she squealed, an ecstasy-induced smile plastered across her face.

When Tierrany took Jewel's champagne flute and splashed some of the ice-cold sticky bubbly across her breasts, she trembled, but giggled and gave Tierrany that look that said she was ready.

"Sssss. Tierrany!" Jewel cried again, as Tierrany sopped up the tangy liquid.

Jewel loved screaming Tierrany's name. It was like an aphrodisiac she simply couldn't get enough of.

"Yeeeessss!" she whimpered.

Tierrany worked every nook and cranny, being extra careful not to miss a spot on Jewel's well-toned body. Tierrany desired to give Jewel pleasure in areas Jewel probably had never imagined. Tierrany believed her attentiveness to that important factor was what kept Jewel coming back for more. Soon, Tierrany had Jewel squirming and begging for more.

When they finished, and lay spooned in the afterglow of satisfaction, Tierrany whispered into Jewel's ear.

"Babe, you had a chance to think about that proposal I sent you?"

Jewel stiffened a bit. She had promised Tierrany that she would think about it, but the truth was, she had no idea how she could remove fifteen thousand dollars from their account and not have to answer to Zeke about it.

"That spa you want to buy into, right?" Jewel stalled.

"Yeah, they're kinda pressing me for an answer, but I don't wanna worry you about it," Tierrany said.

Jewel didn't say another word.

TWENTY

B.J. didn't understand the press. It seemed like the more she avoided their interview requests, the more stories they ran about her! And how the hell did everyone get copies of the lawsuit anyway? She was waiting for the word from her publicist before talking to the media. The publisher wanted them to come up with a plan before she started doing interviews.

When her phone rang, B.J. didn't recognize the number. Was it one of her friends trying to trick her into answering their call? Curiosity was killing her. But she didn't give in.

She was about to write about Mona. The phone started ringing again.

"Who is that? And why aren't they leaving a message?"

B.J. finally grabbed the phone.

"Hello?"

"Bobbi Almond, guurrl, how are you?"

"Who is this?" B.J. asked curtly.

"Oh, my bad, gurrl. It's Saaaasha. I only wanted to tell you, you go, gurrl! What you're doing? Standing up and saying you're not taking this shit laying down. Gurrl, you my *SHERO*!"

"Sasha?"

"Yeah, B.J., what's up?"

"Where do I know you from?"

"B.J., quit being silly! Gurrl, you are too much! Oh, so now you don't know me, right?" Sasha laughed as if she hadn't heard anything so funny in quite a while.

"Sasha Davenport?" B.J. asked like she couldn't believe it.

"I thought so!" Sasha said. "Now, gurrl, if I was you, let me tell you what I would do. First off, I'd find that trick, Ella, and whup her ass! I mean, that was supposed to be your *girl*, and she screwin' yo' man? Oh hell to da' naw. Where I'm from, that's a serious violation, one that can only be remedied with a good ol'-fashioned ass-whupping!"

B.J. listened as Sasha went on like they were old friends. Sure, she knew of Sasha. Pretty much everyone in the professional sports circle did. Sasha had already been through two very high-profile athlete husbands and worked like she was always in search of the next, whether he was already taken or not. But B.J. couldn't think of a time that she had either reached out to the woman or had implied that she wanted to. They had never been friends and B.J. wanted to keep it that way.

"Sasha? I need to go," B.J. said dryly.

"Oh, guurrl, my bad. I didn't mean to hold you. I wanted to let you know that some of us are really feeling what you tryin' to do. And please believe, if I run into that skank hoe, Ella, before you, I'ma bitch slap her ass on GP! Believe that!"

"Oookay," B.J. said, rolling her eyes at the foolishness.

"I'ma check in on you from time to time, but you keep your head up, chicka!"

After they hung up, B.J. wondered what that was all about. Not only did she *not* talk to Sasha Davenport, but the few run-ins they'd had in the past left it pretty clear that she never wanted to. Sasha was loud, flashy, and always looking for a way to promote herself.

B.J. turned her attention back to Mona. She positioned her fingers on the keyboard and got busy.

Now talk about a bag of mixed nuts. Mona Brown was good at what she did. She packed the house when and wherever she spoke. I never understood how her clients looked to her for advice; especially since when it came to her own life, she couldn't fix all that was wrong even if she had magic tools.

Her husband had been steps away from fading completely into the background before he got the job with the Sea Lions. Personally, I think he resented her success. Sometimes coaches wanted to be the only star in the family and couldn't handle it when the little lady began to outshine them. That was my assessment of their marriage.

At times it was a bit confusing about how their relationship worked. Mona needed everything to be perfect at all times. And like the rest of us, Melvin was far from perfect. As a matter of fact, he wasn't even trying to get close to perfection.

TWENTY-ONE

When Mona grabbed the wheel of her convertible Jaguar, her finger inadvertently changed the band on her radio from her favorite FM station to 570 AM. That's when she caught a bit of the Myers and Hartman show and nearly ran off the road.

"All I want to know is whether Coach Taylor's going to be able to handle the upcoming draft with all this drama going on," one of the show hosts said.

"OHMYGOD!" Mona grabbed the steering wheel with both hands and pressed a button to turn the radio up.

Suddenly the near perfect sunny L.A. afternoon seemed dark and gloomy.

"Do these guys not have anything better to talk about? Why aren't they talking about the damned draft?" Mona was so mad at B.J., she felt like she could strangle her. She didn't need this shit right now. What the hell would this mess do to the tour?

As the two hosts went back and forth about whether the Sea Lions drama would be enough to rival those of Tiger Woods and baseball analyst, Steve Phillips, who was fired from ESPN after admitting to an affair with an assistant, Mona considered calling in to the show.

But what would she say? This was surely merely the beginning. She had to do something and she had to do it fast. As Mona stopped at a light, what she heard next made her want to pull over and puke.

"So, did you hear she's going to be on the *Today* show?"

"No, really?"

"Yes, she's supposed to talk about the lawsuit and give a sneak peek at her book, *Blowin' the Whistle!*"

It was too much! Mona was fit to be tied! Before long, everyone would know the stupid title and the damn book wasn't even out yet. B.J. was going on *Today*? A national news program! What would this do to her sponsors? Was it too late for damage control? All of this was racing wildly through Mona's mind. What the hell could she do? She couldn't find B.J.; Taylor was spacing out; and she was trying to avoid a nervous breakdown her damn self.

They were planning to fill the Staples Center. This tour was huge! There was no way they could refund everyone's money. They also had national media scheduled. She couldn't face her backers, supporters, and legions of fans to say there was a problem.

All of a sudden, Mona looked up and couldn't remember where the hell she was going. She turned off Hill Street downtown and pulled over to the curb. This was becoming too much! She had worked too damn hard to have everything destroyed because B.J. was humiliated.

Suddenly, a feeling of desperation washed over Mona. She closed her eyes, and started counting quietly. Then just as quickly, her eyes snapped open and she started laughing hysterically. She felt jittery and her eyes darted around wildly. Her breathing accelerated and she struggled to calm herself.

She finally snapped out of it. Mona exhaled and cleared her throat. She pressed another button on her steering wheel. Instantly, the radio went off and a dial tone rang out through the speakers.

"Hello?"

When her husband answered, she wondered if calling him was a good idea. But it was too late so she tried to play it off.

"Melvin, can you hear me?"

"Yeah, babe. Whassup?"

"I was wondering if there had been any phone messages for me," Mona said.

Her husband sounded a bit lost, but she didn't care.

"Uh, what?"

"I'm waiting on a call," Mona tried to explain.

"Why wouldn't they call you on your cell phone?" he asked.

"I gave the house number," Mona said, but even she didn't believe what she was saying.

"Okay. That don't make any sense, but nobody called the house phone for you," Melvin said.

"Hmm."

"What's going on?"

"Nothing. I'm waiting on this call; that's all," Mona said.

"It's that important to you, but you decided to give them the house number instead of your cell, even though we don't use the house phone?"

Mona wasn't making any sense, but she thought if she called Melvin and he knew what was being talked about in the sports world, he'd say something to her about it. The fact that he didn't gave her a small sense of relief.

"Oh, here's my call coming in now. I'll talk to you later, honey," Mona said and quickly ended the call.

She dialed Lawna's number.

"Hey, girl, what's going on?"

"B.J. is going on *Today*," Mona said.

There was silence on the other end.

"So she's in New York?"

"I don't know. They could be doing the interview by Skype or she could be going to the local NBC station here," Mona said.

"Damn, I can't believe this crap! Mona, she's gonna ruin everything!"

Mona sighed. "We're going to take care of this."

"You keep saying that. You said you had a plan, but guess what? B.J. is still M.I.A. No one knows where she is. I went by the house the other day. Coach looks like a lost zombie and I don't know what the hell to do! I'm so done with this mess! I'm just through!"

"I'm on it!" Mona yelled.

"I'm sick of all this mess! I can't have my business all across the country. It'll ruin my life and my husband's career—"

"Lawna, calm down; I said that I'll take care of it. Let me make some calls. Let's meet later for drinks. Call Jewel and see if she can meet us."

"What are you gonna do, Mona?"

"Don't you worry about that. Just call Jewel and see if she can meet. I should have some news for you guys by this evening."

Mona ended the call with Lawna and dialed a number she should've dialed a long time ago. She finally felt like she was making some progress.

TWENTY-TWO

"What is up with her?!" Ella yelled into the phone the moment Mona answered. "Enough with the damn interviews already! What does she hope to accomplish by going around doing interviews? Mona, I thought you were gonna try and talk to her."

"Not now, Ella," Mona said.

"You got someone there? What's up?"

"We're all upset over this mess. It's all everyone is talking about, but B.J. isn't talking to any of us. I'm not sure what to tell you."

"You can tell me why you sound like that. You've been getting all salty with me lately," Ella said.

"If I'm getting salty, it's because I'm not sure you realize the turmoil everyone is going through right now. I don't understand why it had to be Taylor," Mona said.

"Mona, I told you before, this thing with Taylor and me, it's the real thing. It's not gonna end well for B.J. That's all I can say right now."

"Ella, Lawna told me he's been calling, trying to patch things up to get his family back together. Honey, I think he hopes to go back to his wife," Mona said softly.

Ella didn't linger on Mona's words too long; she didn't want to show the hurt she felt. She giggled a bit, like Mona was telling her a funny little joke instead of the devastating news she wanted to deny. But then, there was still that part of her that wanted to hang on tightly to all the sweet things Taylor had whispered in her ears. Who was Mona to tell her what Taylor felt about her? Had she not lain beneath him? Had their bodies not become one? Had their juices not mixed?

She'd wait to hear from Taylor before she labeled what they had as "over." But Ella knew better than to say that to Mona. She'd allow her to keep thinking that she understood the depth of their relationship.

"Okay, Mona, I see we'll have to show you, too," Ella said with a chuckle.

"Ella—"

"Well, what about Jewel and Lawna? What are they saying about this?" Ella cut her off.

"They're pretty much saying the same thing I'm saying. What can we do? We need to figure out how to stop the bleeding."

Ella rolled her eyes. She never knew what she was getting with Mona. One minute the woman was on a natural high; the next she was as pessimistic as ever. And oh the drama! Ella sighed.

"So what's up with you and Melvin?" Ella was getting more than a little frustrated with Mona. Here she was hoping her friend was working on her behalf, and it appeared Mona was doing nothing.

"Ella, I'm trying to keep my marriage together by finding B.J. so we can try to fix this mess before it gets too out of control."

"Hmm, well, if you ask me, the freak is already on a rampage. She's going around making a fool out of herself by trying to justify suing me and her husband. What is she thinking?"

Mona had quieted down considerably. Ella couldn't wait until Taylor called. She figured they'd put their heads together and map out a way to quiet all the doubters.

Even now, alone in the hotel room, Ella's body still yearned for

Taylor's touch. To say what they shared was an electrifying connection was an understatement. She literally felt sparks when he touched her. And oh, how he knew just how to touch her in all the right places. Now all Ella had were memories. Here she was locked up in this hotel room alone with her thoughts and those haunting memories. One such memory did manage to bring a smile to her face.

The weekly family dinners were a time for the coaching staff and their families to come together and escape the pressures of the season. During one of those outings, Ella and Taylor were nervous. They were extra careful to avoid eye contact out of fear that someone might detect what they were struggling to hide.

Suddenly, Ella pushed her chair back and rose.

"You okay?" Mona asked.

"Yeah, heading to the little girls' room," Ella said as Taylor stood at the opposite end of the long table. She purposely waited until he was quite a ways down the hall before she turned to leave in the same direction.

Before turning, her eyes took in the intense conversation B.J. was having with one of the line coaches' wives. As always, B.J. thrived at the center of the spotlight. She probably never even noticed her husband had slipped away.

On shaky but eager legs, Ella strolled toward the back of the large restaurant. She hoped no one was paying attention to her, although she figured Mona probably was. But Mona would hold her secret.

The hallway that led to the door that closed off the restroom was long and darkened. When Ella reached for the door handle, another hand covered hers. She wanted to melt right there.

"Hurry, we don't have much time," his voice whispered in her ear.

She felt the heat from his breath on her neck and that made her even weaker. Her juices were already flowing and her pulse began to race.

A man walked out of the restroom, still adjusting himself in his jeans as he moved.

"Excuse me," he said.

Once he had passed, Taylor and Ella clumsily stumbled into the men's restroom and went into the last stall. Taylor's hands were moving so quickly, exploring her body as if this were his first time. Ella felt her body tremble in response. She was so excited; she didn't think she'd be able to contain herself much longer. His lips locked on to her lobes and he suckled them before moving down to her neck, then her collarbone. He sucked her skin as if it was his favorite flavor.

Ella's hands explored his body, as if she was trying to remind her brain of what was there. Then, she grabbed his zipper and eased it down to free him. She manhandled his stiffness and savored the sensation of having his bulging veins in the palm of her hands. She squeezed tightly.

"Damn, that feels so good," he said.

They kissed. He sucked her tongue in a frantic and hungry manner. She met his pace. He hiked up her skirt, grabbed her thighs, and lifted her off the floor. Ella's crotchless panties were his favorite; something B.J. would never wear.

With her back up against the wall, she relished the taste of his tongue as it wrestled with hers. When he used both hands to cup her behind, his stiffness instinctively found its way to her opening.

Ella welcomed him with warm wetness and felt him melt into her flesh.

"Oh God," he breathed.

"Hurry," she cried.

"Sssh…" Taylor used a hand to cover her mouth as he bucked his hips and rammed deeper. He moved with a rhythm that seemed perfectly in tune with her body. She loved everything about him—the way he smelled, the way he moved, and especially the way he felt.

It was so intense, so fast, and so passionate. Ella's soul was an out-of-control fire; she needed every inch of him, everything he had to offer.

As the door creaked open, her eyes widened in utter bliss. Taylor grabbed at her mouth again and quieted her as he exploded in ecstasy.

By the time they had eased their way back to the group at the table, Ella before Taylor, no one had seemed to miss them. But the smile that curled at the corners of Ella's lips didn't go completely unnoticed.

Mona leaned over and whispered, "You're playing with fire."

What Ella wouldn't give to be back in that bathroom stall again. She looked at the lifeless phone on the dresser and willed it to ring.

Why wasn't he calling? Why hadn't he gotten in touch? Now that it was out in the open, shouldn't they team up and decide how to handle B.J. and Sterling? They could work this out, but they needed to do it together.

Suddenly her heart began to race. Something was wrong! It had to be; nothing else made sense. He should have reached out to her by now.

TWENTY-THREE

B.J. held the phone as her mother behaved like a kid excited about a trip to Disneyland.

"So, baby, I'm gon' be able to see you on national TV?" Vernice squealed.

B.J. loved when her mother was excited, and Vernice was beyond excited over the news that *her* daughter was going to be on a national TV program.

"I done called everybody I know. I even called Ms. Mary. You know how she's always bragging 'bout her girl and that little picture she had in the *Wave* paper."

"It's not like it's the *L.A. Times* or anything like that."

B.J. behaved as if it bothered her; the way her mother and her friends were constantly comparing their children and grand-children as if they were vying for prizes. But deep down, she was glad her mother had someone to brag about. Lord knows her brother and sister were not worth mentioning.

The only problem was Ms. Mary didn't care for B.J. all that much. It had all started when a huge ticket fiasco had threatened to drive a wedge between Vernice and Mary. Mary's son had promised a group of his friends tickets to the big game between the Sea Lions and the Raiders. When B.J. informed Ms. Mary that she couldn't provide twenty tickets to one person unless they were paying for them, Ms. Mary and her son didn't take it too well.

B.J. was accustomed to it; people always thought coaches and players got free unlimited tickets. Nothing was further from the truth.

Coaches received four tickets to home games; players got two. And there were no special discounts for coaches or players. So when B.J. told Mary what the tickets would cost her son, she started accusing B.J. of forgetting where she had come from. Needless to say, Mary no longer talked to B.J.

"Yeah, but do you know the women's auxiliary still talks about that in church? No big deal to you, but them ol' biddies at church really get a kick outta stuff like that."

"Well, I don't know how they're going to feel about my appearance on *Today*. I'm going on to talk about my lawsuit and the book I'm writing."

"Yeah, about that suit, baby," Vernice began. All of the excitement had drained from her voice.

B.J. cut her off, so Vernice quickly switched gears.

"And, chile, I can't believe my daughter is going to be a published author! Oooh weee!"

"Mom, I already told you, this book is going to make a lot of people upset. Let's assume that I won't win any awards for this one."

"What's that supposed to mean?" Vernice asked.

"I'm just saying, I'm talking about some stuff in this book that people really don't want me to discuss."

"Oooh, like what?" Vernice's voice had lost all of its previous excitement.

"Well, my friends' secrets are about to become front page news." B.J. laughed, despite herself.

"What's that supposed to mean?"

Suddenly, B.J. didn't like her mother's tone. B.J. wasn't the villain. It was Ella and the rest of them who had done *her* wrong!

"Mom, you don't understand and I don't have time to explain it right now. I need to get a good night's sleep, so there won't be any bags under my eyes when I'm on TV tomorrow."

"Yeah, but what's this interview got to do with your friends and their secrets, Bobbi?"

"I don't want to talk about it. Let me go so I can get some rest. I'll call you tomorrow when I'm done with the interview."

B.J. didn't like the sound of her mother's voice.

"Baby, I don't want you on national TV saying bad things about those friends of yours. Baby, what's happenin' with you? I mean, you won't talk to Taylor; now you're tellin' me your friends' business is about to be spread all over the place and you doin' the spreadin'?" Vernice sighed.

"Mom, let me say goodnight to the kids before we get off," B.J. said, unable to stand the lecture any longer.

Her kids were always excited to talk to her. She promised herself to do whatever it took to shield them from the drama surrounding her and their father.

First B.J. talked to her son, then her daughter. She promised them both that they'd spend time together really soon. She felt better after hearing their voices, but the minute her mother got back on the line, B.J. rushed and got off the phone.

Despite herself, B.J. started thinking about her mother's words almost immediately after their call ended. Why should she feel bad? She hadn't done a thing wrong. She was the victim here. The other wives probably felt much closer to Ella, but B.J. was convinced they had hid the affair and, for that, she felt they all had to pay.

Long after their conversation ended, she kept telling herself she was doing the right thing. She wasn't the one who had cheated on her husband. That lowlife had cheated on her, and with a woman she had considered a good friend. No, B.J. had nothing to be ashamed about.

She started going over the notes from her earlier conversation with her publicist. B.J. had spent hours on the phone going through a sort of boot camp for this interview.

Before going to bed, she put a cleansing mask on her face and tied her hair up. As usual, her cell phone was ringing like crazy, but she was trying to gather her thoughts before going to bed. She had already talked to her children, ignored tons of calls from Taylor, and watched in pity as one by one, Jewel, Lawna, and Mona had called her back to back multiple times.

It seemed like one moment B.J. was soaking in the hotel's massive garden tub, then the next, a noise was shattering her world.

After raising her head and focusing on the nearby alarm clock, she realized it was the next day! She banged down on the button to end the noise.

"Oh, God! Did I oversleep?"

Jumping up from bed and rushing to the bathroom, B.J. ran the shower and tried to think about what she should wear.

"Red or cobalt blue really pops on camera, and that's what you want to do," her publicist had said.

B.J. reached into the closet and pulled out a form-fitting cobalt blue Ralph Lauren sweater and a pair of black Dolce & Gabbana stretch slacks that looked like they were made specifically for her body. She finished her outfit off with a pair of strappy, high-heeled Gucci sandals.

The car service the station had sent was there promptly at 4:30 a.m., and B.J. was ready. She felt like royalty, knowing all of this was being made possible because she was writing a book. It helped her to push her mother's words even further back into her mind.

She hadn't done a thing wrong; nothing but trusted a group of women who obviously didn't give a damn about her.

Finally satisfied with her image in the mirror, B.J. walked out and closed her hotel room door. It was pitch dark outside. B.J. looked around as she made a quick dash for the waiting car. It was a black Lincoln Town Car with darkened windows. The driver helped her into the car, after a professional greeting. She eased into the comfortable backseat and prepared for the ride through the dark L.A. streets. Once they pulled up at 3000 Alameda Street in Burbank, the butterflies came to life in the pit of her belly. But B.J. knew how to handle that as well.

"Mrs. Almond?" A young woman greeted her at the side entrance to the studio. She looked more like a teenager playing dress-up than an actual station employee.

"Yes."

"We're so glad you could join us. They're waiting for you in makeup," she said as she guided B.J. into the building. They walked down a long hall and passed several closed doors before entering a room at the end of the hall.

"Here you go," the young woman said.

She turned to leave once B.J. opened the door. Once inside, B.J. realized there were racks of clothes and more makeup than she had ever seen in her life. Two women stood off in a corner, but one approached when she noticed B.J. enter the room.

"Hi, B.J.?" the thin redhead asked. She sported a lopsided bob that B.J. found unique. She was pretty in an odd kind of way.

"Yes." B.J. smiled.

"I'm Helen. Looks like you caught us at a slow point, so choose your chair."

"Oh, thanks, but I won't be needing any of that." B.J. motioned toward the stacks and stacks of makeup.

Helen tilted her head to the side and looked at B.J. as if she was trying to examine her skin.

"Well, I wouldn't advise you going on TV without any makeup at all."

"I did my makeup in the car on the ride over."

Helen chuckled and raised her multi-colored eyebrows. "Yeah, but that's not studio makeup, which is what I recommend. The lighting out there won't do you any justice without some of this."

She rummaged through a drawer, then held up a small compact that seemed to be the perfect match to the color of B.J.'s skin.

"But it's your call," Helen said, half-shrugging her shoulders as if it didn't matter to her one way or another.

B.J. pondered it for a moment, then finally gave in, deciding that since she was about to be the center of attention for all the world to see, she might as well look her very best. When Helen was finished with her makeup, B.J. couldn't believe how good she looked. She had on lots of makeup, but it didn't feel like she did. And when she looked at her reflection, she was happy to see that it wasn't so much that she didn't look like herself. B.J. hated when women wore too much.

Everything seemed to move at the speed of light. After makeup and sitting in the green room, where she watched other interviews that were on before hers, suddenly it was B.J.'s turn. The escort came to walk her from the green room to the set. It was a large, cold room with several mounted cameras and light stands everywhere. B.J. perked up a bit when, off in the distance, she recognized the part of the set that people saw at home when they were watching TV.

She was seated at a desk and told which monitor she needed to look at when the interview started. As B.J. got comfortable in the chair, she glanced over and noticed Matt Lauer in his chair.

Suddenly, he turned to the left, and it appeared as if he was looking directly at her all the way from Studio 1-A in New York. B.J. couldn't help but feel every bit the part of a real celebrity. At first Matt appeared on the screen alone. He was mid-sentence by the time she focused on what he was saying.

"And now, we're living in a time when professional athletes and scandal seem to go hand-in-hand, but very rarely do we hear from that inner circle, the athletes and those who know them best." B.J. wasn't sure where Matt was going with this, but she listened intently. When Matt turned to the right, she realized there was now a split screen and she was in the left box with him in the right.

"Well, all of that is about to change. Our next guest is Bobbi Almond, known to her friends as B.J., the wife of the Los Angeles Sea Lions head coach, Taylor Almond."

Bobbi smiled and nodded like she'd seen other people do as they were being introduced on TV interviews.

"Bobbi, thanks for getting up so early. The sun probably isn't up on the West Coast yet, but we're glad you were able to join us and talk about your newest project, a tell-all appropriately titled *Blowin' the Whistle*."

"Matt, I'm glad to be here," B.J. said. B.J. hoped her nervousness didn't overshadow the interview. She mentally coached herself to remain calm and breathe.

"Well, let's get straight to it, but before we talk about the book, we want to ask about this lawsuit."

"There isn't much to talk about as far as that's concerned," B.J. said sternly. She thought they were going to discuss the book. She did not want to talk about the lawsuit.

"On the contrary," Matt said. "You are suing your husband and the woman you say allegedly caused the breakup of your marriage."

"Matt, I'll let my lawyers talk about the lawsuit. That's not my area of expertise. But if you want to talk about *Blowin' the Whistle*, the hot, forthcoming book that everyone is eagerly anticipating, *that* I can do."

"Well, there is surely a buzz around this book. I'm glad you had time to give us a sneak peek."

"Matt, it's no surprise that there's a buzz. So many people are curious about the lives of professional athletes, coaches, and those of us who are close to them that oftentimes, they have to make stories up. With *Blowin' the Whistle*, I wanted to set the record straight, so to speak," B.J. said.

"Yes, and everything we've heard about this book implies we should brace ourselves for some pretty salacious stories," Matt said, then looked down at his notes as if he was trying to figure out what to ask next.

B.J. took that moment to jump in. "Well, Matt, this is a tell-all book, so if by 'salacious' you mean these stories will be filled with juicy details of all aspects of the lives of my friends and myself, then I guess you can describe it that way." She shrugged as if the comment didn't really bother her.

"See, Mrs. Almond, that's where the confusion comes in. If these are your friends, why would you be writing a book like this in the first place?"

Now B.J. was beginning to get a little irritated. She didn't expect him to ask that question specifically, but the publicist had warned her about being prepared for just about anything. B.J. inhaled deeply, then shifted her body in the chair.

"Matt, all I can say to you and your viewers is, why bother picking up the *National Enquirer*, or *Star*, or another tabloid when I'm willing to give firsthand accounts of true stories that I not only witnessed, but in many cases, took part in myself? The book is titled *Blowin' the Whistle* for a reason."

"I get that, but still, many are probably just as curious about why you decided to write this book. You described these women as your friends. How do they feel about your decision to pen this book?"

B.J. threw her hands up in mock defense; then she giggled. She didn't understand why people kept trying to make her feel bad about writing the book. Where were all of these morality judges when her friends were stabbing her in the back?

"Whoa, Matt, that's quite a bit there. First off, I am a writer. I decided to write what I know and what I know is that your viewers will definitely be entertained when they pick up their copy of *Blowin' the Whistle*."

"Yes, I gather that, but what about your friends? What has been their reaction to this?"

"Matt, I can't speak for anyone else, but I will say my friends are aware of the project and I'm sure that once the story comes out, we'll know a lot more about some of sports' most-noted coaches."

"Okay, B.J., I guess we'll have to be satisfied with that. That's all the time we have," Matt said.

B.J. noticed how dejected he sounded, but she didn't care. She was proud of the way she had handled someone she considered to be one of the best interviewers on TV.

"Thanks again so much for joining us, and we hope you'll join us again once the book is released."

"Matt, it was my pleasure, and of course I will."

B.J. had never felt so hot and nervous, but she figured she did okay. It seemed like the moment she was off the air, it was like a bomb going off. Her cell phone started ringing, vibrating, and dinging to indicate she had missed calls, voicemails, and text messages.

Smiling at the thought, B.J. followed the woman who had guided her through the station out a side door.

"Great job." She smiled as she held the door open for B.J. to pass through.

"Thanks," B.J. said as she gave her a fake smile and stepped out into the pre-dawn air. She slipped into the backseat of the waiting car and beamed with pride. She was so proud of the way she had handled herself.

When she looked down at her phone, she realized her mother had already called four times. B.J. wasn't in the mood. Her mother would start up again about how it was so wrong for her to discuss her friends and their personal business in such a public way. B.J. felt misunderstood. Truth be told, she wished she had never been thrown into this position in the first place.

She eased back in the seat, closed her eyes, and hoped the driver didn't hit too much traffic on their way back to the hotel that now doubled as her home.

TWENTY-FOUR

B.J.'s live interview on *Today* was being scrutinized as if several lives depended on it. And in a sense they did. By the time her friends found out about the interview, the night before, they had quickly put their heads together and planned a viewing party. As they gathered at Jewel's house they didn't know what to expect.

What would she say?

Would she talk about some of the stories she was using in the book?

Was it a done deal?

Would they get anything from her appearance that could help them change her mind?

They were as nervous as B.J. herself. Jewel had ordered breakfast and had quite a spread waiting when her friends arrived.

"It's been so long since I've been here," Lawna said as she strolled in. On any other occasion, Jewel would've proudly shown off all the recent upgrades she had added to the house. But this wasn't the time for that. She had barely slept the night before, worrying about what B.J. was about to reveal on national television.

Jewel even TiVoed the segment. When it was clear that B.J.'s interview was over, she stopped the recorder, then turned to her friends.

"Well, what'd you guys think?"

Mona didn't respond right away. She placed her notepad on the coffee table and stifled a yawn.

Jewel wasn't sure why Mona needed to take notes, even though the segment was being recorded, but she had stopped trying to figure out Mona's actions long ago.

"I think we're in a crapload of trouble," Jewel said.

"Yeah, me too. That's why I've been trying like crazy to get a hold of you guys. I can't believe she went on national television to talk about this book. I guess if there was any doubt about whether she was really writing it, we can forget about that now, huh?" Lawna said.

Mona still hadn't said a word.

She cut her Belgian waffle into perfectly sized pieces. The scrambled eggs were neatly moved to one side of the plate and away from three strips of bacon that sat opposite the eggs.

Jewel looked at her, but dismissed what she was doing. That was Mona, always meticulous with everything. Burgers were cut into four equal pieces, French fries perfectly lined up, and all of her food was in specific sections on her plate.

"I'm going to be ruined if B.J. tells all the shit I've been up to." Jewel shook her head slowly as if her mind had already ventured to the worst possible case scenario.

"You? Now I'm wondering why the hell we trusted her the way we did," Lawna added. "Think about it. We basically told this woman everything. And now that I'm thinking about it, B.J. wasn't all that forthcoming with her own dirt."

"So she's been planning to do this all along?" Mona finally spoke up. But this time when she talked, it was as if she was simply thinking out loud. Her attention was still focused on getting her food right on her plate.

All heads whipped in her direction.

"What do you mean?" Jewel asked.

"What if she planned to write about us and our secrets from the beginning? Think about it. It makes sense. She and Taylor walked into this situation mid-season. She knows that we were already close before she stepped in. It probably felt like she was never really accepted, so we became a case study. It makes sense now. That's the only reason she kept her dirt so close to her chest." Mona was still cutting her food. "Think about it," she added.

As if they were doing just that, both Jewel and Lawna started thinking about the way B.J. had handled them during their times of need.

"Okay, enough!" Jewel screamed, grabbing the sides of her head.

Thinking about all that she had to lose was enough to start her blood boiling.

"I thought I was confiding in a friend. I've never told anyone my business the way I told B.J. And I mean I told her everything!" Jewel said regretfully. "I feel so violated, so let down."

"Listen," Lawna started with a calm voice. "There was no way you could've known B.J. was planning to write a tell-all book. We're not happy about this, but could we be overreacting here? I mean, what if we counter by simply ignoring the book and B.J., too?"

Mona looked at both women. She wasn't planning to ignore a thing. As a matter of fact, she was already hard at work trying to get a lead on where B.J. was hiding out. And the minute she found out, she wasn't about to take her idea before any committee. She knew what needed to be done and she was going to get it done.

If Mona understood anything, she understood people and she felt like everyone had a price. The way she saw it, B.J. had no idea what she was in store for. Divorce could get nasty and costly, and if B.J. really was serious about leaving Taylor, she'd need a war-chest to fight properly.

"I plan to offer her a little check with a whole bunch of zeros," Mona finally said, quoting one of her favorite songs.

Mouths dropped and eyes grew wide. Was she joking?

"This thing is getting way out of hand but—" Jewel started.

"Maybe it is, but I'm not about to take any chances. I'm willing to pay her off, and as soon as I find out what that publisher is offering, I'm going to triple, or quadruple it if I have to, whatever they offered."

Just then, Lawna's cell phone rang. It pulled her attention away from the conversation. She frowned at the number she didn't recognize. But she answered anyway.

"Hello?"

"Is this Lawna Carter?"

"Yes, who's calling?"

Mona and Jewel looked at Lawna.

"Lawna? Heeey, guuurrrl. It's me, Saaasha. I wanted to reach out to you and the other ladies to tell y'all how bad I feel about this thing with y'all and B.J.," Sasha said.

Lawna's frown deepened. She hated when Sasha felt the need to stretch out the *a* in her name.

"I can't imagine what I would do if one of my gurrls threatened to dish all the dirt she had on me. Gurrl, you must be sick," Sasha said.

"Uh…" Lawna was still trying to wrap her mind around the fact that Sasha was calling *her*. How had she gotten her hands on her cell number? They weren't close, nor did they speak to each other beyond a forced hello in passing while in public.

"Between me and you, this ain't nothing but B.J. being hot over Ella fucking Taylor," Sasha said easily, like they were good friends shooting the breeze. "Umph, umph, umph. What in the world are y'all gonna do?"

"There's nothing for us to do," Lawna said, shrugging her shoulders at Jewel and Mona, who were both still looking at her.

"Who's that?" Jewel mouthed.

"Sasha, I don't know what to say," Lawna said, to let the others know whom she was talking to.

Jewel and Mona frowned at the mention of Sasha's name. Knowing she was now in the mix made Lawna that much more uneasy. Sasha's reputation preceded her wherever she went. No one wanted their names mixed up with hers.

"So, you tryna tell me, y'all not gon' do a thing? Ya'll gon' let her put all your business out there on blast like that?" Sasha seemed flabbergasted.

"Sasha?"

"No, I mean, quite surely she's done some dirt herself. Girl, start tellin' her business, even if you gotta make some shit up! That'll teach her ass a lesson! I always thought it was funny how y'all followed behind her like she's some sort of queen bee or something. She's so rigid with her plain Jane-looking ass!"

"Sasha!" Lawna tried again to interrupt her. This time she was more forceful, but it didn't help.

"I'm just sayin', Lawna, you can't tell me she ain't done shit while y'all was wilding out like that. She got a lotta balls, if you ask me. But still, cardinal rule number one, you don't go spillin' shit 'bout your gurrls."

"Sasha, I need to go!" Lawna finally yelled.

"Oh snap! Guurrl, my bad. You know what? I really like you. I ain't too fond of those other chicks you hang with, but we could really shake things up. Since B.J. out doing her thang, we should kick it some time."

"Um, I don't know about that," Lawna stammered.

"Now look here, you ain't gotta worry about me judging you.

I'm not like that. And I damn sure won't run around blabbing your business. I don't even roll like that. But anywhoo, I wanted to reach out to you after seeing B.J.'s interview and let you know that people like B.J. always get theirs. Keep your head up and whenever you ready, call me and we can go raise some real hell. Give B.J. some more shit to add to that book of hers!"

Sasha started laughing. Lawna pulled the phone from her ear and frowned at it before ending the call.

Jewel dismissed her with a roll of her eyes. But Mona never lost her cool.

She was too busy trying to work out the details of her plan in her head. Someone had to stop B.J. before everyone's life was spinning out of control.

TWENTY-FIVE

B.J. couldn't believe all of the interview requests that were pouring in. Forget the fact that after her appearance on *Today*, snippets of her interview had already gone viral. She had seen herself on ESPN, *Extra*, *Entertainment Tonight* and E! And her agent was as happy as she could be.

But now it was time for B.J. to get back to work. She did have a book to write and she needed now more than ever to get this first draft done and turned in. After seeing all the reports over what's to come, she finally realized the full scope of what she was doing.

People really were curious about what she had to say. And there was that part of her that knew Mona, Jewel, and Lawna were somewhere losing their minds. B.J. kept pushing her mother's words to the back of her mind and she constantly reminded herself that it was her "so-called" friends who had done her wrong and not the other way around.

As if she had summoned her up through her thoughts, B.J.'s cell phone rang and it was her mother.

"Hey, Mom, I was just about to call to talk to the kids," B.J. said.

"They're right here," Vernice said.

"Mommy," her son whined.

"Hey, baby." B.J. genuinely missed her kids. She missed her

family life as well. Why did Taylor have to mess up the way he did? Outside of helping the other wives out of whatever mess they'd landed in, she was totally devoted to her family. Taylor's infidelity had completely blindsided her.

"When are you coming to see me?" he asked.

B.J. closed her eyes and fought back tears. She burned with fury when she thought again about what Ella and Taylor had done. She talked with her daughter after her son, then labored through a conversation with her mother.

After talking with her mother, B.J. pulled herself together, and fired up her laptop. It did bother her that her mother wasn't supportive of the book, but B.J. told herself she had to do whatever she had to do. For her, this book was the best way to show Taylor and her friends that she was going to have the last laugh in this embarrassing situation.

Each time she sat down to write, she faced the same struggles. What to keep in, and what to leave out. Considering she'd been thinking about this particular story for quite some time, she figured she needed to write it and get it over with.

B.J. started typing.

Chapter 21

I remember our STD field trip as clear as day. It was the week the Sea Lions and the Redskins were the featured game on Monday Night Football. By that time in the season, our husbands couldn't have cared less if we decided to miss a game. It was all they could do to keep the players focused on winning instead of the fact that the entire world would be watching.

We all decided that would be the best time to make the trip; it would give us an entire weekday to handle the problem. The drive from L.A. to Bakersfield had to be one of the most boring ways to spend three hours. Once you passed Magic Mountain and made it through the grapevine, a dangerous patch of mountainous terrain that offered the shortcut between Kern County and L.A., you were lucky if you weren't bored to tears by the deserted rural area along the path.

I remember how nervous Jewel was about making the trip. I actually had to talk some sense into the girl. That fool acted like just because the symptoms had gone away (even though she hadn't received any treatment) everything was okay.

Jewel couldn't believe how cool Mona was about the entire situation. Jewel was embarrassed, but it helped to have friends who weren't judgmental.

"I'll find a doctor far enough away so you can get the treatment discreetly," Mona had assured Jewel over lunch. "That way we can put this behind us and move on."

That was Mona; always putting things away in a neat little box.

They were at the Cheesecake Factory in Redondo Beach.

"I can't believe this," Jewel said.

"Let's look at the bright side," Lawna said.

Everyone looked at her in astonishment. Lawna truly believed there was a silver lining to every dark cloud.

"The bright side?" B.J. asked.

"Yeah, there is a bright side, even in this situation," Lawna said confidently. "Think about it; we're deep enough in the season that she ain't gotta worry about Zeke wanting sex. You know how they get during the season."

Eyebrows went up, and heads nodded in agreement. Lawna was right. Jewel's symptoms popped up three days after she'd had a tryst with a guy she had met on Facebook, but because her husband was so engrossed in the season, he had tunnel vision. She didn't have to worry about infecting him. He was too tired, and too grouchy to want sex. Often, he'd leave the house before dawn and come back completely worn out from the day's grueling practice.

Sometimes he'd fall asleep in his media room, the day's practice on the big screen, his clothes unchanged, and his whistle still around his neck. Yes, football season was intense.

"I don't like feeling like this. I can't believe that bastard gave me a germ," Jewel said. "No matter how much I bathe, I don't feel clean."

"You should've used a condom," B.J. said before stuffing her mouth with salad. B.J. rarely realized her lack of sensitivity.

Jewel rolled her eyes. She didn't mean to, but she hated when people stated the obvious.

"We did use a condom, but it broke. As a matter of fact, he had to go fishing between my legs to scoop it out when we were done."

"Sounds like that was a serious romp," Lawna said.

"That's the thing. It's unfortunate that he wasn't clean, because he was hung, and boy, did he know how to hit my spots. I hate that I had to pick up something from his nasty behind."

Three days after that lunch meeting, they had piled into B.J.'s rented BMW SUV and hit the road for Bakersfield.

"I'm so nervous," Jewel admitted.

"Don't be; everything is set up. We'll go, get the diagnosis confirmed, receive treatment and we'll be back on the road in a flash," Mona rattled off, like this was merely another task on her ever-so-busy to-do list.

Two–and-a-half hours later, B.J. turned to Mona and asked, "Where are we going? What's the address again?"

"It's 2020 F Street. We're going to the Community Action Partnership of Kern County. A friend of mine works there; he's waiting for us, knows all the details."

"Okay, cool."

At the office, Dr. Gordon Miller, a tall, light-skinned, black man with a thin frame and a friendly face greeted Mona and her friends personally. He hugged Mona for a long while.

"It's been too long," he said as they finally broke from their embrace.

"Yes, it has. You look good," Mona said. "And thank you so much for understanding about this."

"Not a problem," he said.

Mona went around the group and introduced Dr. Miller to each of her friends.

"Okay, who's the patient?" Dr. Miller asked.

Jewel raised her hand like a student unsure of the answer in class.

"I'm Jewel Swanson," she said.

"Okay, ladies, I need a few minutes alone with her and we'll be back shortly."

Jewel couldn't believe she was in this predicament. How could she have been so stupid? But then again, she had done it all right. They'd used a condom. Who could be blamed because it broke?

"Usually this is a process that takes a few days, but because of the special circumstances, I'm going to streamline it for you. Once we check everything out, I'll let you know your options."

He must've thought the worst of her. What kind of married woman needs to leave town to be treated for a sexually transmitted disease?

"Okay," Jewel said.

After a thorough interview, the doctor was ready to examine Jewel. Once she heard they were about to take to the road to drive far enough away so she could be treated for a sexually transmitted disease she had picked up from a one-night stand, she thought she had hit rock bottom. Jewel couldn't imagine a time when she had felt more embarrassed as she eased herself onto the examination table and put her legs into the stirrups.

When she caught a whiff of the odor that came from between her thighs, she suddenly felt more embarrassed than before.

"Just relax," he said, "and take a deep breath."

Dr. Miller hardly flinched, and for that, Jewel was grateful.

Hours later, after enduring a very painful injection in her left butt cheek, Jewel sat in the backseat as B.J. drove them back to L.A. This she told herself was her last straw, as far as men were concerned. There had to be something better out there.

TWENTY-SIX

W hat if Mona's foolproof plan didn't work? What if the truth about what she'd been doing came out and really rocked her world? She couldn't afford to lose Zeke, regardless of what all he had done. Even a bad day as an NFL coach's wife was better than most days as a working-class fitness teacher. Jewel now worked only because, and when, she wanted to. She mainly worked to keep her own body in shape. It was tough knowing your husband was constantly surrounded by younger, harder, more eager bodies. The cheerleaders and groupies were enough to make any wife rethink letting herself go.

Tierrany called and Jewel tried her best to ignore it, but she couldn't. Their connection, the bolt of electricity that sparked when they touched, all she felt couldn't be denied and it couldn't be ignored.

"The heart wants what the heart wants," Jewel said as she dialed Tierrany's number. She felt weak giving in and calling her back so soon, but she wasn't good at playing hard to get.

As soon as Tierrany answered, Jewel couldn't downplay the happiness she felt. She was torn by what they were doing, and the bliss that usually made things seem so clear and so possible, even though she knew they weren't. If Zeke had any inkling about what was going on, there was no way their marriage would last.

With B.J.'s threat hovering over her, Jewel realized that it was only a matter of time before she and Tierrany would have to face the music. But still, that wasn't enough to keep her away.

"Jewels, what's going on? Is everything okay?" Tierrany asked.

The concern in Tierrany's voice was evident, and that really touched Jewel. Tierrany had a way of making her feel special. The way Zeke used to. But lately, if he wasn't locked in his media room watching porn flicks, he was fast asleep when she was ready to be touched and loved. And if he was awake, he soon made her regret ever wanting his affection. The last time they were together, Jewel had to bite down on her lip so hard to prevent herself from crying out in pain, she thought for sure she had broken skin.

"You like it rough, don't you?" Zeke grunted in her ear.

He was oblivious to the fact that he was actually hurting her. Either that, or he simply didn't care. She couldn't be sure which was true, but as the side of her body smashed up against the wall again, all she could do was close her eyes and beg for it to be over.

"Yeah, that's right, don't try to run now," he said.

Jewel was on all fours, struggling with her husband's full weight as he rammed himself into her with no mercy. The moment she tried to ease the impact by twisting her hip to the side, he'd grab her around the waist tightly and hold her in place. That shoved the whole side of her body and face right into the wall. It was not a good feeling. She couldn't remember the last time having sex with her husband had felt good.

He'd spent most of the night pounding on her from behind, grabbing fists full of her hair or spanking her with his massive hands, and somehow that did it for him.

"C'mon, be still, quit runnin'!"

The sex talk was always a one-way conversation. She never responded and he always ignored her pleas to stop. He never cared whether she reached orgasm, and most times she was silently praying he got what he wanted so she could recover. Tierrany was a welcomed change from what she was used to with Zeke.

"Yeah, just—"

"Just what? You still there?" Tierrany asked.

"Yes, I'm here, I was thinking."

"Well, I saw that interview B.J. did. Baby, you can't let it stress you. She's gonna do what she's gonna do," Tierrany said.

"I know, but I can't help but think about what's gonna happen when Zeke finds out about us."

"You think he'll try to hurt you?"

"No, nothing like that, but Zeke's a super-macho man. He's not the average man who would probably go somewhere and lick his wounds, then get back in the race. He's gonna take this extra hard."

"See, that's what I like about you. Here you are still thinking about him after all he's put you through."

"But look what I'm doing. You know what this is gonna do to him?"

"Stop thinking about him. Let's meet so I can help relieve some of that stress I hear in your voice."

It started innocently enough. Tierrany came over to the house to help Jewel when she was thinking about doing some bodybuilding. They grew closer, with Tierrany being very complimentary of Jewel. They talked quite a bit; Tierrany even confided that she was trying to save up enough money to open an upscale spa.

Jewel decided against the whole bodybuilding thing in the end, but by then, she and Tierrany had developed a close bond. Jewel had no defenses when it came to Tierrany. If someone had told her years ago that she'd be involved in an intimate relationship with another woman, there's no way she would've entertained the thought.

But here she was, struggling to find a way to turn Tierrany down, and she couldn't. Deep down inside, she really didn't want to.

"I'll run you a nice hot bath, the way you like it. We could share a bottle of icy cold champagne. I'll even put our favorite CD on repeat."

Jewel smiled.

Why couldn't Zeke say and do these things? All he wanted to do was chase skirts. She knew what she was getting herself into with him, but she had no idea it would be this hard. She had all but stopped answering their home phone because of all the hang-ups. It was his silly girlfriends, but what could she say or do?

Jewel was tired of not being enough for her husband. Based on the pornos he watched, she deduced that he preferred someone who was more voluptuous than her. The women on those porn flicks had big, round, bodacious booties that often looked fake.

Tierrany didn't care that Jewel's buns of steel were average, or that her B-cups were just Bs.

This is the last time. One more taste, Jewel lied to herself.

"Where do you wanna meet?" Jewel asked.

"The usual spot. You coming or you want me to come get you?"

"I'll be there."

"Okay, see you in a bit, oh, and can we talk about the proposal?"

Jewel had already disconnected. Her mind drifting to thoughts of how badly she needed to get out of the house, but she had to wait for Zeke to get home first. He'd be good and tired, so there was no doubt she'd be able to get out to see Tierrany.

A bit later, she heard her husband before she saw him. Jewel still loved him, and if only he would change his ways, they could be happy together again. But Jewel had been down this road so many times, she started feeling like a domestic violence victim who couldn't leave her abusive man.

Zeke was talking on his cell when he walked through the door. And, as usual, he was loud.

"Hey, how was practice?" Jewel asked as she rounded the corner and greeted him.

He nodded, but the phone stayed at his ear.

"Yeah, Coach, that shit was rough. Well, I'm about to watch some film, then call it a night," he said into the phone.

By the time he stepped all the way into the kitchen, Jewel was putting a loaded baked potato onto his plate. Zeke was a steak and potatoes man and he loved a hearty meal after practice every night.

"Mmmm, smells good, but I'm eating in the media room," he said. He spanked her on the ass, then walked over to the refrigerator, opened the door, looked inside, and closed it without taking anything out.

"Oh, I'm going to meet Lawna and Mona for dinner and a movie tonight," she said over her shoulder. Jewel knew he'd be asleep in front of the massive screen in his media room less than an hour after he inhaled his food.

"Okay," Zeke said. He picked up the stack of mail, flipped through the envelopes, then yawned.

He put the mail down when Jewel passed him his plate.

Once he was taken care of, Jewel went upstairs to change. She'd shower at the hotel, but she wanted to wear something sexy.

She couldn't help feeling like some love-sick teenager getting ready for a date. She was excited and anxious at the same time. To avoid suspicion, she rarely left with any additional clothes or toiletries. Jewel had this down to a science. Once she left the house, but before arriving at the hotel, she'd stop at Rite Aid and stock up on travel-sized toiletries that she would leave in the hotel room at the end of their stay.

Tierrany never complained when she had to slip out in the middle of the night. She was very understanding about Jewel's situation and always behaved as if any time she got was sufficient.

"Zeke, I'm leaving!" Jewel yelled from the front door. When she didn't hear a response, she figured he was already asleep, and that was fine with her.

That meant she could stay with Tierrany literally until the sun threatened to pop up and start a new day. It would be risky, but Jewel knew for certain, once she left Tierrany, she'd be completely satisfied.

As she prepared to back out of the driveway, she caught a glimpse of her eyes in the rearview mirror. "What is happening to me?" she asked aloud. But just as quickly, she shook the question off and took off toward her meeting with Tierrany.

TWENTY-SEVEN

B.J. was gearing up for one of two interviews she had scheduled for the day. One of the stations wanted to do a Skype interview with her later and she was excited, but the first one was going to be at a station in Burbank.

Because it was a cable station, there was no fancy driver to pick her up, but she was still excited nonetheless. B.J. wore a black Halston Heritage halter jumpsuit with a fuchsia half-sweater trimmed with ruffles, and a pair of fuchsia platform sandals.

She arrived at the studio, and was rushed right onto the set. She sat on a lumpy sofa next to a desk. No makeup, fancy hair-stylist, or posh green room to relax in. But luckily, after her *Today* appearance she had bought some of the studio makeup Helen had used on her.

"How are you?" Cindy Croft asked. Cindy was a masculine-looking woman but she seemed friendly as she smiled at B.J. Cindy sported a blunt blonde pageboy haircut, with green eyes that seemed awkwardly placed too far apart on her flat face. She hosted a popular local talk show that was on the edge of the hottest news stories. Cindy started flipping through a stack of papers on her desk.

Suddenly, two assistants approached and began to fumble around B.J. to get a small microphone attached to her clothes. Then it was time to begin. B.J. cleared her throat and straightened her back as she tried to get comfortable on the sofa. The set-up reminded her of the late-night talk shows with the host behind a desk and she, the guest, on a sofa.

"I'm Cindy Croft and we are discussing what all of you are talking about. It's the story of a woman who said, enough is enough! When her husband decided to take a mistress and she found out about it, she decided to get even. Lara Thomas has the story."

As B.J. sat listening to the story about herself and the lawsuit, she was struck by how odd the entire situation sounded. A reporter's voice started as a collage of pictures flashed across a small screen.

"It is expected to be one of the messiest divorces in Tinseltown, and that's saying a lot in a city where even a breakup is a major production. Now the contentious battle has taken a turn no one expected. NFL Head Coach Taylor Almond's estranged wife has filed a lawsuit, claiming his relationship with Ella Blu, the wife of one of his assistant coaches, caused Mrs. Almond and the Los Angeles Sea Lions head coach to drift apart. Taylor Almond won't comment on the lawsuit, but his lawyers say it is completely 'meritless.'"

Now there was video of Taylor on the practice field. B.J. didn't know if this was good or bad for her case. He looked powerful, blowing his whistle and yelling at some of the players as they scrambled through their workout.

"Mrs. Bobbi Almond filed suit in Los Angeles two weeks ago. It's the latest chapter in what's expected to be a nasty divorce saga between the former college sweethearts who separated nearly a month ago. She and Taylor Almond have two small children, ages three and two, who are also listed as plaintiffs in the suit."

Now pictures of Samantha Sloan were on the screen.

"Bobbi, who is represented by celebrity attorney Samantha Sloan, says she's tired of women who have a complete disregard for the commitment shared between a married couple. Among other things, the lawsuit alleges Blu 'engaged in sexual activity' in the couple's marital bed, which 'severely impacted the plaintiff emotionally and mentally.' It also claims that while carrying on this affair, Taylor was dipping into the family's finances to hide and continue the secret affair, thereby threatening the financial stability of his family's quality of life."

The reporter's voice seemed to fluctuate as she read some of the details of the lawsuit.

"The defendant obviously befriended the plaintiff with the intentions of easing into the home of a married man, Taylor Almond. Damages in excess of four-point-five million dollars are being sought by Bobbi Almond."

Once the story was over, the host turned to B.J.

"We're now joined by Mrs. Almond herself. Bobbi, thanks for being here with us. Everyone is talking about this case, so I can imagine how busy you must be."

B.J. smiled uneasily. She was getting a bit tired of these interviews.

"People have been weighing in on this as if it somehow impacts them and their own relationships. The question everyone is asking is, why sue the mistress?"

"Marriage is an agreement, similar to a legally binding contract between two people. If that agreement or contract is broken, then that's a breach. In this case, Taylor didn't act alone."

"But what do you hope to gain by this lawsuit?"

B.J. paused before answering.

"We live in a money-driven society. People don't really feel pain unless it's measured by something tangible. It's not about the money. It's about alienation of affection and the source of that alienation."

"But isn't it more or less your husband's fault? Mrs. Blu didn't enter into that agreement with you; he did," the host said.

"Yes, that is true, but what's also true is that it takes two. If my husband approached her, all she had to say was no. And let's not forget, this is a woman who was in my inner circle. She was a family friend."

B.J. did a half-shrug. "I don't want to try this case in the court of public opinion. I want to go in front of a judge, have him hear the facts of the case and make a ruling based on the facts, not on the parties involved, and certainly not on what the public thinks."

"So you think you have grounds for a legitimate case here?"

"Oh, absolutely; someone should be liable for helping to break that contract I entered into with my husband. That's all I'm saying."

The host turned back to the camera, smiled, and said, "We'll have more with an NFL coach's wife who is suing both her husband and his mistress for the breakup of her marriage and we're taking your calls and comments, too! Stay with us."

During the commercial break, the host didn't really talk to B.J. A couple of assistants brushed up Cindy's makeup, fussed with her hair, and then it was time to go back to the interview.

"Caller, you're on with Bobbi Almond. What are your thoughts?"

"Mrs. Almond, I feel like what you're doing is a good thing! It takes two and if she entered the relationship knowing he was married, why not sue her? She knew what she was doing and by suing her, she won't be so quick to want to ruin another home. I say good for you! And good luck!"

"Thank you," B.J. said.

"Thank you, caller. Let's take another call. Hi, caller. You're on with Bobbi Almond, the NFL wife who is suing her husband's mistress for the breakup of her marriage. What are your thoughts?"

"Mrs. Almond, at first I thought you were on to something, suing this woman for cheating with your husband, but then I learned about this so called tell-all book you're writing, something about *Blowin' the Whistle*. Now I'm wondering if you're not just another scorned wife?"

B.J. took the question head-on. "Thanks for that question, but here's what I have to say. I have every right to feel scorned. I was faithful to my husband. Being a coach's wife is stressful enough. Knowing that I was giving my all and he was giving far less because he was otherwise occupied, well, I'd say that's enough to piss anyone off. Wouldn't you?" Cindy looked like she was about to say something, but B.J. quickly added, "And the title of my book is *Blowin' the Whistle*, as you indicated."

"We're going to have to leave it there and go to a quick break." The host smiled into the camera, then added, "When we come back, more with an NFL coach's wife who's suing her husband's mistress!"

There was a mixture of calls for the rest of the show. Some of the callers agreed with B.J.'s decision, others were very critical. Some men called in and complained that they were worried about how this would impact the coach's ability to win during the upcoming season. One even accused Bobbi of possibly working for one of the Sea Lions' rivals.

B.J. didn't care about the negative comments. She wanted to be the poster child for why you shouldn't give in to temptation.

Unfortunately for B.J., this particular interview, which was held at a studio in Burbank, was in the middle of the afternoon. So when she walked out of the doors, she was greeted by a sight that literally stopped her cold in her tracks.

TWENTY-EIGHT

Ella was tired of hiding out. She wasn't tired because she was alone, but because her mother, Tabitha Davidson, kept calling to complain about Ella's kids. This time Ella answered the phone.

"When are you coming back?"

"I dunno," Ella said. "Why, what's wrong?"

"They keep crying and whining for you. I don't know what to tell 'em."

Ella didn't respond.

"I don't know what to say about these two." Tabitha sighed. "I mean, they act like they ain't got no home training!" She sighed again. This time it sounded as if she was really overwhelmed.

Did it really take all of that? Ella wondered. Her kids couldn't be any worse than her sister's, but she wasn't about to get into that with her mother.

She should've packed her stuff and taken off for a deserted island. Why not lay low until this mess went away? Her husband kept calling, and so did her old friends, minus B.J. of course. But the way that woman had been making the rounds to all of the TV, radio stations, and internet shows, Ella wondered how she even made time to write her so-called masterpiece. She still hadn't heard a word from Taylor and that agitated her.

"I'm gonna come by there in a few hours," Ella said. She wasn't sure if her mother was telling the truth. She had a feeling the woman wanted to get all up in her business. You had to be living up under a huge rock not to know what was going on; especially the way B.J. was going around talking about it to anyone with a microphone. If the kids were so bad and whiny, why didn't she hear them in the background?

Ella knew her mother could be such a drama queen at times, but she could also imagine the older woman was probably getting inpatient because she wanted some answers.

The truth was, Ella wasn't ready to face anyone. She had been talking to Mona and trying to figure out if Mona had made any progress with convincing B.J. to drop this whole mess. Ella's life would never be the same, so she wasn't really in a hurry to get back to the mess. She couldn't see a single bright angle in this situation. How could Sterling continue to work for the man who had been secretly sleeping with his wife? If he quit the Sea Lions, where would he go? What would become of their family, their lifestyle after Taylor chose her over B.J.?

She looked around at what had been her hideout for weeks and glanced out at the magnificent view of the ocean. She hadn't even used the in-room Jacuzzi.

Ella wished she could stay. Everything about the room was so serene, the complete opposite of her life. Painted in bright powder blue, with crown molding done in sea-inspired green and bright white, it was inviting. The massive bathroom had sleek, modern fixtures, including counter-mounted sinks with black granite countertops and stylish glass shelves.

There was even a fifty-two-inch flat-screen TV and a DVD player. A fireplace faced the iron, king-sized bed. The room's walls were adorned with artwork that depicted nautical scenes. She didn't want to leave. She wanted to stay right there and let this mess boil over.

"Oh well," she said out loud.

Ella had really screwed up this time. Now, she had to go face her mom and get the third degree. She had seen B.J. on TV; she'd heard people on the radio, read the papers, and she wondered how long it would be before most, if not all, of her secrets came out.

There was so much more to her relationship with Taylor and she wasn't quite ready to face the music. What could she possibly say to Lawna, Jewel? Mona was upset over what she had done, but Mona had a way of thinking any problem was solvable through a good long pow-wow. When it came to B.J., Ella knew a snowstorm would have to blow through hell before B.J. would talk to her ever again.

But they all used to have such great times together. Ella wished she'd had the power to say no, but she hadn't.

"I'd better go see about my kids before my mom tracks me down," Ella said to herself as she eased up from the bed. If she had to be honest with herself, she'd admit she was running out of money.

When Ella first decided to get away, she pulled a bunch of cash from the safe, stuffed her bag, packed up the kids, and didn't look back. Her hope was that she'd be close to a decision about what to do next before the cash ran out.

Sterling surely missed her and the kids, but she had no idea how she was going to face him ever again. He had been good to her. He had made sure that she and the kids had more than she could ever imagine. At times she had wondered if he suspected anything, but she would shake those thoughts from her head. She never thought about hurting Sterling; she never really thought about anything other than when she could see Taylor again.

By the time Ella arrived at her mother's house, the panic and sheer hysteria with which Tabitha had called seemed to have calmed considerably.

Ella rolled her eyes as she stepped into the modest little home. Her mother still had thick plastic covering the sofa and loveseat. The black- and gold-trimmed, three-piece coffee and end table set looked as shiny as it had when she was growing up in the house.

"Where are the kids? Thought they were driving you mad?" Ella said upon entering the darkened living room.

"Oh, they're down for a nap. Keep your voice down; ain't no sense in waking them," said Tabitha. She was a short and petite woman who had sported an Afro for as long as Ella could remember. Her lips were dark purple and her eyes were small and beady. There was nothing attractive about Tabitha as far as Ella was concerned.

Ella pursed her lips and looked at her mother cockeyed.

"You had me rush over here thinking my kids were on the verge of stringing you up and you got them to sleep? In the middle of the afternoon?"

"It's like riding a bike," Tabitha said with ease.

Instantly on alert now, Ella suddenly wished she was back in her hotel room. She should've known her mother was trying to get her over to the house so she could get all in her business.

"Sit. It's been so long since we've talked," Tabitha said, patting the empty spot next to her on the sofa.

"What's up, Mom?"

"I wanna know what's going on... The news, the papers, they even talkin' about it on the radio. I'm so confused."

Ella hung her head low. How do you look your own mother in the face and confess to cheating with your good friend's husband? Then *said* friend files a lawsuit against you and the entire world seems hypnotized by this drama. Not to mention, most people seemed to be applauding B.J.'s lawsuit. Ella looked and felt like the world's biggest fool.

"It's all a huge misunderstanding," Ella lied.

"Is it now?" Tabitha asked. Her voice was dripping with sarcasm. By now her hands had flown to her hips, her face was twisted into a frown, and Ella suddenly felt like it was her mother's own man she had slept with.

"Well, why are you asking me if you've been sittin' up here watching the news, listening to the radio and reading the papers?" Ella snapped.

Her mother gave her that "check your tone" look and Ella simmered down a bit. But she was pissed because she now confirmed what she had thought. Her mother was plotting to get her to the house so she could get the details straight from the horse's mouth.

"I'm under a lot of pressure right now. I don't have time to sit and try to play the guessing game. If you've got questions, just ask," Ella said.

"Fine. Did you or did you not stab your friend in the back by sleeping with her husband like she says you did?"

Ella swallowed hard.

It sounded even worse than she'd imagined. She had been spending too much time by herself.

Just as she was about to answer her mother's question, her cell phone rang. The ring tone told her who it was, but still Ella's eyes focused on the caller's name and number. In spite of herself, she couldn't help the smile that began to curl at the corners of her mouth.

"Hold on a sec, Mom," she said as she pressed the button to answer the call. She turned her back to her mom.

"Ella, this is Taylor. We need to talk. Can we meet?"

Ella closed her eyes. Maybe this thing wouldn't turn out as badly as she expected.

"OHMYGOD! Of course, I can meet you in say an hour or two?" She couldn't help how giddy she felt.

Her mom and the kids would have to wait!

TWENTY-NINE

Normally the NFL Draft weekend was a time of great anticipation, not just for the college hopefuls, but also for the wives of the coaches. Of course the coaches had a vested interest in the draft. Months of careful planning went into deciding which representative would be present at Radio City Music Hall in New York, and which would stay back to negotiate during the draft for the right to pick an additional player in a given round. All of this played out on a very public stage.

Tickets to the NFL Draft are free and made available to fans on a first-come, first-served basis. The tickets are distributed at the box office the morning of the draft. Most fans who want to get a live glimpse of their team's high-profile picks wind up waiting in long lines, but few seem to mind. Each year, the main event is hosted at New York's Radio City Music Hall, but all across the country smaller draft parties have become a tradition.

On the West Coast, none of those parties were more coveted than the one hosted by B.J. Almond and the rest of the Sea Lions coaches' wives. But this year, due to all of the drama going on, there would be no party and no celebration hosted by either of the Almonds.

The first year B.J. held the party, it was sort of a spoof on the way the men were all consumed by the importance of the weekend. But it had taken off unexpectedly, the press had shown up, and soon it became an annual event. That was, until this year, when B.J. walked in on her husband and her so-called good friend, Ella.

This year, weeks before the draft, Sasha saw an opportunity and decided to take full advantage of all the chaos that was surrounding the Sea Lions wives.

She would have the mother of all draft parties, and she knew just what to do to get the press out in full force. Sasha had noticed all of the buzz surrounding B.J.'s lawsuit, and her forthcoming tell-all, *Blowin' the Whistle*. She had been dying for a way to get in on some of that spotlight so she started dropping hints that her upcoming party would be the ultimate backdrop for what was bound to be the hottest photo opportunity for the press.

Sasha started contacting all of the L.A. sports-related blogs with what she was calling a news tip. She started name-dropping to imply which reporters had already committed; then made getting on the list seem urgent and close to impossible.

As she dialed the last number on her lengthy list, she smiled to herself, thinking how great she had been to come up with the idea.

The minute someone answered, she disguised her voice and said, "I need to speak to a producer or whoever takes press releases about sports-related stories."

Sasha knew by calling the bloggers and asking for real sports reporters that would immediately get their attention. At no time did any of the people admit they were not whom she asked for.

"Uh, okay, you're speaking to 'em," the guy who answered the phone lied.

"I wanted to follow up on the press release we sent last week. It's about the Fantasy Draft party going on at the Villa this weekend," Sasha said.

"Oh, yeah, what about it?" The person on the other end didn't sound all that interested.

"Well, we wanted to make sure you guys got it, since B.J. Almond and Ella Blu are going to be there. Security is gonna be tight, and both Fox and CBS have already scheduled interviews, so we're trying to make sure we have a spot for you as well."

"Oh, interviews?" the guy asked.

Sasha knew there was a rift between real journalists and bloggers who wrote stories but weren't held to any kind of journalistic code of ethics. In the L.A. sports world, some bloggers were feared more than actual reporters. If one of their stories went viral, it could seriously impact a player's worth. And in most cases, bloggers had no one to answer to, so they were free to write whatever they wanted.

"They'll be there? And they're talking to the press?"

"They've agreed to hold a brief presser, but if you don't sign up early and register as press, you may not get in."

It worked exactly as she had suspected when the idea first struck. By the time Sasha was done, just about every, radio, Internet, and TV station's sports department had been put on alert.

This was bound to be the most talked about party this side of the Mississippi. Sasha had it all set up; she had even secured sponsors for the event.

Just then, she had an even better thought. There was no way in hell B.J. or Ella would show up, but what if she extended an invite to the other ladies. All she needed was to be seen with them a few times. Paparazzi would be out in force. Then she could really execute her master plan. Sasha was getting tired of the way these athletes were treating her. So what if she was older; so what she had a couple of kids; her best years were still ahead.

She dialed Lawna's number and waited for an answer.

"Hey, Guurrrl, what you know good?" Sasha sang, as if she and Lawna were good friends.

"Who is this?" Lawna sounded irritated, as if she was being interrupted.

"It's me, silly…Saaasha."

"Sasha, look, I'm real busy right now—"

Before Lawna could finish, Sasha cut her off. "Oh, I won't hold you long. I was wondering if y'all had gotten in touch with Ella yet. I wasn't sure if you had, but I wanted to let you know she'll be at my draft party this weekend."

Silence hung between them, but that was fine by Sasha; that's when she knew for sure that she had Lawna's full attention.

"I'm not trynta get all up in y'all's business or nothing like that, but when she RSVP'd, I instantly thought about you. I think y'all can work this thing out. Why not do it at a party? You know ain't nobody in they right mind 'bout to act a fool at a party."

"You talked to Ella?" Lawna asked.

"Yeah, not about all this stuff that's going on, but I did talk to her, told her she was welcomed and well, I wanted to let you know she'll be there."

At first Lawna didn't say anything. Sasha wasn't sure if she was losing her. But suddenly, Lawna asked, "Where'd you say this party was being held again?"

Sasha grinned as she rattled off the information. Before long, she'd be coasting along on Easy Street, and she didn't have to keep chasing these damn athletes to get there either. Besides, deep down she realized that she was getting too old for that.

THIRTY

This shit could not be happening! As B.J. stood with the April sun bearing down on her like it was mid-August instead of the very beginning of spring, she wondered how in the hell they had thought to find her here of all places. She hoped the people from Cindy's show weren't gawking at them through the windows.

"We only wanna talk," Mona said. As usual, her voice was as calm and soothing as can be. B.J. hated being handled by Mona. It really got under her skin, and this time was no exception.

B.J.'s eyes narrowed, and her jaw tightened. She had nothing to say. She didn't appreciate being cornered like this. She didn't give a damn how slowly and deliberately Mona spoke. If B.J. had wanted to talk to any of them, she would've returned one of their many calls. Couldn't they take a hint?

"We want you to think about this; that's all," Lawna said.

B.J. whipped around and looked at her, then shook her head.

"There's nothing to think about," she said through gritted teeth. "I can't believe you guys tracked me down and decided to try and gang up on me like this."

"No, no, B.J. that's not what's going on here," Mona offered.

She was starting to work B.J.'s nerves, and if she didn't watch out, B.J. would tell her what she could do with that damn olive branch she was trying to extend.

"You won't return calls; you ignore emails and text messages. We simply didn't know how else to get in touch with you."

"I even tried to send you a card, but I don't know if it ever arrived. We only want to talk," Lawna said.

B.J. planted her feet and put her hands on her hips. She had defiance written all over her face, and her friends had known all too well that once she made up her mind, she wasn't the easiest person to talk to; especially when she was mad.

"Okay, well, you've obviously been stalking me. Ain't no telling how long this is going to go on, so get to talking. Let's get this over with."

All of a sudden, no one had anything to say. The three women looked as if they were waiting for each other to start.

"Yeah, that's what I thought," B.J. said, rolling her eyes. She huffed, then moved as if she was about to leave.

"No, wait," Mona said. "I have plenty to say, and for starters, we don't wanna talk here. It's too hot out here, and people are walking by. This is not a good place. Let's go find a nice restaurant so we can sit and try to figure this whole thing out."

B.J. looked at her, but she didn't say anything.

"We could go to the Grove," Mona offered.

But B.J. never budged.

Mona wasn't sure if she had finally gotten through to her, but she was hopeful. She thought about all of the messages she had left on B.J.'s voicemail and couldn't understand how she could be so callous. If it were her, she would've broken down long ago and at least called back to leave a voicemail.

"I told you guys before, nothing has changed. I'm going through with the book. I'm suing Taylor and Ella and it's just that simple!"

"What about us?" Jewel asked.

For the entire time they'd been standing there, Jewel hadn't said a word. Once B.J. let her secret out, her world would be as good as crumbled. She didn't think she had the right words, much less the power, to try and change B.J.'s mind.

"What about you?" B.J.'s eyebrow began to twitch. She was frowning as if standing there was pissing her off even more. "Did any of you stop to think about me when you were harboring information that kept Ella's secret safe?"

Jewel didn't have an answer. She turned to Mona, wondering why the voice of reason hadn't stepped in and said something to make B.J. see things differently. Where were Mona's great counseling skills? Why had this thing been dragged out for so long anyway?

She finally spoke. "B.J., I wish you wouldn't look at it like that. That's not how things happened. We didn't mean to hurt you. We were in the dark, just like you. We didn't plot with Ella to hide that affair from you. Hell, we didn't even know for certain that it was going on. You've gotta believe what we're trying to tell you."

"I ain't gotta do a damn thing but breathe and one day die!" B.J. snapped.

"You're absolutely right. I said that the wrong way," Mona quickly interjected. "I didn't mean to imply that I was telling you what you *had* to do. I was hoping that if you realized we did not set out to hurt you, you'd be willing to sit down and talk about it; that's all."

"Don't fucking patronize me, Mona. I'm not one of your damn frail patients you can play word tricks on," B.J. snarled.

Mona exhaled. She needed B.J. to get on board; she needed B.J. to stop acting like a brat and put forth some effort. But she didn't want to piss her off even more.

"I need to go. I have a three-thirty interview to get ready for, so if you'll move the hell out of my way..." B.J. said.

"Wait, B.J.," Mona said.

"No, I'm done here. And stop following me around before I have to add all of your names to the lawsuit for harassment!"

Without another word, B.J. shoved her way past the three of them.

"Is that how you plan to handle everything from here on out?" Mona asked. "You're planning to settle all of your differences by suing everybody?"

"If I were you, I wouldn't wait around to find out. My best advice is that you all leave me the hell alone. That way you can get a sense of peace before my book hits the shelves."

The three stood there and watched as B.J. stormed off, and climbed into her car. She slammed the door, cranked it up and careened out of the parking lot like she was racing to put out a fire.

THIRTY-ONE

"I am so over her stubborn behind!" Jewel said. "You know what, let her tell my secrets. This is ridiculous! She thinks somebody's gonna kiss her ass so she won't go and embarrass us all?" Jewel huffed.

"Well, she's hurting right now. Try to put yourself in her shoes," Lawna said. But that comment didn't do anything to calm Jewel down. It seemed as if it riled her up even more.

"Her shoes, my ass!" Jewel snapped. "Enough is enough. We didn't do shit to her! We didn't screw her man! Why should we be punished for something we didn't even get any pleasure out of? I'm tired of hoping she'll change her mind!" Jewel threw her hands up and turned to leave. But that's when she realized that she and Lawna had ridden with Mona.

She stopped and turned back to face the other ladies. Now she was mad. Mad at herself for letting Mona talk her into coming along, mad for standing out in the sun, begging someone who had her mind made up, and mad that B.J. wouldn't listen to anything they had to say.

"Don't you guys see? She's getting some sort of sick pleasure out of torturing us. She knows we didn't do a damn thing, but this is so B.J. She's a sadistic, control freak! She was embarrassed; her feelings were hurt, so now we all have to suffer! It's that simple. I don't think this is really about us not telling her about something we knew absolutely nothing about! Think about it!"

"Well, I don't want to focus only on the negative. I'm gonna try and look at the bright side here," Lawna said as they started toward Mona's car.

"The bright side?" Jewel balked. She started laughing. "You have got to be kidding me! Were you even at the same intervention turned confrontation? Did we not try to appeal to this woman's sense of empathy? We were so damned apologetic, even though I don't think we have a damn thing to be sorry about, and still she all but spat in our faces!" Jewel frowned. "She couldn't care less about us. If she cared, she'd at least try to see where we're coming from, hear us out, something!"

"She's scared, lonely, and she's not sure whom she can trust right now. Think about it. For the past four or five years, we've all been so close. We've been each other's confidantes..." Lawna started before Jewel cut her off.

"Whoa! Hold up a sec," Jewel said. "No, she may have been our confidante, but let's face it, we now know the bitch was using us as research for her book!"

"Okay, Jewel," Mona said.

"Okay what? Seriously, don't tell me you're like Ms. Sunshine over there." Jewel motioned in Lawna's direction. "B.J. is mad as hell and she ain't trying to hear nothing we gotta say! She wants revenge."

"Yes, that's obvious, but that doesn't mean we start turning on each other," Mona suggested. "That's definitely not the answer. We'll get through to her."

"Are you kidding me? How are we gonna get through to somebody who has nothing but hate in her eyes and probably in her heart when it comes to us? Nothing we can say or do will stop her from writing this book."

"I'm not so sure," Lawna said.

"I'm not so sure," Jewel mocked, with her head twisting.

"I'm with Lawna on this one, Jewel."

Jewel rolled her eyes and wondered if she was being punked. A camera crew was bound to jump out of the bushes at any moment now! Those two were acting as though B.J. simply needed more cooling-off time. Forget the fact that she looked like she was ready to fight when she had first seen them standing there. Jewel didn't know if they were about to be maced, pepper-sprayed or something worse.

Mona hit her alarm and opened the car doors. They all climbed inside. "We're going to work this out."

"I didn't want to go this route. I was really hoping that we could talk some sense into her, but now that I've had a chance to see her, I mean really take a good look at her, I have a better idea of just how angry she is," Mona said as she backed out of the parking space, turned her wheel, and headed for the exit row.

"Oh, so you didn't think she was really angry before?" Jewel asked sarcastically.

Mona glanced at her through the rearview mirror. When she did, Jewel's eyebrows went up.

"Seriously, you're trying to tell me you learned something different from her in the ten minutes we stood out there baking in the sun?"

"All I'm saying is, she's far more upset that I first thought. This gives me somewhat of an idea of how to approach her next time."

Jewel started laughing as if she was talking to one of the Original Kings of Comedy.

Lawna looked worried, but Mona had a look of determination on her face as she headed for the freeway that led back to L.A.

"Well, y'all can have this mess! I'm done!" Jewel clapped both hands in a washing motion. "I am done! I don't give a flying—"

Mona exited the freeway and turned down the street that would lead to Jewel's house.

"Jewel!" Mona yelled.

"Jewel, what? I'm serious. This is too much for me, and I'm tired. As a matter of fact, when I get home, I'm gonna go to Zeke, and I'm gonna tell him everything my damn self!"

Mona slammed on her brakes, forcing everyone's body to jolt forward. She nearly ran through a red light.

"Uh, I don't know if that's a smart move," Mona said, looking at Jewel through the rearview mirror. As she waited at the stoplight, she tried to convince Jewel to think about what she was about to do.

"Hey, girl, don't waste your breath on me," Jewel began. "'Cause, remember, I was right beside you when you were trying to reason with B.J. You got your work cut out for you with that one, so let me handle mine, and y'all do whatever you gotta do!"

THIRTY-TWO

Ella had been on cloud nine since she floated out of her mother's house and back into her car. She was finally going to meet with Taylor and that meant the possibilities were endless. What if he finally decided *they* should be together? What if he too finally realized B.J. wasn't the woman for him?

It was hell getting out of there without giving her mother the answers she wanted, but Ella lied and told her Mona needed her help for a few hours. Only after she promised to return immediately after meeting with Mona, did Tabitha allow her to leave.

Ella drove back to her hotel room and quickly fixed her hair and makeup. They'd probably make love when he first arrived, so she used some scented body wash and lotion to make sure everything was perfect.

When she was showered, moisturized, and dressed in the daintiest outfit she could find, she dialed Taylor's number to see where he was.

"I'm about fifteen minutes away," he said.

Ella was so excited. She even forgave him for not reaching out soon after B.J. caught them in bed. Now she understood how shocked he must've been. She figured they'd put their heads together about how to handle Sterling and deep down inside, she knew everything would be fine.

"You want room service or anything?" she purred.

"Nah, I'll see you soon," he said, and hung up.

Ella found that kind of odd. But she told herself she needed to stop looking for problems where none existed. Nearly an hour after their last phone call, Ella was still waiting on Taylor to arrive.

She was trying not to get too upset, but she wanted him to hurry. In hopes of helping the time to pass faster, she turned on the TV and eased back onto the bed. He knew her room number so she didn't have to worry about whether he'd be able to find her. She just needed him to hurry. Ella had conjured up all sorts of steamy images of them in her mind and she was eager to make most of them reality.

Another hour passed before she heard the faint knock at the door. Her head snapped in its direction, and that's when she realized she had dozed off.

"Oh, just a minute!" she yelled.

Ella rushed up from the bed and checked her reflection in the mirror. She tousled her hair and puckered her lips, then rushed to open the door.

She was not prepared for the vision that greeted her, and the smile quickly fell from her face.

"Hey," Taylor said as he rushed into the hotel room.

Closing the door behind him, but unsure of what to make of his appearance, she took a deep breath and leaned against the closed door.

"Taylor, honey, is everything okay?" she asked sweetly.

He looked disheveled. She had never seen him look so un-attractive in all the time they'd been together. His beard looked rugged and unkempt. He was in desperate need of a haircut or at least a trim; nothing about his appearance was appealing to Ella.

"You gotta fix this," Taylor finally said, sounding desperate.

Ella's eyebrows inched up a bit. She knew what he needed, but she also knew it would take some work to convince him. Why was he even still talking about B.J.? They should do what they did best. Why were their clothes still on?

"I'm so glad you finally called. I was worried," Ella said.

But her words didn't seem to register.

"I was thinking if you called her, and explained to her that it meant nothing, maybe she would listen to me," Taylor blurted out as if he hadn't heard anything she said.

Ella decided to remain calm.

"Just tell her it meant nothing," Taylor added.

That hurt more than Ella wanted to admit. What did he mean, it meant nothing? Wasn't he here so they could work it out? Weren't they going to make love? He just needed a moment.

Ella forced the smile back to her face. Maybe it was her approach. She needed to let him know she was willing to help him get over B.J. That's what it was.

"Taylor," Ella said sweetly. "Let's talk about us. B.J. is still pissed, but truthfully, what can we do to change her mind?"

When Taylor looked at her with his dark and faraway expression, Ella's heart nearly skipped a beat. He looked as if he couldn't comprehend her words. What had happened to the raw passion they had shared? When had he been unable to resist her?

"Ella, you've gotta help me fix this. I can't go on without B.J. She's threatening to take my kids; she's suing us; she wants a fuckin' divorce!"

This was not the same man who had ravished her every chance he had gotten. This was certainly not the man who had worshiped her body and made her feel things no other man had.

"I can't lose my family," he said.

Ella frowned. She didn't know quite how to handle this situation. Did Taylor really think she would help him get back with B.J.?

Here she was ready to dump Sterling in a heartbeat and he wanted *her* to help him get his wife back?

"I, uh, I don't understand. I mean, what about us? What about the great sex we shared? Our chemistry. What about everything we meant to each other?"

Taylor looked at her like she was speaking Arabic. He shook his head as if he was warding off confusion.

"Us," he muttered like the thought disgusted him. He frowned. "There *is* no us. Did you hear me say I'ma lose my wife? My children?"

Ella didn't bat an eye.

Taylor's frown deepened.

"Ella, I came here to beg you to help me get my wife back. You and me, that was nothing. It was all good while it lasted, but you knew what was up. Shit, you're married, too. I need you to play your position. I wasn't trying to mess up what you got going, and I damn sure didn't think you were gonna mess up my family."

The lump in Ella's throat felt like it was the size of a boulder. There was no way she could save face. She felt like the biggest fool ever.

"You thought I was coming over here to—"

Ella raised her hand to stop him. She was still trying to hold on to the stinging tears that threatened to fall from the corners of her eyes.

"What makes you think *I* can talk to B.J. for you?" she managed.

"I've tried everything. I'm desperate! I don't know what else to do. I figure since you two were such good friends..." Taylor's voice trailed off.

Ella felt like she was going to be sick.

How was she going to admit to Mona that she had been right all along? Ella thought she was taking a gamble by giving into

Taylor's advances. She thought she had given him the kind of attention B.J. never could. Was his memory really that short?

Now Taylor was crushing her heart into a million pieces by all but admitting that sex didn't mean I love you, or that I even care enough about you to leave my wife!

THIRTY-THREE

B.J. was so rattled when she finally arrived back at the hotel that she thought her nerves were shot to hell. How dare they try to gang up on her after all they had done to her? She couldn't wait to get through this last interview.

Once she finished it, she'd get on that computer and try her best to write as much as possible. The nerve of them!

"I've got to chill out. I can't do an interview like this." B.J. was so wired, her hands were shaking. As usual, after she was on the freeway and racing toward home, she started replaying the afternoon in her head.

There was so much she should've said. They'd acted like she was the one who'd kept something from *them*. They were lucky, all three of them! If B.J. could, she'd get Samantha to add their names to the damn lawsuit.

Shouldn't they also be held responsible for this mess? B.J. was so humiliated; she didn't want to see anyone who were reminders of her old friends or her old life.

Things were going downhill, but when Sasha called her up like they were, or could ever be, friends? Well, that's when she realized for sure, each and every one of those heifers had to pay. As she patted her face with the sponge from her compact, she suddenly looked at her reflection in the mirror.

"Who says I can't add their names to the lawsuit? Maybe I

need to discuss that with Samantha." If there was a way to do it, Samantha would figure it out. Right now she needed to get ready for this Skype interview.

She flicked her wrist and glanced down at the time.

"Damn!" She quickly painted her lips, puckered them, and rushed to the desk where her laptop sat idle.

B.J. logged on to the site and entered the station's Skype number. She hoped her head didn't look too distorted, but at this point, there wasn't much she could do if it did.

"Bobbi Almond?" the producer greeted as B.J. tried to adjust her monitor to see him better.

"Yes," B.J. answered.

"Great. I was getting a little worried."

"Sorry about that. I had an appointment that ran over," she said.

"No, it's fine. I'm glad we've got you now. Okay, you're actually at the bottom of the B block. Our anchors will both introduce you; then they'll switch to one person when it's time for the Q and A."

"The what and A?" B.J. asked.

"Oh, sorry, my bad, question and answer section. They'll run a short story first, then come back and ask you some questions. You can see me clearly?"

"Yep," B.J. said.

"Good, then we're just about ready to go. Good luck, and thanks again for joining us."

B.J. sat through all of the crime-related stories and a few about the city council and a weather tease before they finally got to her. She shouldn't have been at this point already, but she was starting to get burned out on these interviews. None of them asked anything outside of the normal: Why are you suing the mistress? What do you hope to accomplish? What are your friends saying about the book stuff?

She was bored before they even started.

After the anchors read a story about her and the fact that she was suing her husband and the mistress, B.J. actually had to stifle a yawn. Now that would've been funny. What if they came to her and she opened up with a big, hearty yawn. The thought made her smile. And just as she did, the female anchor said, "B.J. Almond, thank you so much for joining us."

"I'm glad that I could be here," B.J. said.

As B.J. suspected, the woman asked the same damn questions she had answered on all of the other shows. She told herself she didn't see why they simply didn't record from one station and play it back on their own.

As they were wrapping up, the woman said, "What do you say to those who consider this another frivolous lawsuit that's going to help clog up our legal system?"

"Frivolous?" B.J. countered with attitude, despite herself. "I'd tell them that until they walk into their bedroom and find their good friend sharing their bed with their spouse, they shouldn't write me off! I hope no one ever finds themselves in that position, but I tell you what, I'm not about to sit back and lick my wounds. No, not at all! I refuse to go down without a fight!"

"Wow!" the anchorwoman said. Her eyes grew wide. "Well, B.J. Almond, we will definitely keep following this case and we hope that you come back and visit with us when it wraps up."

"Thanks for having me," B.J. said. "Oh, and I'd also like to add that my book, *Blowin' the Whistle*, will be out soon. I want to make sure that people think twice before they cross those who consider them a friend."

"And that has to be the last word. Again, B.J. Almond, thanks for your time today."

When they went to another story and her monitor went blank, B.J. disconnected. She'd had quite a day.

Her cell phone rang as she was about to go run a hot bath. It was her agent.

"B.J., you've been all over the place! We've been going crazy, trying to keep up with all of the press."

B.J. hadn't heard that much excitement from her agent since they'd inked the original deal.

"Darlene, things are getting kinda crazy," B.J. admitted.

"Oh? What's going on?"

"Well, some of my old friends confronted me outside of a TV station earlier today. It completely rattled me. For a moment, I thought I was going to have to cancel my last interview."

"Do we need security to escort you to these events?" Darlene asked. She was truly concerned for B.J.'s safety. "I'm sure the publisher would understand that added expense."

"No, I don't think we're there just yet, but I did want to make you aware that people are starting to make their feelings known about this project."

"Oh, B.J. you're not having second thoughts, are you?"

"I wouldn't say second thoughts, but I'm wondering how bad it will get once the book is out. I mean, this is just from the few interviews I've given. What will happen when people get their hands on the book and start reading all these details?"

"Hopefully, they'll tell all of their friends about it, and they'll all run out and buy their own copies," Darlene joked.

B.J. wasn't really in a laughing mood. She was serious. She hadn't thought about her safety before. She didn't think there was any reason to worry. People wrote tell-all books all the time. Look at that guy who wrote the book about Terry McMillan, or the slew of rap star girlfriends. That Video Vixen girl was on her third or fourth book, wasn't she?

B.J. sighed. No one would prevent her from writing this book, that was for certain, but she did have to think about her safety. She did have two small children and they didn't ask to be brought into this mess.

Why did her stupid friends have to cause such a mess? And even though Mona would never admit it, B.J. had a gut feeling that she had helped Ella hide the affair. Ella and Mona were too close for Mona not to have known what was going on. At times, B.J. was torn over her decision to get back at her friends with the book, but when she thought about how Mona and Ella must've made fun of her behind her back, that made the decision much easier.

"I don't want you to start worrying about stuff like that," Darlene said. "Focus on your writing. I'll speak with your editor and we'll figure something out."

"I'm not sure it's at the point where we need to devote more than a conversation to it," B.J. protested. She didn't want them thinking she scared easily.

"I've got it under control, B.J. You do what you do best. Get us a first draft of that manuscript and let us get it out in time for football season."

"But the season is right around the corner," B.J. said.

"I know, but isn't it wonderful? The publisher has agreed to fast track it. That's why we need you to buckle down and get it done. Bobbi, that's almost unheard of, so, not to add any pressure, but, I'm sure this is going to be huge!"

B.J. didn't realize the book was coming out this year! How the hell was that not going to add pressure? She sighed. There was so much she needed to do. First, she needed to call her mom and explain that she'd have to keep the kids longer. That was something B.J. didn't look forward to. She really missed her kids, but she needed to get busy and she couldn't write if they were around.

THIRTY-FOUR

Nearly a week later, the strangest thing happened when B.J., her mother, and the kids were getting out of the car in front of the Four Seasons Hotel in downtown L.A. She could've sworn a man snapped her picture.

"This has gotta stop," B.J. muttered. She laughed at how paranoid she was becoming. Okay, so now paparazzi were following her to the hotel? She chuckled to herself.

"Everything okay?" her mother asked.

"Yeah, I'm fine. A little stressed over this book; that's all."

Her mother's features tightened and her lips pursed. B.J. knew her well enough to realize that was her way of biting her tongue. There was something her mother wanted to say, but she was holding back; she didn't want to feel her daughter's wrath.

It was rare for Vernice to disapprove of anything B.J. did. She was the one child who always made her proud. B.J. had noticed the strain the disagreement over the book was having on her relationship with her mother. Just the other day, as she hovered over her laptop, she had asked herself it this was truly worth it. But B.J. told herself she needed to move forward. What would she look like if she suddenly threw in the towel? She had done so many interviews; just about everyone interested in sports knew about her drama and the forthcoming book. No, there was no way she could abandon the project now.

They were returning from dinner after spending the entire day together. B.J. had missed her kids, but if she was going to meet that deadline, she needed to be away from them so, when she could, she spent quality time with them and her mother. They were going to spend a few more hours together before she sent them off to Pasadena.

For the most part, their time together had been nice, except every now and then her mother would make snide little comments under her breath or B.J. would catch her staring.

"I wanna be sure you know what you doin'," Vernice would say when B.J. asked her what was going on.

B.J. was getting tired of it. In her mind, she was already counting down the minutes until her mother was headed back to Pasadena. The only downside was that her kids would have to leave, too. Spending time with them only proved to her how much she missed them.

Hours later, B.J. felt like she'd been typing nonstop for days. If she wasn't mistaken, her fingers were even starting to cramp. But she was so happy with herself. The story was coming along better than she had hoped it would. After she stopped to do two telephone interviews, she was right back at it.

Being in the Pro-Prime light wasn't easy. The athletes on the field weren't the only hard bodies in the stadiums. NFL wives were under incredible pressure to look sexy at all times, and maintain hard bodies of their own.

So it was no surprise that a coach's wife might catch the eye of one of those young studs on the field. It was like one of the ultimate taboos. And the way Lawna told the story about the cub she had snuck away to Hedonism with, it made us all feel like we had been a fly on the wall in that room. What it did for me was confirm that Lawna was growing increasingly wild. She admitted she'd always had a thing for rookies.

Yes, of course I'm still naming names. So when LeMarco Warren was traded from the team, they met up and behaved as if they were never going to see each other again.

The Sea Lions were playing the Eagles and while we didn't have plans, Lawna had plans of her own.

I have to admit, I'm not sure what all he did to her, but I'd be damned if she didn't look like she was eighteen again when he was done. You could see happiness all over her face as she told the story.

They had just arrived at the all-adult resort, Hedonism II, situated on the tip of legendary Negril Beach. The resort is known for its wild theme parties, a nude water slide that snakes through the disco and its nude beach and nude pool. Lawna was so excited; she didn't know how much longer she could act as though they were two strangers who happened to have arrived at the same time.

After he left the registration desk, she discreetly followed him to the elevator and down the hall once they reached the right floor.

Lawna all but glided into the cool ocean view suite LeMarco had reserved for their romp. She could see why the resort was so successful. Everything was lavish, with stylish furnishings and an atmosphere that promised something exotic for everyone—nice, naughty, nude, or prude. Lawna was so excited.

The moment the door closed behind them, they charged toward each other and started kissing. There was so much panting and clawing at each other's clothes, she thought she'd die from the anticipation alone. LeMarco's body was magnificent.

"Oh, God, I don't think I've ever wanted someone so badly," she said, pulling him onto the four-poster, king-sized bed.

"Damn, I feel you; I feel you," LeMarco said as he allowed her to lead him. "This shit is tight. I hope you'll still feel like that after I'm done with you."

Lawna giggled. "You know I will."

"Good." LeMarco was now on top of her. He pressed down a bit harder, careful not to put the entire weight of his body on her. They kissed some more. He sucked her neck, and palmed her breasts. He squeezed hard, just the way she liked it.

Suddenly, she moved her head away from him so that she could look upward.

"OHMYGOD!" Her mouth gaped open. "Is that a mirror up there?"

LeMarco turned to see what she was talking about. Then he started to laugh.

"That's gotta be the biggest mirror I've ever seen. It's the size of this whole bed, directly above us!" She giggled.

"It is!"

"This is really nice; I mean, really really nice."

LeMarco's mouth suddenly covered hers. He eased more of his weight onto her body and Lawna braced herself. She loved the feel of his muscular frame on top of her. There wasn't an inch of fat anywhere on his lean body. Everything was so hard and tight, she'd be reliving this moment long after they were done and had gone their separate ways.

The room was done in a bright aqua color with chocolate crown molding. Flat-screen TVs were hoisted up in one corner of the bedroom and in an opposite corner of the living room.

"I've wanted you from the moment you walked into Coach's office," he said.

Lawna had been attracted to rookies before, but never had she acted on that attraction. There was something about LeMarco that she couldn't resist. He was all of twenty-three years old, but she didn't care.

"Oooh, I need to pee," Lawna said as she wiggled beneath him.

"Now, I'm not into no golden showers or anything like that," LeMarco joked.

Lawna pinched his sides, and was in awe when her fingers could hardly grab his skin. His body was that tight. He eased up and watched as she ran into the bathroom.

Inside the bathroom there was a Jacuzzi tub, big enough for two, and a massive glass-enclosed shower with a multi-head position for the top and the bottom of one's body. A few feet away was the patio door that showed off the hot tub that overlooked the beautiful Caribbean sea.

After using the bathroom and washing her hands at the sink, she eased back into the room. She was glad she hadn't walked out talking; he had just hung up the phone.

"Is everything okay?" she asked. She leaned against the bathroom's doorframe.

LeMarco turned to her and smiled. "Oh yeah, it's all gravy."

She walked over and they started kissing again. She allowed her hands to travel all over his body. He felt so good, so hard, and so perfect beneath her touch. She was so eager, she felt like a five-year-old on Christmas morning.

"Are we gonna make it out of this room this weekend?" he asked.

Lawna pulled back and used her fingers to wipe at her lips. She giggled.

"I'm not complaining; just let me know. We can order room service and we ain't never gotta step foot outside until it's time to go. What you think?"

He smiled as he looked up at her.

"You mean you don't wanna prance around in your birthday suit? I figured you'd want to show everybody what you're working with," she joked.

"There's only one person I wanna show anything and she's right up in here, so what's up?" LeMarco shrugged.

He was sexier than a chocolate-covered Calvin Klein model and she loved everything about him. Everywhere her eyes wandered, they took in perfection.

"You sure do know how to make a girl feel special."

"Oh, you ain't seen nothing yet. I wanna make you feel real special, excited, relaxed, then satisfied to the fullest. Believe that!"

"Your commitment to excellence?" she asked, grinning.

When he started undressing, Lawna wanted to pinch herself to make sure this was real and not some fantasy dream. She should've been taking off her clothes, but she wanted to see everything he was doing. She wanted to take mental pictures so when she returned home to her life with her intense husband, she could escape back to this place and be with LeMarco; even if it was only in her mind.

Naked now, LeMarco walked over to her and started to take her clothes off. She felt so sexy with him.

"I'm gonna give you a little taste. Then we'll enjoy champagne in the hot tub, before I finish you off after dinner," he said.

"I love a man who knows how to plan, and how to execute his plan," she teased.

As promised, he ravished her body with such precision, it was as if he'd been loving her for years. He used his tongue, his teeth, his fingertips, the palms of his hands, and his muscled legs.

Lawna was brought to tears. She'd forgotten such bliss still existed on Earth. Suddenly, she realized that the knots that had found a home in her shoulder seemed to have vanished. Her legs couldn't stop trembling, and the way he kissed and suckled her inner thighs wasn't helping matters.

LeMarco ordered a feast. They ate, watched a movie. Then he

reached over and kissed her again. She was wet all over again, from one kiss.

"Let's go relax in the hot tub."

When she followed him out to the patio, the mild breeze hugged her skin and she felt like she was truly in heaven. He offered her a hand and helped her step into the hot tub.

There was a tall silver wine bucket nearby and it was sweating. Lawna noticed there were two bottles chilling inside.

LeMarco grabbed one, popped the top, and took a healthy sip from the bottle. When he passed it to Lawna, she took a sip and giggled.

The powerful jets kept the water's rays strong, hitting all of the right spots for Lawna. She eased down into the water. She felt so free, soaking naked in a hot tub at dusk with a sexy man.

"You are so beautiful," he said.

LeMarco moved closer to her and took the bottle. He took another swig, then held it up to her lips. She drank as much as her mouth could hold and moved her head back.

"Sorry, babe. Just wanna make you feel good," he said.

She swallowed, then smiled at him.

If only he knew; if only he knew.

THIRTY-FIVE

"How did you get this number?" B.J. screamed into the hotel's phone for the umpteenth time. "Don't call here anymore!"

She was beginning to get frustrated. The damned reporters seemed to comprehend no boundaries. She was under pressure to finish this book and now people were crank-calling her hotel room!

It had been the same caller each time. A scruffy voice or some kind of computer-altered voice that said the same thing over and over again.

"B.J., I know your secret, so if you think you're going to get away with this, you've got another think coming!" That was followed by a wicked laugh.

B.J. didn't know who the hell was trying to throw her off her game, but it wasn't going to work. She thought about how the caller kept talking about knowing her secret. She told herself she didn't have to guess too hard to figure out it was probably Mona trying some of that reverse psychology bull crap.

B.J. was not a weak woman. She didn't care what people thought of her as much as she let on that she did. No, B.J. was extremely smart and calculating. Unlike her gullible friends, she didn't need to get the approval of others before she decided what to do.

And she certainly wasn't foolish enough to go telling people her business. She had learned her lesson long ago. B.J. wasn't supposed to be married to Taylor. She had a high school sweet-heart long before she found one in college.

Bryant Soloman was the epitome of a perfect man. He and B.J. had gone steady from her sophomore year up to a month before prom. Back then, she was tight with Tamera Smith. She and Tamera were closer than sisters. They shared all kinds of secrets. B.J. had told Tamera everything—how she had finally given her virginity to Bryant, how they were going to get married and run off together after high school.

Tamera had also shared her secrets with B.J., but there was something Tamera didn't admit. She didn't tell B.J. that it was her and not B.J. that Bryant originally wanted to talk to when they all first met.

B.J. remembered it like it was still as fresh as the heartache she suffered for years.

Not only had Tamera been keeping that secret, but she'd also decided that maybe she'd acted too hastily when she'd decided that she wanted Bryant's best friend, Trey Blake, instead of Bryant.

Trey turned out to be a dog, so Tamera decided to start telling Bryant everything B.J. had told her. She also told how B.J. had slipped up and slept with this college guy when they went to a frat party. It didn't take long for Bryant to decide B.J. really wasn't the one for him. He didn't get with Tamera either, but that experience was enough for B.J. to learn that it didn't make sense to share your secrets with anyone. She kept hers close from that day forward.

Years later, when B.J. and Bryant ran into each other, he admitted that he had never stopped loving her. He told B.J. he was young back then and didn't think he could move beyond what she had done, but he was grown now and wanted to try again.

It was too late. B.J. was already married to Taylor. They were newlyweds at the time. But Bryant always stood as a reminder of that valuable lesson she'd learned from Tamera.

"Too bad Mona, Jewel and Lawna didn't have a Tamera in their lives," B.J. said to herself as she turned back to her manuscript.

She wondered if she should use a digital voice recorder to speak into so she could crank out chapters faster.

Chapter 30

Mona's fans would lose their mind if they realized they were following a nut case. Seriously, the girl is a freak! All she needs to do is avoid stepping on cracks in the sidewalk and she'll be fully certifiable.

It's a good thing she's self-employed; there's no way she'd be able to hang on to a nine-to-five. While she never really cheated on her husband, Melvin, she does talk about his lack of skills in the bedroom quite frequently. I always wondered, why any woman would marry a man whose penis didn't satisfy her before she got married. Did she think he'd grow a few inches over the years?

To hear her tell it, Melvin is so small that, at times, she fantasizes about those big hunky studs in the locker room. It's like the fixation she had with that movie Any Given Sunday. *The movie was good. Jamie Foxx has always been one of my favorites. I loved the intensity and how Cameron Diaz played the hell out of that owner role. But Mona loved the infamous locker room scene. Cameron walked into the room and one of the players walked by completely naked, showing how hung he was.*

Believe it or not, Mona became so obsessed, she even thought of tracking down the actor! We finally talked her out of it, explaining there was no reason to hunt him down; it wasn't like she was going to hop on for a ride. We knew her well enough to know that was something she wouldn't do.

Fans or patients of hers are the ones I really feel sorry for; don't even think we don't know all your business! Seriously, Pamela Johnson, we know that you've been to sex rehab three times and your husband, David, is just about ready to throw in the towel.

And, Geneva Bradshaw, how are you going to be an executive at Capitol Records and think your kleptomaniac ways aren't going to cause problems both at home and at work? And I heard your husband, Kevin, is fine as all get out! Yeah, when you go to Mona Brown for any kind of counseling, expect your business to be well-discussed in great detail with her friends.

B.J. laughed as she sat back and read that paragraph. She didn't know if the publishers would allow her to leave Mona's clients' real names in there, but what the hell? She'd let them take it out if they wanted. For now, that's how she felt. And besides, she hoped her editor realized it wasn't good to mess with an artist's work!

THIRTY-SIX

Mona used one hand to hold the phone to her ear and the other to hold her head. She was devastated, and for her, a critical situation was hovering over her. Her head was thumping louder than her racing heart. She was so pissed she didn't know what to do.

"I have this f'ing thing under control, believe me. I'm so sorry and the minute we get off the phone, I'm going to find a way to put a muzzle on her!"

"Listen, two sponsors isn't that bad, but we've gotta cut this thing off before it bleeds out of control. It's one thing for sponsors to pass on you, but if people start asking for refunds…"

Sean Hughes was the promoter for Mona's upcoming conference. Mona had spent nearly an hour trying to assure him that things weren't going to get any worse with the media. So far, every day, more and more details were being leaked about the Sea Lions coaches and their personal lives. Most of the stuff wasn't even true, but it was becoming more difficult to separate the truth from the rumors.

"Don't even throw that out there. I'll get on top of this. I was already working with my team to figure out the best approach," Mona lied, cutting him off.

"I hope you know what you're doing; we all stand to lose a lot of money over this. Not to mention, your credibility is at risk, and we can't have that."

"Sean, I've got this under control; seriously. Now let me take care of this," Mona said. She wanted to get off the phone and out of the hot seat. They were weeks away from her major event at the Staples Center and now there was concern over some of the stories leaking from B.J.'s book.

"This is all too damn much!" Mona screamed and hurled the phone across the room, where it crashed into the wall and fell to pieces.

"B.J. has got to stop this now!"

Did this woman really not care about ruining everyone's life? Could she really be that vindictive? Mona didn't have the time to sit around and wait to see. She needed to do something and she needed to act fast. Her plan to pay B.J. off never really got off the ground because she couldn't find the cow!

She walked into her master suite and plucked the phone from the nightstand. She dialed the number and when a voice answered, she exhaled.

"I was just looking for your number, Mrs. Brown," the man said.

Cedric Bryant was the private investigator Mona had hired to find B.J. Up to this point, she was somewhat okay with him working at his own pace, but now the stakes were higher. She needed results, and she needed them fast.

"Were you?"

"Yes, your girl has been living at the Four Seasons downtown," he said.

"Great!" Mona was so thrilled.

"If you like, we can meet up so I can give you everything I've got so far," he said.

"Cedric, that is music to my ears. I can meet you anywhere in the next thirty minutes."

"Okay. Well, I'm over here off Manchester. How about Roscoe's?"

"Is that on Florence and Manchester?"

"Yup, say in thirty minutes?"

"I'll be there, Ced. Thank you!"

Mona knew hiring this guy was her very best option. There was no way she would've found B.J. without him. She changed out of her lounging clothes, grabbed her checkbook and her bag.

On the drive over, she started going over in her mind what she would say to B.J. She had to be effective. She was running out of time and she couldn't run the risk of losing everything behind this mess.

A part of her wondered what B.J. had been saying on all these damn interviews to get sponsors to drop her like that. But she figured she'd get all of that later. For now, she needed to get with Cedric, check out his information, and decide what to do next.

Roscoe's House of Chicken and Waffles was a South Central staple, and each time Mona ventured over there, she told herself she needed to come more frequently.

The only thing that pissed her off was the tiny parking lot that was shared with several other businesses. But today, when she pulled up, there was a spot on the street right next to the building.

"This must be a good sign," she mumbled as she parallel-parked expertly.

Mona jumped out of the car and walked into the dark little restaurant. Cedric was waiting at a corner table usually reserved for parties of more than two. But Mona was glad he was able to pull that off.

While Mona loved the food at Roscoe's, what she didn't like was the cramped area, the rickety tables and chairs, and she certainly didn't like their flatware. Pushing all of these thoughts from her head, she reluctantly took the soiled menu the waitress passed to her.

"Let me know when you guys are ready." She smiled. "I'll be right back with two waters."

"I'll take coffee," Cedric said.

The waitress looked at Mona as if she thought Mona might want coffee as well. At first Mona was so eager to get on with their meeting, she figured she could skip the drink, but thought better of it.

"Do you have to-go cups?"

The waitress looked baffled. "Yes," she said.

"Okay, please bring me a large glass of orange juice, but put it in a to-go cup and bring me a straw, please."

"Okay."

Mona pulled her hand sanitizers out and carefully wiped her hands. Then she used a Clorox wipe to clean her section of the table.

Cedric opened his large manila envelope and jumped right in. He had various pictures of B.J. arriving and leaving several places. He had pictures of her with her kids and her mother outside the hotel and pictures of her walking outside her room.

"Wow, you're thorough," Mona said.

"Just doing my job." Cedric pulled out a log that showed a list of places B.J. had visited over a two-week period. He left nothing to the imagination. Most of the stuff was routine. B.J. visited several TV stations, studio00.s in Burbank, radio stations, the nail shop, hair salon, drugstores, nothing out of the ordinary until an unfamiliar building caught Mona's eye.

"What's this?" Mona asked.

"Uh, it's a luxury apartment building where B.J. rents a place."

The answer made Mona frown.

"B.J. doesn't live in an apartment," she said.

"No, of course not," Cedric said. "But she pays the rent there faithfully every month."

"For who?"

"Her sister."

Mona was a bit disappointed that there wasn't any real dirt on B.J. That made the fact that she was in on the whole affair between Ella and Taylor even more difficult to stomach.

She wanted the three of them to come together so everyone's lives could return to normal. Mona thought back to the last tearful phone call from Ella.

"He never wanted me. I was such a fool," Ella cried.

Mona didn't enjoy saying *I told you so*, and she'd resisted as she listened to Ella describe how Taylor had tracked her down only to try and enlist her help in getting his family back together.

"Did you really think he was going to leave his family for you?"

"I know this sounds stupid now, but why wouldn't I? Mona, she's so mean. She complains about having sex with him. It's so obvious she only likes the lifestyle she's able to live because he's an NFL head coach," Ella complained.

"Yeah, but if that's how their relationship works. Who are you to judge or decide he needs or even wants something different?" Mona asked.

Ella was still devastated, but Mona simply wanted the mess to be over. She wanted to remind Ella that she had quite a bit in Sterling, too, but it was clear that Ella needed time to get over Taylor's rejection.

"So what are you gonna do, Boss Lady?"

Cedric's question brought Mona back to their table and helped her push Ella further away.

"I don't know yet," Mona said.

"Well, sorry I couldn't dig up any dirt on her. She seems to really be devoted to her husband, children, and her extended family."

Mona still had to try something. She had far too much to lose, so she'd have to regroup and decide on the best course of action.

THIRTY-SEVEN

"Guurrrl, I'm so glad you could make it!" Sasha squealed like a robot programmed to deliver those exact words. She wore a royal blue, barely there, sequined tank minidress that made her legs look like they were extra long. Her look was topped off with a pair of five-and-a-half-inch, come-hither stiletto slippers.

On draft night, 8623 Melrose Avenue in West Hollywood was the place to be. The crowd was a mixture of young Hollywood stars and professional athletes. And although she was neither, Sasha Davenport greeted each guest personally with a set of air kisses to their cheeks, whether they wanted them or not.

With help from her sponsors, Sasha had transformed The Villa, a dual-level top nightlife hotspot, with an exclusive and A-List guest list, into the mother of all draft parties.

The Villa had a stucco façade with dark wood and marble floors, as well as a long, marble-top bar and a fancy centerpiece of a golden globe, meant to resemble a library of the old rich with hundreds of books stacked on wall shelves. For tonight's event, a long table was moved into the center of the first level.

On either end of the nightclub were huge football goalposts made of colored, sculpted ice. Between them was a spectacular seafood wonderland. Massive appetizer trays were stacked in a series of cascading towers. Each contained an array of chilled colossal king prawns, clams on the half-shell, mussels, and lobster tails, along with oysters and crabmeat. There were also boneless, wild Copper River salmon fillets, caviar, and Alaskan king crab legs. Scallions, along with lemon wedges and herbs, nestled in the crushed ice bedding that lined the edge of the display.

Most of the crowd was gathered in front of the seventy-five-inch, double-sided plasma screen that hung from the upper level.

"Could this place be any more fabulous? This party, it's so live. I can't take it!" Sasha yelled at one of her friends as she looked around the room.

"How the hell did you get all this press out here?" the girl asked through her fake smile.

Suddenly, a group of people cheered at the announcement of another draft pick.

"OHMYGOD! Is that the sports reporter from Fox?" the girl asked.

"Yup, all the stations are going live from here tonight," Sasha bragged. "I've already been interviewed twice." She winked.

"Okay, Sasha Davenport, what the hell did you do, and how come you didn't hook me up?"

Sasha hunched her shoulders and started dancing around seductively. "Don't you wanna be me right now?!" Sasha teased.

"Sasha, you tell me what you did. How you got all this press here? The way paparazzi has the place staked out, you 'bout to be in *People* magazine or something!"

Sasha grinned a toothy grin, and started wiggling her hips. She loved being in the spotlight. Talking to her friend, Gigglez, kept her mind off the fact that she hadn't seen any of the Sea Lions coaches' wives and she needed those bitches to at least show their faces.

She already had a photographer lined up to take as many pictures as he could. The plan was for her to leak them to the tabloids the next morning.

"I need to go mingle; more people are coming in," Sasha said as she danced away from Gigglez.

Her timing couldn't have been better. Just as she arrived back at her post near the door, Lawna walked in.

"Lawna, guurrrl, you look delicious! Just fab as always. Didn't you use to model?" Sasha asked.

Lawna was wearing a dusted gold-colored Gucci shorts set. The single-button jacket revealed just enough of her full breasts and a hint of her flat stomach.

"Thanks, and yeah, I did," Lawna said. She wondered where this sudden interest had come from, but this wasn't the time to talk about it. "Sasha, looks like you've got quite a crowd here."

"I do. Come on in and enjoy yourself." But as soon as Lawna stepped all the way inside, a photographer seemed to appear out of nowhere.

And if that wasn't strange enough, Sasha shoved a chilled champagne flute into her hand, grabbed her by the shoulder, and said, "Say cheese!"

It all caught Lawna completely off-guard. She didn't have time to smile. Instead, she gave what must've been a deer-in-the-head-lights glare as the camera's flash clicked off continuously.

"What the?"

"Oh, gurrrl, be careful. Paparazzi are all over the place. They're like cockroaches," Sasha whispered to Lawna.

The photographer was still snapping away.

Lawna quickly rushed away and tried to find the others.

When Mona arrived, she received the same treatment as Lawna. When it was over, she looked down at the text message Lawna had sent.

I'm upstairs. Where's Jewel?

Mona rushed up the stairs and found Lawna who looked more like she was hiding out than having a good time.

"You seen B.J. or Ella yet?"

"No, but everyone else and their mamas seems to be here," Lawna said.

"Yeah. How the hell did Sasha pull this off?"

Lawna shook her head. She had been wondering the same thing from the moment she walked up and noticed paparazzi lined up like they were at the Shrine Auditorium for the Grammy Awards.

"I doubt Jewel is coming," Mona said.

"You know if she told Davon?"

"I asked her to give me a few more days. I gotta tell you something," Mona said.

"Oh, God! I can't handle any more bad news," Lawna said.

"No, nothing like that. Well, not completely. I hired a private investigator to find B.J. She's staying downtown at the Four Seasons."

Mona rattled off B.J.'s room number and what appeared to be her daily routine.

"Wow! You actually hired someone to find her? So, now that you know where she's staying, you going over there?"

"I am now; especially if she doesn't show up here tonight," Mona said.

After sitting around for nearly an hour, Mona and Lawna started to think that Sasha had just said Ella and B.J. were coming. They couldn't imagine what would've been taking them so long to get there if they were really coming out.

"You think Sasha lied?" Lawna asked.

Mona turned her head. "I didn't want to say anything, but I was thinking the same thing!"

"You know what, before we go jumping to conclusions, let's move around a bit. We've been sitting here in this one spot. For all we know, they could be downstairs mending their differences and doing the Cupid Shuffle," Lawna joked.

"I seriously doubt that," Mona said, laughing as she got up.

Downstairs, the party was in full swing. But Mona did notice a couple of the reporters huddled in a corner. They didn't look too happy and the target of their anger seemed to be Sasha. Sasha moved around the room, apparently oblivious to the reporters' building fury.

Mona wondered what was going on, but she was more curious about whether B.J. and Ella had finally made an appearance. She had been calling Ella ever since she had heard she was coming to the party, but there was no answer. Mona turned to Lawna and said, "Let's break up. You go over to that side. I'll take this side. Let's meet back here in fifteen minutes. We know neither of them are upstairs. If we can't find them down here, they're not here."

"Okay, cool."

By the time Mona and Lawna met back up again, they had already figured out the truth. Neither B.J. nor Ella had promised Sasha they'd come to her party.

"That lying…she's such a social climber," Lawna said.

Mona frowned a bit. She noticed two of the people who had been near the reporters were now looking around as if they were searching for someone.

"Wait here. I'm about to go find out what's going on," she said.

As Mona approached the two young ladies, they looked at her like she was crazy.

"Hi, I'm helping Sasha. She asked me to make sure you guys had everything you needed. Is everything okay?"

"Absolutely not!" one of the women yelled. Her complexion started to redden. "We were told the wife of the Sea Lions head coach was going to be here and she and the woman she's suing were going to make statements! We've been here from the beginning; this is nothing but a party promoting Sasha Davenport!"

"Well, let me go find out what's happening and I'll come and let you guys know what's going on, okay?" Mona smiled.

"That would be so helpful. Every time we try to talk to her, someone comes and rushes her away."

"Yeah, I could see how that would be irritating."

Mona walked away from the women, who turned and headed back to the corner where the reporters were still huddled. They looked even more pissed than before.

"Let's go," she said to Lawna without even stopping.

"Wha-what's going on?"

"Put the drink down and let's get the hell up out of here. I don't know what kind of game Sasha is playing, but we don't need to be any part of it!"

Lawna put down the glass of Nuvo she was drinking, grabbed a crab leg from a platter, and rushed to catch up with Mona.

"Bye, ladies. Thanks for coming," Sasha had the nerve to say on their way out.

THIRTY-EIGHT

B.J. understood the publicist from her publishing house knew what she was doing in regards to getting her as much exposure as possible, but damn if her actions didn't leave B.J. confused. She was getting tired of all the interviews.

Not only was B.J. still giving interviews, but the publicist had her dropping little segments from *Blowin' the Whistle*, which B.J. did not agree with. She felt like telling people so many of the stories before the book's release wouldn't help sales one bit. But she did as she was told. Publicity and marketing were not her forte and she'd tell anyone who wanted to listen.

By the time she had finished her interviews, four for today, she didn't even feel like writing.

"Don't get discouraged; you're almost done," B.J. told herself. And she was. She had been doing so well.

Samantha had finally called to say they had a deposition date. They talked a little about the kind of press she should expect and what she should wear. They also set an appointment for B.J. to come meet with Sam before the deposition. Even that was going well.

She was still getting those phone calls, but B.J. knew how to handle her business, so she wasn't the least bit worried. Each year of her marriage, her rainy day account had gotten fatter and fatter and she had Taylor by the balls. Even if they agreed on a settlement, she and her children would be comfortable for the rest of their lives. And that was all that really mattered.

B.J. was considering taking a break for the night, but she wasn't sure if that would put her too far behind.

When the phone rang again, she didn't even bother answering. She didn't know who the caller with the computerized voice was, but she wasn't about to keep playing his game.

B.J. started thinking about the information they were strategically putting out in the press. She had talked about Ella nearly killing Sterling with those bootleg Viagra pills. She talked about Lawna's whorish ways, and Melvin's substandard penis, Jewel's decision to switch teams after she contracted an STD. As she thought about all the drama and juicy details she had outlined in the book, she had a good feeling about sales.

Then something made her chuckle out loud. She started typing.

I can remember watching the game in one of the team-sponsored suites. The wives usually shared it with charity organizations and local business leaders. Although we were glad we weren't out there on the 50-yard line or tucked in corners of the end zones, you had no control over who was in the suites and they were always packed.

I overheard a conversation and I swore it so reminded me of Zeke and Jewel. Now tell me, what kind of man doesn't realize that his wife and her so-called friend are screwing right under his nose, sometimes in his own damn house?! That's what I mean about football season. These coaches are so disconnected from reality during the fall that a woman could do just about anything and his simple behind wouldn't even know it. That's what happened with Jewel.

And really, who can blame her? Zeke was relentless with the way he chased after women. I had heard about him and a couple of the cheerleaders, and Jewel even found some papers that pointed to him being arrested in Pittsburgh for having sex with a hooker! I mean, c'mon!

You can't really blame her for saying enough is enough, can you? The only thing is, I'd have to go through every man on the face of this earth before I turned to the extreme she did.

When B.J. heard the guys on "Mike and Mike in the Morning," talking about that one earlier, she couldn't help but laugh. At this point, people all around the city were trying to match coaches or players to the stories she had carefully allowed to leak during interviews.

The two hosts were arguing about whether having a bisexual wife was really a problem. It may have been something about their deep discussion, or maybe it was Vernice's nagging voice, but for a split second, B.J. wondered would ruining everyone really make her feel better about what had happened?

THIRTY-NINE

"Jewel Swanson!" Zeke screamed.

She didn't even need to see him to tell that he was drunk. She rolled her eyes at the thought of having to babysit his ass tonight!

"Jeeewwwwel!" Zeke hollered.

Jewel sat up in bed and pulled her sleep mask from her eyes. She wasn't in the mood. It seemed as if every day there was some new drama and she was ready for all of this to be over. B.J. had been talking but it was almost like someone else was keeping this drama going. Jewel couldn't make any sense of it and this wasn't the time to try and figure it out.

What was he going to do, go through every room of the house yelling her name?

"Jewel Swanson, where the fuck are you?"

He was really drunk. Okay, the moment she got him settled down a bit, she'd go make a massive pot of coffee. She didn't feel like being up all night. Jewel figured, the only thing worse than a loud sloppy drunk was one who refused to pass out, and when her husband got like this, he was the worst kind imaginable.

He burst into their bedroom, nearly knocking the door off the hinges.

Zeke could barely stand, much less walk. She wondered how the hell he had made it home like that.

"Are you gay?"

Jewel sat starting at him blankly. She was stunned speechless.

Was he really asking her the question she herself feared the most? How did he find out? What should she say? He was drunk; she smelled the liquor seeping from his pores as he stood at their bedroom door.

"Tell me now!" he stammered, and nearly stumbled onto the foot of their bed.

Was this her moment of truth?

"Don't fuckin' lie to me! Why are all the guys saying this shit! Are you gay?" he asked.

Now Jewel knew for sure this crap had gotten way out of hand. Every day, on sports radio, on the local news, everyone was talking about some new information B.J. had leaked from the book. It was like the city was now obsessed with trying to figure out which of the NFL coaches fit some of her descriptions.

"The shit's gonna come out, so you'd better take this ass-whupping now!"

Was he for real? Jewel still hadn't said a word. He wobbled every time he moved. And when he pointed his finger, it was more toward a spot on the wall next to her head than at her.

"You're drunk," she said.

"And you're gay!"

"I'm about to go back to sleep. You want me to make you some coffee? I can smell you from way over here. You reek of alcohol," she said.

"Don't try to fix the subject," he stuttered. "You've embarrassed me for the last time."

PLOP! THUD!

And just like that he was on the floor. A few seconds later, Jewel heard him snoring harder than any human being ever should.

She started to get up and make the coffee, but decided, what's the point? It was probably best to let him sleep it off.

Jewel turned off the lamp on her nightstand, pulled her mask back down and tried to go to sleep herself. But guilt hung heavy on her heart. She had talked about telling Zeke herself, but she couldn't imagine what that conversation would've been like.

At first, she used to justify what she was doing with Tierrany by saying Zeke had brought it on himself because of all the dirt he had done. But more and more, she started to think about what finding out would do to him. Deep down inside, she didn't really want to hurt Zeke; she wanted him to realize what he had in her and be more attentive, more gentle and more loving. She didn't intend to get so caught up in her emotions with Tierrany. Now that her husband knew, she wasn't sure what would become of their marriage or her relationship with Tierrany.

Jewel didn't think she was gay, yet she was attracted to Tierrany. For sure, she was confused. She closed her eyes and tried counting sheep.

Maybe her curiosity had been fed. Maybe she wasn't all that attracted to Tierrany at all. During their time together, she was always on the receiving end of the pleasure. Then there was that whole money thing Tierrany struggled not to bring up. Jewel didn't have the heart to flat out tell her no, but that was something she couldn't do. Things were so complicated.

What if Zeke decided to leave? Was she ready to live her life as a lesbian? She cringed at the thought of public display of affection with another woman. But if she didn't love Tierrany, was this simply lust? She wanted her husband, but she also wanted everything about the way Tierrany made her feel.

The guilt was preventing her from sleeping. She wondered what it would be like once Zeke woke from his drunken stupor. She wondered what the future would hold for her. Would time help her decide which side of the fence was right for her?

FORTY

B.J. couldn't believe what her eyes were seeing. Was she really looking at a picture of Lawna and Sasha hugged up at a party? Sure, Lawna looked a bit confused, but when did those two start talking to each other?

B.J. typed the last of what she was going to do for the rest of the night.

Wasn't it funny how karma worked? Lawna was the whore, and those aren't my words. What else do you call a woman who uses social networking sites specifically to pick up men to have sex? But Jewel was the one who kept getting the STDs. Lawna didn't know these men. If they looked good, that's all that mattered. She'd hook up, handle her business, and move on.

I know what she was doing was wrong, but I blame him for the way she is. Why a man would turn his wife on to swinging, then expect her to be faithful is beyond me. But that's how she started.

I didn't think Lawna would ever leave Davon, but it made you wonder, why people like that get married. She doesn't merely have someone on the side. We could pretty much understand that if, it was simply one person.

But this girl seems to get off on a new man each and every time. The other day I was thinking, her coochie must be so worn out, how does anyone even get any pleasure out of that? I'm only saying, that's how much the girl is out there!

I can remember her telling me about these sleazy parties she and

Davon used to attend together. Now I'm not into judging people, but when she told me she started enjoying that stuff, I was at a loss for words.

B.J. leaned back and admired her work. And to think, they thought she needed a ghostwriter. B.J. had managed to get most of the book done alone. She had the last two chapters to go and she was confident she'd coast right through those.

"This calls for a celebration," B.J. said. At first she was going to order room service, but then she remembered there was a nice restaurant with a bar in the lobby. Why shouldn't she go down and have herself a celebratory drink? She deserved it. She had worked hard enough.

B.J. jumped up. She'd shower, change, dress up a bit, and get a feel for what life was going to be like as a single woman.

Once she was dressed and her makeup was to her satisfaction, she headed for the door. But when she pulled it open, her clutch purse fell from beneath her arm.

As she stooped, her eyes focused on a pair of Fendi wedges that stood in her doorway. B.J. slowly stood up and snarled at the person in front of her.

"What the hell are you doing here?"

FORTY-ONE

L awna tried to tell herself she needed to slow down. She at least needed to wait this thing out with B.J. She didn't know what Mona was going to do, but since they knew where B.J. was staying, all three were hopeful that the woman would finally come to her senses. She also didn't know what to make of the pictures that were popping up of her and Sasha. But she had other, more pressing issues.

She realized that she had a serious problem when she pulled into the parking lot of the old hotel on Figueroa. Now she knew for sure she couldn't fix that problem alone. The fact that her husband needed external stimulation to touch her didn't make it any easier; especially when so many men saw her as a sexy, irresistible woman.

The one standing in front of her now was the latest in a string of men who didn't have a problem stroking her ego. This one was eye candy in its rawest form; so handsome he could be considered man-pretty. They had been playing goo-goo eyes since she'd walked into the restaurant earlier and spotted him from across the room.

Lawna knew she was going to fuck him the second he smiled at her. She didn't even lie and tell herself this was the last time anymore. Really, what was the point?

It didn't take long for them to connect and agree to go someplace where they could be alone.

His name was Shane, and hers was Trixie for the night. She didn't care whether he was giving an alias, too. Ten minutes after they arrived at the room, they were in each other's arms.

"Damn, you feel so good. You feel real good," Lawna said as she stroked his muscled body.

"And so do you, Trixie," Shane told her.

They fell into a deep and passionate kiss. With heat rising all around them, their body temperatures soared even higher.

As Shane caressed and explored her body with his hands, Lawna could feel his excitement building. He began to suck her neck, then allowed his lips and tongue to travel down to her chest. His tongue followed his hands' lead, and he played with her nipples, suckling them just right.

Lawna was on the edge. The more he touched, the more he kissed, the more she wanted. It was as if everywhere she moved, his stiffened hardness seemed to follow, poking at her like it was speaking directly to her.

Unable to resist anymore, Lawna reached out and grabbed him. She was pleased with his width and his length. He turned her around and she turned him back until she had Shane pinned up against the wall.

The excitement had her blood boiling. She felt like her skin was on fire, and it was nothing compared to the blaze that he had awakened deep inside her.

"Wow!" Shane yelped.

When she backed up for air, he grabbed her head between his hands and kissed her hard.

"C'mon, I wanna love you right," Shane said.

Lawna followed his move. She was completely naked, and so was he. But when he stopped at the bed and stood stroking himself as if he was waiting on her, she cleared her throat.

"You need your condom," she said.

"Damn, I wanted to do you raw," he whined.

"No can do." Lawna held up her left hand. "I'm married."

A smile curled at the corners of Shane's lips. "I should've known," he said. "Y'all are always wild, like your old men done forgot how to hit it right." He smiled. "On the dresser?" he questioned, with his eyebrows nearly touching his hairline.

"Yeah, right there on the dresser."

"You're not scared, are you?" he asked.

"Me? Scared?" He found a condom. "Oh, never ever that!" Lawna said.

Lawna eased herself onto the top of the dresser. He moved over to the dresser, where Lawna sat with her legs spread wide.

Shane stood back for a second, admiring her.

"I don't think I've seen anything so beautiful in a long while."

"It feels even better than it looks," she teased.

FORTY-TWO

"W hat the hell?" Jewel pulled her naked body away from Tierrany and frowned as her eyes met with a set that promised to kill her. The door was barely hanging on its hinges, and a menacing barracuda of a man stood in the doorway, smoke coming from his flaring nostrils.

"I knew you bitches was into some dyke-ass shit!" he growled angrily.

"Wait, I can explain!" Jewel stuttered, scrambling to cover her own naked body.

She didn't intend to make love to Tierrany after Zeke's drunken accusation the night before. But when he didn't wake, she took that opportunity to leave the house and keep herself busy all day until she could hook up with Tirerrany. The original plan was to talk to her, explain for once and for all that there was no way she could help her with the money she wanted, then try to explain why they probably needed to slow down a bit.

"Oh shit!" Tierrany screamed, despite herself. Zeke, Jewel's once unsuspecting husband, had obviously found a clue and they were caught in the act.

Jewel's eyes grew wide as she sat unsure of what to do. Tierrany, obviously having seen her own life flash before her eyes, wasted no time jumping up and putting on some clothes. Jewel, on the other hand, was temporarily stunned frozen.

"I trusted your nasty ass, thinkin' you bitches were friends! Friends my ass!" he roared, his rage seemingly building right before their terrified eyes.

"Call nine-one-one," Jewel finally managed in Tierrany's direction, keeping her eyes on her enraged husband. He was a mountain of a man, six feet four inches, at least 240 pounds of muscles and rage, with veins threatening to pop at his temples.

Jewel had no idea what Tierrany was doing at this time, but she hoped Tierrany was looking around for a weapon; her husband wasn't about to be talking for too much longer. He had fire in his eyes and obviously Tierrany was his target.

Jewel managed to ease herself up slowly. Forget the clothes; no point in being shy now, Jewel told herself as she gently raised her hands up into a non-threatening stance.

"Now, Zeke, calm down," Jewel said softly.

Tierrany looked like she was trying to ease out of the door. But Zeke quickly turned his attention to her.

"You fucking bitch!" he spat. Spittle gathered at the corners of his mouth as he slowly moved toward them. "I trusted your dyke ass, all up in my goddamn house, and all the damn while you've been fuckin' my wife!"

"Zeke, it's not what you think." Jewel wasn't thinking or she would've reconsidered those words.

"It's not," Tierrany added.

His face contorted into a twisted mess. "Bitch, your head was buried between her thighs! And you trynta' tell me it's not what I think!" He actually laughed. It was a deranged-sounding laugh, but a laugh nevertheless.

"Y'all must really take me for some chump-ass clown!"

Jewel shook her head, trying to erase what his eyes had seen.

Her husband was now looking at her, his eyes focused as if he was contemplating his next move.

"OHMYGOD! OHMYGOD!" Jewel heard Tierrany cry. "I'm so sorry," she sobbed.

That's when Zeke turned back to her. Jewel prayed the girl had done what she was told and called the police, because when Zeke pulled out a .38, Jewel almost fainted.

Certain she was running out of options, Tierrany started making deals with her maker.

God, if you help me out here, I swear I won't fuck with another married woman! Ooops on the f-word, but still you know my heart.

Just like a sinner, always turning to God when we done fucked up, Jewel thought, the minute Tierrany finished her pseudo prayer.

"You made a fuckin' fool outta me," Zeke growled toward Jewel. But this time he had steel to back up his words. "Neither of you bitches better not make a move!" He pointed the gun at Tierrany, then back at his crying wife.

"No use in crying now, bitch. You weren't crying two minutes ago when ya'll was all but bumping coochies, were you?"

"Drop your weapon now!"

Jewel released a huge sigh of relief. The cavalry had finally arrived, and not a moment too soon.

FORTY-THREE

"I have given you the proof; we hang just like I told you and I'm the closest one to all of them!" Sasha yelled into the phone. She was tired of trying to explain her close connection to the entertainment show's producers. Either they wanted her on, or they didn't. She was already in negotiations to sell a story to *In Touch* magazine. This thing was turning out far better than she had hoped.

"I've sent you the pictures from my party, and I faxed over the phone records. I don't understand why you guys are trippin'," she said, then rolled her eyes.

"We want to make sure you'll be able to talk to us in great detail about this; that's all," said the producer.

"No one else is talking so I would think y'all would be trying to jump all over me."

"Yeah, well, let's work this out. So are you going to be able to try and help us figure out who she's talking about? This is some pretty specific stuff," the producer said.

"I told you, I can. Did you read the article about me in *Star*?"

"No, I didn't, but let's talk more about your appearance on our show."

Sasha had a slew of interviews lined up. She was making her own rounds on radio, TV, and even some of the Internet programs as well. It was all part of her plan, and so far everything was falling into place. Lately, she had kept all of the stories B.J. dropped from the book alive.

It was Sasha who confirmed which coach needed to double-check which lane his wife was rolling in. She had also confirmed that another coach needed to rein his wife in because she was screwing rookies and strippers alike. Yes, Sasha was on a roll, and the stuff she didn't know personally, she'd made up. She decided early on, since the major parties weren't talking, she could tell the press whatever she wanted; it wasn't like they could do any kind of fact checking.

For instance, when the story about the STDs leaked, she had done simple arithmetic. Since Lawna was sleeping with a bunch of men, it only made sense that it was her who got the claps. It wasn't like anybody was going to challenge Sasha anyway. She had finally found her calling and this hustle was the best she'd had in quite a while.

She even threw a few nuggets of her own in there. For instance, B.J. had never said anything about anyone binge fucking, but it sounded good to Sasha, so she pinned that little gem on Jewel. She couldn't stand her any damn way. The tabloids ran with that story so fast, Sasha couldn't believe how much they were willing to pay. She was already living lovely and the future only promised even more riches if she played her cards right.

Later that afternoon, Sasha made her debut on one of the city's top-rated entertainment programs. Many more were still clamoring for her.

She was a sight to behold. She was all made up. Her long tresses sat atop her head in a cascading bundle of lustrous curls. Sasha was dressed in a sequined tank top that was so tight, her cleavage looked like it was spilling over. She rounded out her look with a pair of designer skinny jeans and high-heeled, thigh-high boots. She was over the top with excitement.

At the first sight of Sasha, the anchorwoman looked confused. Her eyes widened a bit, but she quickly refocused, adjusted her expression, and glanced down at her scripts. Once the camera's red light came on, the anchorwoman looked up, smiled, and started talking.

"The saga continues. While the Sea Lions first lady is preparing to battle her husband in court, some of her closest friends are beginning to speak out. Sasha Davenport knows all about the high-stake lives of professional sports. Not only was she married to a couple of high-profile athletes, she is a personal friend to Bobbi Almond and the other ladies embroiled in this very messy drama."

The anchorwoman turned and smiled at Sasha.

"Sasha Davenport, welcome." She smiled warmly. "You know these women on a personal level. Can you tell us, what's going on in their camp right now?"

"Shelly, this is nothing but a hot, funky mess; we all know that. But what many of y'all don't know is that these women's lives are near ruin. Not only has B.J. filed this lawsuit, but she's doing this tell-all book about our other friends, and nobody knows how to get past this."

"So it's safe to say a rift has arisen between this tightly knit group of friends?"

"Oh, that's an understatement! I'm sure you've heard some of the stories that are gonna be in the book. For example, the couple at the center of the tiny penis claims. Can I say penis on TV?"

The anchorwoman looked flustered. But before she could answer the question, Sasha jumped back in.

"Shelly, gurrl, how would your husband feel, especially if he was a coach, and his players heard about how he's lacking in an area that counts the most. But how would he feel if all of America was about to find out he ain't packin'? I mean, that ain't his fault! You know God had to spread it around, so He gaveth to some more than He gaveth to others!"

Shelly looked like she didn't know what to say. She awkwardly asked, "So you know which coach this is?"

"Oh, of course it's gotta be Coach Brown," Sasha said with no hesitation. "Look at that beer belly of his. If you ask me, it looks like he's a good six months' pregnant."

Shelly tired to get control of the interview by interrupting, but Sasha quickly shut her down by raising her voice and shaking her head.

"No no, no, lemme add this. Now you know doggone well, if a woman looked like that, ain't no way in Hell…" Sasha frowned. "Oooh, can I say Hell, on TV? Well, anyway ain't no way in the world she would be married to anybody connected to the NFL." Sasha looked directly into the camera "We're talking the *N.F.L.* I'm just saying what y'all thinking out there, America!" Sasha leaned back and nodded knowingly.

Unfortunately for Shelly, Sasha's interview went on for another five minutes. She was only supposed to have a three-minute segment, but the producers in the control room were having a ball. So they kept telling Shelly, in her ear, to ask another question.

It didn't matter that Shelly seemed a bit aloof and uninterested. Sasha more than made up for that. She was animated, lively, and seemed to be a natural in front of the camera.

She felt good, and this was only the beginning. Another show had already booked her as a guest celebrity correspondent to cover the Almonds' deposition next week. Sasha was so proud of herself and the way she had salvaged a bad situation and completely turned it around for herself.

FORTY-FOUR

Mona was nowhere to be found, and Jewel wasn't answering her phone. Lawna stood in front of the TV with her mouth hanging wide open.

She couldn't believe Sasha. What a sleazy opportunist! Now *she* was going around doing interviews? And she was passing herself off as a close friend and confidante of theirs? What was next?

"That's why she had us posing for pictures like we were family." Lawna was pissed. Now they could add Sasha's name to the list of people they needed to worry about. This thing was growing crazier by the day.

Lawna also realized that since the deposition for B.J.'s lawsuit was next week, there was no question about whether she'd had an epiphany and come to her senses.

"And how the hell did Sasha know B.J. was talking about Melvin? We all know, but Sasha is nothing but a lowlife, gold-digging skank."

Lawna tried again, with no luck, to call Jewel. She especially wanted to tell Jewel what Sasha was up to. There was already bad blood between those two. The last thing she wanted was for Jewel to see those pictures and get confused into thinking something that wasn't there.

At least she now knew who was responsible for all the stories that were popping up. They knew B.J. was talking, but in addition to her, apparently Sasha was also. And the real problem was people seemed to want to hear everything the little gold digger was talking about!

"Uuurrrggh!" Lawna wanted to scream.

FORTY-FIVE

B.J. had been holed up in her room for the last three days. She had no idea how things had gotten so out-of-hand. Why was she in such a bad situation? Her friends had betrayed *her*. *Her* husband had committed a crime that any jury would've found him guilty of. He had brought another woman into their home, into their bed. But now B.J. was the one trying to figure a way out of the latest mess.

This time when her cell phone shrilled, she looked over at it with horror in her eyes. What would she do? What could she say to Darlene? And would she have to pay that money back? It was an advance, but now that she wouldn't be able to deliver the manuscript by next week as promised, could they sue her?

Just as she suspected, it was Darlene again. B.J. didn't answer. How could she tell Darlene that a mistake she had made had now come back to bite her in the ass?

B.J. flopped down on the king-sized bed and closed her eyes. She couldn't handle another drink; regardless of how badly she needed one.

She had been trying to shake the horrible thoughts from her mind, but couldn't do it. As a matter of fact, any odd sound still caused her to jump and she was right back in the middle of what had been the worst night since she'd caught her husband and Ella in bed.

B.J. had been on her way down to the lobby when she opened her hotel room door and came face to face with the barrel of a gun.

"What are you doing here?" That was all she could think to say. She wasn't trying to make matters worse; she was so stunned.

"You have ruined everyone's life. We tried to reason with you, but you wouldn't listen. I was going to pay you three or four times what that publisher had paid, but then I realized, this isn't about money to you. I left message after message. Still you wouldn't budge."

"Mona, you don't want to do this," B.J. had said.

"Get back into the room! I'm in charge now!"

B.J. felt like a fool. She should've taken Darlene up on the offer to provide her with security. She had never had a gun pulled on her before so she did what she had seen in the movies. She threw her hands up in surrender and tried her best to follow Mona's instructions.

Although Mona spoke calmly, B.J. didn't want to give her any reason to accidently pull the trigger.

"We can work this out," B.J. said.

"Soo, now you wanna work things out, huh?" Mona's eyes looked glazed over. She started laughing hysterically, and B.J. was suddenly afraid.

"Do you know how many times we called you? I personally dialed your f'ing number until my fingers felt like they were going to fall off! You never even bothered to call back. You probably never even listened to a single one of those messages. While we lived in constant fear, you were up here relaxing and spilling our secrets. Well, I for one, am on the verge of losing everything. So guess what, B.J?"

B.J.'s eyes began to mist. She was struggling not to cry. She knew long before this exchange that what she was doing was wrong. Lately, she'd been fighting with herself, her mother's words and the thought of all of it, but she didn't know how to take it back. Still, she couldn't deny the anger she felt over what had happened to her. Even with a gun aimed squarely at the center of her forehead, she didn't want to give Mona the satisfaction. Why shouldn't they have to pay for what had happened to her? It was like Mona and the others simply wanted her to turn the other cheek and forget all about everything. Didn't anyone deserve to suffer for her pain? She had done nothing wrong.

"I said, guess what, B.J.," Mona snarled.

"I, ah, I don't know," B.J. finally said. She hated that her voice came out sounding so weak. If she was going to take a bullet between the eyes, then so be it! She wouldn't beg Mona. She wouldn't beg anyone. They had done her wrong!

"I've been up for the past two days," Mona said before she broke into tears. "Why the fuck are you making me do this?"

The tears went from a stream to a gush and B.J. wasn't sure what she should say. She didn't want to get shot, and she didn't want an emotional Mona to accidently pull the trigger.

B.J. sighed. "What do you want me to say?"

"I want you to show me where you write, let me see your set-up," Mona said. The crying had stopped. She used the back of her free hand to wipe tears from her face.

"Okay, fine," B.J. said. She turned to lead Mona into the sitting room where her laptop sat opened and on the desk.

"Can you put the gun away?" B.J. asked over her shoulder as she walked around the laptop.

"Pull up your manuscript," Mona said. "But wait, let me see exactly what you're doing!"

B.J. sighed. She only had one copy of her manuscript. She hadn't emailed it to herself or anything. She was so afraid of what Mona was about to make her do.

Mona walked over to the side of the desk where B.J. stood. She kept the gun pointed at the side of B.J.'s head.

"Sit down!"

"You don't have to do this," B.J. said.

"You've left me no other option. I have tried everything to reach you. Until now, nothing has worked."

B.J. opened up the Microsoft Word document and watched as her page and word count appeared at the left bottom of the screen. Mona was paying attention to the same thing.

"So you've got forty-eight thousand words; forty-eight thousand words that describe some of your friends' deepest and darkest secrets." She tsked and shook her head sorrowfully.

"I was angry," B.J. said.

"We tried to tell you; we never turned on you. Taylor and Ella, I can understand, but us, we were caught off guard as much as you were. But remember, B.J., you didn't want to hear any of that."

"I was wrong," B.J. admitted. And she meant it. All she had wanted in the beginning was for the other wives to accept her the way they had obviously accepted each other. But no matter how hard B.J. had tried, they all seemed to be closer to each other than to B.J.

"Oh, now that I have my gun here, you can finally see the other side, huh? You must think I'm some special kind of fool."

"What do you want me to do?" B.J. asked. She felt the warm tears burning in the corners of her eyes, but she tried her best to suck it up. If it was meant for her to die tonight, what could she do to change that?

"Here's what I want you to do. Go to 'Select All,'" Mona instructed.

B.J. did as she was told.

They watched as all of the document's text was highlighted.

Instead of telling her what to do next, Mona reached over and hit the delete button.

B.J. gasped. She didn't know how to explain it, but a sense of relief suddenly washed over her. However, the gun was still pointed at her. She didn't want to make any sudden moves. Mona was unstable and anything could happen.

Mona pressed the button to confirm that she did want to save the changes and closed out B.J.'s manuscript.

A series of mixed emotions washed over B.J. She was relieved, but also sick. All of her hard work was gone. When Mona's eyes glanced toward the stack of journals next to the laptop, B.J. swallowed hard. It felt like dry rocks mixed with pebbles were gliding down her throat.

Now she was ready to cry. A couple of stray tears escaped and raced down her cheeks before she could catch them. Luckily Mona was still behind her.

"Okay, what are those?" she asked.

B.J. knew Mona was talking about the journals. Everything was about to be ruined. With the gun still pointing at B.J.'s head, Mona reached over and flipped through one of the journals.

As her eyes took in the words, she started getting more upset.

"I'm taking your computer," Mona said. "It's going to be recycled, with the hard drive completely destroyed."

B.J. didn't respond.

"Actually, I want you to put the computer and the journals into this bag right here."

Without uttering a word, B.J. unplugged her laptop, gathered the four journals and a manila folder, then placed them all into Mona's bag.

"Now, let's take this over to the door."

Mona followed closely behind B.J. as she headed for the door.

"Drop it right there," Mona instructed.

Once that was done, she turned to B.J. and said, "Now, I want you to sit down and listen to what I have for you."

FORTY-SIX

It had been a turbulent three days for Jewel. Sure she had gotten Lawna's warning about what Sasha had been up to, but that was the least of her concerns. Now things were starting to make sense. So it was Sasha who had beat her to the punch.

Jewel was now kicking herself for not following her first instinct. Jewel was going to confess everything to her husband herself, but she was talked out of it. Then Sasha went and told the world that Zeke Swanson was the coach who had no clue that his wife was cheating on him with another woman.

It didn't take long for all hell to break loose. When Zeke actually caught her and Tieranny in the act, the police had come just in time.

After Zeke was arrested and hauled off to jail, Jewel finally felt the gravity of what she had been doing. There was such a huge double standard here. Her husband had cheated on her so many times and no one cared, but she got caught cheating and her entire world instantly began to dissolve. Still, she was wrong. She should've tried to work it out with Zeke before taking such drastic measures.

The loud boom at her front door literally made her jump. She couldn't imagine who was at her door. After seeing Zeke's mug shot plastered all over the news and in the newspaper, she was on pins and needles at all times.

"Who's there?" she yelled.

When there was no answer, she considered not going to the door at all. What if it was one of the reporters who had started staking out the house? Everything was a huge mess. She used to lose sleep at night, imagining the worst that would happen once the book came out, but never in her wildest dreams did she figure her husband would wind up in jail.

And to imagine, they were afraid of the stupid book, but never once did she think the worst would happen even before the thing hit the shelves. This was a huge mess. Jewel dragged herself to the foyer and took a deep breath. Lord knows she didn't need any more drama for now.

Jewel pulled the door open and was stunned to see two huge men standing there.

"Are you alone?" one asked.

Her heart was thumping so loudly in her ears, she swore her eardrums were about to pop. No way in hell was she about to tell two strange men she was home alone. Just as she was about to slam the door shut, a door swung open on the SUV that was parked out front. She hadn't realized it before.

Suddenly Zeke stepped out of the vehicle and the two guys pushed their way past Jewel and into the house.

"Bitch, I want you gone. They're here to help you pack your shit! I don't care where you go, but you gotta leave here today!"

Jewel didn't know what to say. She frowned; her lips began to quiver.

"Zeke, I'm sorry. Let's talk about this," she begged.

"Ain't shit for us to talk about. Go talk to your girlfriend. I'm done!" he said.

"You can't just put me out!" she screamed.

"Like hell I can't! C'mon, get your shit. It's time to go," he said.

"Zeke, let's talk about this, please. Let's go to counseling," she sobbed.

"Ain't shit a counselor could say to fix this! And I don't give a fuck!" he screamed. And when he screamed, the two guys rushed to his side.

"You okay?" one of them asked.

"Yeah, dawg. Just help get her shit together so she can bounce!"

And just like that, Jewel's husband washed his hands of her. She threw most of her things into bags and boxes, with the help of the two guys she had never seen before, and looked around one last time.

"I am so sorry, Zeke," she cried.

"Yeah, bitch, since you got caught, but you didn't look sorry when that dyke was..."

He cut himself off and dismissed her with a wave of his arm. Zeke stared at her and shook his head as if he was looking at the most pathetic thing in the world.

Jewel didn't know what she would do. As she turned to leave, Zeke yelled after her. "Oh, by the way, you have thirty days, then you can either buy me out of the car or I'll send someone to pick that up!"

Jewel felt sick. She simply turned and walked out the front door and away from the secure life she'd known for the last five years.

Unable to reach Tierrany, she drove to Lawna's house. But her mind kept thinking about why Tierrany was not available. The last time they had talked, Tierrany came right out and asked her for the money. Jewel felt so uncomfortable and caught off guard she quickly changed the subject. Tierrany didn't press the issue, but Jewel could tell she was upset.

As she approached Lawna's house, she decided not to call. It was just too much to try and explain over the phone.

When she pulled up there, and knocked on Lawna's door, she suddenly wished she had called first.

FORTY-SEVEN

"I'm outta here!" Davon yelled.

The fight between him and Lawna had escalated to an entirely new level. Lawna wondered how the hell all this had happened so quickly. She was still waiting for Mona to find a way to get through to B.J. What had happened to that plan? Didn't Mona say she had a plan? And why couldn't Mona talk to her girl and get this thing worked out? Lawna didn't believe for a moment that Mona hadn't known all along about Ella and Taylor. Those two were far too close for her not to know.

"You started this mess!" Lawna yelled back.

"You treated me like I was some kind of sexual deviant when all along you were out there fuckin' any and everybody." Davon looked at her with such disgust, Lawna felt like she was about to be sick.

"What the hell is wrong with y'all? You mean to tell me all you bitches didn't have shit else to do while we were struggling to make a good life for y'all?"

Davon's anger quickly turned to rage right before her eyes. And he was scaring the hell out of her. Spittle gathered at the corners of his mouth and the frown on his face made him look evil. She had never been afraid of her husband before.

Lawna didn't know what to say. Most of what he was saying was completely true and she couldn't dispute any of it. How the hell he'd found out about her being left naked and alone at a sleazy motel in South Central was beyond her.

That was, until she remembered Sasha. Sure, it started with B.J., but it was Sasha who was making the rounds and playing connect the dots like it was her duty to pair each coach with every scandal as it was leaked.

Lawna wanted to wring that girl's neck. Who gave her the right to get all up in their business and make a bad situation even worse?

After not hearing her husband's voice, Lawna decided to go and investigate. When she found him, he was in their master bedroom packing his bags.

"What are you doing?" she asked.

"Packing, what the hell does it look like?" He was as nasty as could be when he spoke to her.

"Davon, no, wait," she pleaded, reaching out and grabbing his arm.

He jerked and pulled himself away from her grasp. "Bitch, if you put your nasty hands on me again, I'll make you sorry!"

"Why are you talking to me like this?"

Davon stopped what he was doing, turned and looked at her as if he was finally hearing her for the first time. With his face twisted into the same menacing frown, he cocked his head to one side and lit into her.

"Lemme see. You've been running around hooking up with strangers you met on the gotdamn Internet and fucking them like some dog in heat. Hell, if that's not a bitch, I don't know what is!"

He turned back to his packing as if what he said made complete and logical sense.

Lawna's shoulders began to convulse. She was crying so hard she fell to the floor. Suddenly, she curled into the fetal position and cried some more.

Davon simply stepped over her as he went back and forth to the dresser and the closet. He behaved as if she wasn't even in the room with him.

"You think you got something to cry about now? Think how I feel. Ain't no telling who all you done fucked!" he spat. Suddenly, he stopped again. "I'm the laughingstock of the coaching staff!" He cocked his head to the side ever so slightly again. "Wait, have you fucked any of my players?"

Lawna was still crying so hard she barely heard what he was saying.

When the doorbell rang, they both looked toward the bedroom door. She welcomed the distraction, even if it was only for a moment.

"Now what?" Davon asked. "Lemme guess, maybe one of your Internet hook-ups followed you to the house. Maybe he had so much fun the last time, he wants to hit it again."

Again, Davon stepped over Lawna, but this time, he headed for the door. Lawna pulled herself up from the floor and followed behind her husband.

It wasn't until he had the front door wide open that Lawna realized it was someone for her.

"Oh shit, the dyke's here!" Davon yelled over his shoulder. His laughter was so wicked it sent a chill down Lawna's spine.

Jewel stood at the front door with an expression of sheer bewilderment across her face.

"What's this, a hoe meeting?"

Jewel didn't move. She was frozen right where she stood.

Davon left the door open, turned, and walked back into the bedroom.

"Birds of a feather," he said as he passed Lawna.

"Oh God, Lawna!" Jewel cried at the sight of her friend. "Are you okay? Did he hit you?"

"Girl, everything is falling apart. This friggin' book!" Lawna sobbed.

Jewel came inside and looked around.

"Zeke put me out," Jewel said in a hushed voice. She was trying her best not to let Davon hear her.

Lawna's eyes grew to saucers.

"You've got to be kidding me," Lawna said, using the backs of her hands to wipe her face.

"No, it's over. That's why I came here. I don't have anywhere else to go. But what's going on here? I should've called."

"No, no, Davon is packing his shit as we speak. He's leaving me!"

"Oh, Lawna, no!"

Just then, Davon walked out pulling two massive duffle bags behind him.

"I'll be back to get the rest of my shit in about a week. You two hoes try not to have too much fun," he said, before slamming the door shut behind him.

Jewel sighed. Lawna stood there, stunned. Was this really her life? Had her husband really walked out?

"I still don't understand how things spiraled out of control so quickly. I needed to make it to ten years. Didn't even make half of that," Jewel said.

Lawna didn't say a word.

"What am I gonna do?"

"Well, I know we're gonna be fine. It won't be easy, but let's try to look at…"

"If you mention a bright side, I'ma sock you!" Jewel said.

At that, they both burst out laughing.

FORTY-EIGHT

It had been three days since Mona thought she had taken care of the problem. At gunpoint, she had confiscated B.J.'s laptop, all of the journals and the folder containing a ton of emails, receipts, and phone records.

She couldn't believe B.J. had compiled so much information about their lives. Sure she knew B.J. was the newcomer to their little circle, but they all thought they knew her very well. Mona's plan was simple. She'd stand by and watch with her own two eyes as the computer and its hard drive were completely destroyed. Once that was done, she'd assemble a fire in the backyard. She'd used the portable pit near the pool and burn every page of those journals.

Mona didn't know where their lives would go from here, but there'd be no tell-all book, and for her, that was a good place to start. She didn't know what would happen with B.J. and Taylor either, but she planned to have a serious talk with Ella.

"I have one question to ask before you go," B.J. had said. Mona had the laptop and all of the journals and was preparing to leave.

"Would you have really shot me?" B.J. wanted to know.

That's when her bottom lip began to quiver. But Mona wasn't done yet.

"I've gotta give it to you, B.J. I wouldn't have wanted to," Mona confessed. "But you had to be vindictive. You couldn't leave well enough alone. You were already suing Taylor and Ella, but that wasn't enough. So I had to protect myself and the others. We did nothing wrong, but you didn't want to hear that."

B.J. closed her eyes and swallowed hard.

"You know what?" B.J. asked. "I'm glad it's over. I really am. All of this stuff, the embarrassment, the betrayal, I'm glad it's over."

Mona laughed. She had finally gotten to B.J. She may have had an icebox for a heart, but like everyone Mona knew, she had a weak spot.

"So what are you all planning to do now?" B.J. asked.

"Nothing yet, but with all the havoc you've wreaked on our lives, I'm thinking many of us will have to figure out how to pick up the pieces. As long as this book never sees the light of day, I think we'll be fine."

When B.J.'s left eye began to twitch, Mona tasted victory.

For B.J., this was a huge defeat. If she had retracted the manuscript herself, it wouldn't have been a big deal, but the fact that she was forced to, and at gunpoint; Mona knew B.J. well enough to know that was very difficult for her.

Yes, she had worked hard to make sure they wouldn't have to worry about B.J. and her book. It was mutually agreed before Mona left the hotel that there would be no book after all.

So days later, Mona didn't understand why despite all of her efforts, her world had still crumbled.

It was her turn to ignore calls. Her cell phone had been ringing like crazy. The promoter, Sean, had called two days earlier to say it was best for all parties concerned if they postponed the Staples Center event.

That had been a difficult pill for Mona to swallow.

"Was that when the shit started?" she muttered. "Naw, maybe it was the shit B.J. leaked."

Mona had been questioning and answering herself for the past seventy-two hours. She hadn't showered, brushed her teeth, or attempted to groom herself in any way. For the first time in years, she didn't meditate, do yoga, or any kind of exercise.

Her usually meticulous house was in a state of complete and utter disarray. Books from the library were scattered all over several rooms in the house. Some of her prized, framed articles lay shattered on the floor with glass all over the place.

"Who did all of this?" she asked. "That fucking B.J., she's responsible!" Mona answered.

One side of Mona's head was matted since it hadn't been combed. But she didn't care what she looked like. Her house simply hadn't been the same since Melvin walked out. It took two days for that scene to stop playing over and over again in her mind.

"You told people about our private life?"

"It's not what you think," Mona tried to explain.

Melvin's features registered pain more than embarrassment. He wasn't loud or even aggressive. But she knew him well enough to tell that he was hurt. Now Mona regretted all she had said about her husband over the years.

"Isn't it your job to keep people's private lives private?" he asked. He looked confused, like he couldn't make sense of her betrayal.

"It's not what you think; it didn't happen the way you think."

"You keep saying that, but here again, I'm confused. So you supposed to be helping other people, but instead, you sitting up making fun of us and spreading our business around for everyone to make fun of us?"

Mona denied his words, shook her head until it felt like it was going to fall off.

"That's not what happened, I thought I was talking to a friend. Everyone needs someone to talk to, I'm no different. I didn't expect—"

"You didn't expect me to find out that I was the punchline for jokes with you and your friends, huh?"

"It wasn't like that."

"I've been nothing but supportive of you and your career. I've always listened as you complained without passing judgment. I thought we were equally yoked. I thought we liked the same things, enjoyed similar beliefs. I would've never thought you weren't happy with our sex life, and if you weren't happy, I don't know why you didn't trust me enough to come and talk to me."

The day Melvin walked out of their house with a few of his things in bags, Mona stopped caring about everything.

Mona had tried her best to use her counseling tools. She tried to tell herself this could be worked out. He simply needed time to cool down. But why did he have to leave their home in order to cool down?

When she got up to use the bathroom, something crunched beneath her feet, but she didn't care what that was. She needed to relieve herself.

The cell phone rang again, but she wasn't in a talking mood; not today.

On her way back from the bathroom, there was a knock at the front door.

"Who the hell?" Mona was curious. Maybe it was B.J., trying to wheel and deal again.

When she pulled the front door open, Jewel and Lawna stood there with their mouths hanging wide.

"Jesus! Mona, why aren't you answering the phone? You scared us shitless!" Jewel screamed.

"And what's this notice attached to your front door?" Lawna snatched it off and followed Jewel into Mona's house.

"What tornado blew through here?" Jewel said, suddenly watching her step.

"Ever since Melvin left, I haven't gotten around to cleaning up," Mona said. "I'd offer y'all something, but I don't have anything!"

"Wow!" Lawna said as she took in the sight. Everywhere she looked, there was complete destruction. Plants were overturned and their dirt spilled right where they lay. Pictures and magazines were scattered on the floor and Mona herself was a mess.

She was padding around in a pair of dusty-looking house shoes that had lost their fluff long ago. Her pajamas were soiled with visible stains and they couldn't figure out where the stench was coming from.

"Oh, shit!" Lawna said. She looked up from a letter she had found on the coffee table when Jewel and Mona looked in her direction. "What time is it?"

"Five after eleven," Jewel said. "Why?"

"Because according to this letter, Mona has until noon on the thirtieth to get a check over to this address to return the deposit she was paid for the Staples Center event or she's going to have to refund money to her investors and the promoter."

"What the hell? I can't do that. That's a lot of money," Mona cried. "We have to get the key to the safe deposit box."

"Okay, where is it? We have less than thirty minutes," Lawna said, shaking the letter for good measure.

"Shit! Melvin!" Mona said. She had a faraway expression on her face.

"Where is he?"

"Call the Coach's office," Jewel suggested.

"Wait, I need to get something out of the garage," Mona said.

Lawna and Jewel tried to track Melvin down while Mona rushed out to the garage.

"Hi, Taylor, we need to get in touch with Melvin. This is Lawna."

"Oh, they just went to eat," Taylor said.

He sounded so distant, like he still had the weight of the world bearing down on him.

"They're at M & M's," Taylor said.

"Damn, M & M's Soul Food? Which one?"

"On MLK, up the street," Taylor said.

"Okay, thanks." Lawna hung up and looked around. "He says the coaches went to eat at M & M's. Where the hell is Mona? We've got less than an hour to get to West Martin Luther King Junior Boulevard. That's the location closest to Exposition Park."

Exposition Park was where the Sea Lions practice field was located.

Jewel looked around at the mess. "I don't know. I think she's still in the garage."

They rushed there and started screaming when they flicked on the light.

"Mona, what the fuck are you doing?"

The car was running and Mona was behind the wheel.

"Is she trying to kill herself? What the fuck!"

Luckily, Mona had only been gone for a little while before they realized what was going on.

"Girl…" Jewel pushed her out of the driver's seat. "What the hell is wrong with you? The clock is ticking and you're sitting up here trying some dumb shit?"

Lawna removed the old rag from the tailpipe and pressed a button to open the garage door. They escorted Mona out to Jewel's Range Rover.

After they piled in, they told Mona they were headed to M & M's to get the key from Melvin. They'd rush to the box and get the information to the promoter.

Thank God they were able to use the commuter lane. On the drive over, they talked to Mona and tried to convince her that everything was going to be okay. Jewel didn't do that much talking; looking on the bright side wasn't her strong suit.

When they pulled up at the restaurant, Mona moved to get out of the car.

"Whoa, lady, where you think you going?" Jewel asked, gently pulling her by the shoulder.

"Listen, Melvin is so pissed, he'll refuse to talk to both of you. We can waste time or I can go in there and get the key so we can go."

"But you're in your pajamas, and they're not, uhm, clean."

Without any more arguing, Mona got out of the truck and waltzed into M & M's Soul Food restaurant as if she was dressed in the latest couture outfit, instead of filthy pajamas.

Eyes followed her from the moment she walked in. A hostess approached her.

"Ma'am, are you okay?" the young woman asked. She looked confused.

"I'm looking for my husband. He's a coach." Mona looked beyond the girl and toward the back of the restaurant.

"Uh—"

"That's okay, I found 'em," Mona said and strutted to the back like the people pointing and gawking had no impact or her.

Again, as she passed, all eyes followed her, but she didn't care. Unfortunately, as she walked up to Melvin, his back was to her, but the other coaches saw her approaching and started looking at her like something didn't quite register.

"Melvin, I need the key to the safe deposit box," Mona said. "Hey, guys," she greeted the other coaches.

Melvin whipped around at the sound of her voice. All of a sudden, his eyes looked like they were about to explode.

"Wha...what the hell are you doing here? How'd you even know where I was?"

"Not important; I need the key," Mona said in a no-nonsense tone.

"You need to lower your voice. I ain't even sure I got the damn key," he said.

Mona knew what this was. Melvin was apparently trying to show off in front of his buddies. She had neither the time nor the patience.

"Eh-hem," a voice cleared from behind. "Uh, is everything okay over here?"

Mona turned to see a man dressed in a suit, standing behind her.

"Yeah, everything is okay. What's your problem?"

"Ma'am, we need you to lower your voice. Our customers are trying to enjoy their meals."

"And I need you to mind your own damn business!" Mona turned her attention back to Melvin, who had turned back to face his friends.

"Are you ignoring me?" she asked the back of his head.

"Naw, I'm done. I ain't got your stupid key," he said without looking at her. When the other coaches chuckled, she started fuming.

Before she realized what was going on, her hand was wrapped around a water pitcher and she had already turned it upside down on top of Melvin's head.

He jumped up out of his chair and hollered so loudly, they quickly became the center of attention. The chair tumbled beneath Melvin and his wallet and keys fell to the floor.

Mona reached down, picked up the key ring, examined it, and pulled the one she wanted from it.

"That's all you had to do in the first damn place," she said as she sashayed out of the restaurant like nothing had happened.

FORTY-NINE

By the Fourth of July weekend, B.J. had checked out of the Four Seasons Hotel and was settling in back at home. Taylor decided it was best that he leave and allow his kids and wife to be back in familiar surroundings. Since she couldn't deliver the manuscript, her agent was now talking about the publisher's options in situations like these.

Whatever the hell that meant. It had been nearly a month since B.J. had gotten the courage to take her agent's call. By then, Darlene had already figured something was terribly wrong.

"I've decided I can't write this book," she had said to Darlene the last time they talked.

"But the ghostwriter—"

"I'm not going to be able to do it," B.J. persisted.

"Did someone get to you?" Darlene asked.

"I need to go. I'm moving back home and I've got tons to do before the kids get there," B.J. said.

"Jesus! Moving back home? B.J., what's going on?"

As B.J. pulled into her driveway, she pushed thoughts of that last call to Darlene out of her mind. In the first few days after they'd talked, she kept anticipating being served with papers. She thought for certain the publisher would be suing to try and get their advance money back.

B.J. was going to dig into her rainy-day fund and pay back the advance, but she needed to see how this thing with Taylor was going to play out.

There was a part of her that was relieved about the book. The more she thought about it, the more embarrassed she was by her behavior.

The deposition was horrible. B.J. thought by suing Ella she would get some sort of satisfaction, but instead, all that had done was cause her more heartache. She wished Samantha had told her that they would have to get all of the explicit details surrounding Taylor's affair with Ella.

B.J. didn't need to know that a couple of weekends when B.J. was gone, Ella was walking around her house naked as if she owned the place.

She also didn't need to know that during weekly staff dinners, Taylor and Ella would sneak off for a little romp, even if it was a ten- or fifteen-minute quickie inside a restaurant bathroom.

When she was face to face with Ella, B.J. still couldn't fathom how she had grown to trust Ella the way she had.

The details of their affair were so outrageous, that B.J. didn't know how long she could take it. During day three, while Samantha was asking questions about other affairs, Taylor had suddenly had enough.

"Let's stop," he said to his lawyer.

The attorney looked at him like he had lost his mind.

But Taylor seemed undeterred. He looked B.J. dead in the eyes and said, "I'm sorry. I was wrong. If you agree to drop Ella's name from the suit, I'll give you everything you're asking for as long as we share custody. If you agree, Ella and Sterling will leave for good. We're working out a deal for him to go coach in San Diego, with the Chargers," Taylor said.

Before B.J. could answer, Samantha reached for her arm and

whispered in her ear. "Let's take this, avoid court and spare the kids additional problems."

"You'll pay my attorney fees, too?" B.J. asked Taylor.

He sighed. "Yup, whatever you want."

That quickly, the deposition was over. B.J. felt good about their agreement. The truth of the matter was, she was worn out. She was sick and tired of being tied to this whole mess. If she could go back in time, she'd do things so differently.

It was mid-July and the Sea Lions were gearing up for training camp. Much of the bad publicity surrounding the team and its coaches had died down considerably. It had been a rough few months, but everyone involved was trying to pick up the pieces and move forward.

FIFTY

Mona was finally getting the help she needed. After her nervous breakdown, she agreed with her counselor that a residential facility would probably be her best option. Unfortunately her friends never made it to that promoter in time for her to return the check as agreed.

She was still trying to work out an agreement to pay the Staples Center deposit back, but would probably go to court over money the investors wanted outside of their initial investment.

Mona still talked to Lawna and Jewel. And since she was going to be in treatment for forty-five days, she agreed to let Lawna stay at her place since Melvin refused to come back.

During her last conversation with Melvin, she realized they probably shouldn't close the book on their marriage quite yet.

"I only wish you had been out there cheating instead of telling the world that I couldn't satisfy you," Melvin had admitted.

"But that's not what I said," Mona told him. "You have to remember, B.J. had to spice that stuff up. Then by the time Sasha picked it up, you might as well have been asexual."

"I just need some time," he said.

They talked once a week. At the treatment facility, Mona received intense counseling, and was even put on medication for severe depression. She felt good about her decision to get help; she really didn't want to hurt herself. She had counseled enough to realize her failed suicide attempt was more a plea for help. She had been at the house alone for days before Jewel and Lawna showed up. If she wanted to really end things, she'd had ample opportunity to do it when she was alone.

Her friends were very supportive. They wrote letters and sent cards and pictures every week. Mona planned to piece her business back together once she got out.

But for now, with no TV, no visitors, or any other distractions, she'd been working on a book of her own. This one was nonfiction and it was focusing on women and their need to take on too much.

The title of her book was *It's All Just Too Much!* The writing made her feel like she had something to look forward to.

She was taking time out to make sure that when she checked back in, she could live life to the fullest.

FIFTY-ONE

On the drive back to her old house, Jewel thought about the irony of her situation. A week had gone by before she'd actually caught Tierrany on the phone and even then it was because she'd called from Mona's house phone while she was visiting Lawna, and not her own.

"Wow, so this is what we've been reduced to?" Jewel said the minute Tierrany answered the call.

"Who's this? Jewel?" she asked.

"Don't even know my voice anymore?"

"Oh, naw, it's not like that at all," Tierrany said. "I've been busy."

"So busy that you ain't even had time to check up on me? You knew my situation," Jewel said.

"Listen, I thought you and your ol' man were gonna work things out."

"Work things out?" Jewel screamed. "He was hauled off to jail after he caught you eating my pussy! Did you really think there was any chance of salvaging what we had?"

"I'm not tryna get you all worked up," Tierrany said. "Besides, once you didn't lend me the money, I pretty much knew what time it was between me and you anyway!"

"Hmm, oh, is that what this is about? The money? That's funny. Used to be a time when all you wanted to do was get me worked up," Jewel said. She started to add something else until she heard a woman's voice purring in the background.

"Just a sec, babe," Tierrany said.

A massive lump suddenly lodged itself right in the center of Jewel's throat. "Wwwho's that?" she managed.

"Oh, nobody," Tierrany lied.

Before Jewel could say anything else, Tierrany said, "Hey look, you take care of yourself, okay? I need to run. Guess I'll see you around."

And that was it. That was the last time Jewel had spoken to Tierrany, the very woman who had her questioning her sexual orientation. She remembered the good ol' days, when Tierrany made her feel like she didn't know what good love was until she was loved by her, another woman. Tierrany had Jewel convinced she had put a hex on her that no man walking could undo.

Now the thrill really was gone and Tierrany had moved on. Jewel didn't want to feel sorry for herself, or think Tierrany was trying to use her for money, but the thought did enter her mind. Then, to add insult to injury, Jewel was questioned by the police. It seemed that after Sasha went running her mouth like she had diarrhea between the lips, the police wanted to talk to Jewel about Penny Jones, the woman who'd had a miscarriage after they had convinced her to take the pills. They had questioned Lawna, too. Luckily for Jewel, the officer who came to question her apparently didn't believe Penny's story, or they didn't have any evidence to pin anything on Jewel.

She was questioned, denied knowledge of Penny Jones, and that was that. Jewel considered herself lucky but she wasn't brave enough to ask what had happened to Penny. That question, she decided, would accompany her to her grave.

And this time, she was certain none of her friends would be quick to talk. They'd been down that road before.

When Jewel faced entering her old house for the rest of her

things, she was surprised to realize Zeke had calmed down considerably. He was no longer cursing and throwing a fit and his two bodyguards were nowhere to be found.

Their greeting was cordial and she was grateful for that; she wasn't in the mood to fight.

But the biggest surprise came when she decided to get busy and take care of the task at hand. She turned to leave Zeke in the living room.

"Well, I'll get the rest of my stuff, and get out of your way," she said, as she prepared to walk out.

"Wait, what's your rush?" Zeke asked.

"Oh, not rushing, just thought you would want me to hurry. I really didn't expect you to be here. I could come back, you know, when you're not here," she offered.

"No, that's not necessary. I um, I need to tell you something anyway," Zeke said. "I owe you an apology."

Jewel was stunned; his voice sounded sincere. The anger was no longer there, and when he looked at her, she didn't see hatred or rage in his eyes.

"Sometimes, hanging out with all those guys can really play a number on you," he said.

Since she had no idea what he was talking about, Jewel didn't interrupt. She merely sat and listened.

"Those young guys in the locker room, they've got all that money. They can have anything they want and they talk about all their sex-ca-pades like it's the norm. I allowed myself to get caught up."

Jewel smiled.

"I shouldn't have been running around on you like that; half the time I needed Viagra to even keep up. But there was a part of me that was scared one of those young, hard-bodied jocks would turn your head, and I'd be stuck looking like a fool."

Never had Jewel heard her husband talk so honestly and freely.

"When I heard about all that shit you and the other wives have been up to while we were out there busting our asses, it made me crazy. But the wild part is, when the guys started busting my balls about you and that..." He stopped talking and swallowed hard before continuing. "Honestly, I was more pissed by how it made me look."

Jewel's eyes widened at that admission. Still, she just sat and listened.

"In a room full of testosterone, you don't want to come off like you can't handle your business at home," he admitted. "And your woman turning to another woman?" He chuckled.

That's when Jewel moved closer to her husband.

"I could've tried a lot harder. I don't need to be trying to keep up with those kids. They're grown-ass men, but with all that money and ass thrown in their laps, they act like oversexed children. Shit, I'm too old for that crap. Been there; done that!"

Zeke stretched a beefy arm around Jewel's shoulders and pulled her close.

"Sometimes I wondered what would've happened if I wasn't so busy trying to hide my own dirt. I mean, would you have even felt the need to go and be with someone else, much less another female?"

Zeke shook his head.

"Yeah, and the funny thing was, the other guys were tripping off me. They were like, dude, join the party. It was wild. A few fist bumps and high-fives later, nothing had changed. I always think about what would've happened if you'd been with another man. Either way, thinking about it made me realize how wrong I was to be doing all that I had done."

Jewel couldn't believe her ears. She didn't even know he thought about the way he'd run around on her. His words were so sincere and she felt, for the first time since she'd caught him cheating, that he was being honest.

She turned to look up at her husband and smiled at him.

"Baby, I'm glad you're back home. Let's work this out," Zeke said.

Those words were music to Jewel's ears.

FIFTY-TWO

After getting her life back on track, Lawna realized she didn't need all of those men to feel good about herself. She also realized how lucky she had been to escape all she had done with no sexually transmitted diseases. For a while, she missed the closeness she had shared with B.J. and the other ladies.

Lawna didn't think about the serious nature of her situation; she was constantly surrounded by people who were reconciling. Mona was getting the help she needed; Jewel and Zeke were working things out; even Ella had resurfaced. She and Sterling were moving to San Diego. A part of Lawna held out hope that her situation would also work itself out.

So the day that she was served with divorce papers, it all still seemed somewhat unbelievable. She didn't want to wrap her mind around the fact that Davon really wanted out of their marriage for good. Look at all he had done while they were married. He'd had so many affairs on her, she'd turned looking the other way into an art form. Then when he'd come to her and asked that she agree to have sex with other couples, she'd stood by him during all of that and then some. She couldn't believe this was what she'd gotten for trying to please her husband. Sure things got out of hand, but she'd simply made a mistake.

"Wow," she said as she flipped through the paperwork. Every day she picked it up, it was like she was just served yesterday instead of nearly a month-and-a-half ago. She simply couldn't bring herself to sign it.

Life was kind of funny. When Lawna was married to Davon, she thought she hated being married. She felt so unappreciated, disrespected, and completely unloved. Those were the emotions that sent her into the arms of others. The new men knew just what to say, how to say it, and it all made her feel sexy and irresistible.

It was several weeks after Davon had walked out when she discovered the electricity she thought hooking up with strangers sent surging through her blood might've been something else.

Lawna eyed the divorce papers but left them right where they sat. She got up and turned on the TV. It was turned to a cable channel, and as she was about to change the station, something caught her eye.

"Welcome to *The Sasha Davenport Show*, where you're thirty minutes away from the most delicious dirt Tinseltown's got. So sit back, get comfy, and let the new Queen of Talk whisper in your ear."

"Jesus! Are they giving talk shows to anybody these days?"

Suddenly, the music went up and Sasha strutted out on stage. She looked even trampier than Lawna remembered, but her audience was full of fun-loving people, jamming to a new hip-hop song a DJ was mixing, and it looked like everyone was having a great time.

When the music faded, the camera focused on Sasha's face. She smiled and sang, "Welcome to *The Saaaasha Davenport Show*! Hello, babies, how y'all doin'?"

Lawna pressed the button on the remote and turned the TV off. She was suddenly more interested in listening to a CD.

ABOUT THE AUTHOR

By day, Pat Tucker Wilson works as a radio news director in Houston, TX. By night, she is a talented writer with a knack for telling page-turning stories. A former television news reporter, she draws on her background to craft stories readers will love. With more than fifteen years of media experience, the award-winning broadcast journalist has worked as a reporter for ABC, NBC and Fox affiliate TV stations and radio stations in California and Texas. She also co-hosts the literary talk show, "From Cover to Cover," with ReShonda Tate Billingsley.

Known as one of the fastest writers in the country, Pat has wowed editors with her ability to turn out five to ten thousand words a day. But it's not just quantity that has Pat at the top of her game. The quality of her stories is what keeps the readers coming back. A much sought-after ghostwriter, Pat gets her greatest joy in creating her own stories. She is the author of six novels and has participated in three anthologies, including *New York Times* Bestselling Author Zane's *Caramel Flava*.

A graduate of San Jose State University, Pat is a member of the National and Houston Association of Black Journalists and Sigma Gamma Rho Sorority, Inc. She is married with two children.

Pat Tucker is the author of *Daddy by Default*, available from Strebor Books. Her next novel is *Party Girl*.

Visit the author at www.authorpattucker.com.; Facebook-Pat Tucker; Fan Page-Author Pat Tucker Readers; Facebook-Sylkkep PL Wilson; Myspace-Author PL Wilson; Myspace-Author Pat Tucker; Twitter-cauthorpattucker; www.fromcovertocovershow.com.

IF YOU ENJOYED "FOOTBALL WIDOWS," BE SURE TO LOOK FOR

PARTY GIRL

BY PAT TUCKER

COMING SOON FROM STREBOR BOOKS
ENJOY THIS SNEAK PREVIEW

PROLOGUE
HOPE

When the car fluttered, and seemed to making a clunking sound, the next thing I knew, I was pulling over to the side of the road. My heart was racing.

"Uh-oh!"

As I steered the car off to the side of the road, I bit down on my bottom lip. I allowed it to slow before I brought it to a complete stop. By the time I jumped out of the car, it had started smoking. I didn't know if the thing was gonna blow or not.

"Dammit! Now what?" I sighed.

I glanced around in both direction and could barely see a few feet in front of me. The hiss from the engine had me completely spooked. It was pitch-black outside and besides the sounds from the engine, the only other sounds I heard were crickets and grasshoppers for miles. What little I could see was only visible because I didn't turn off the headlights.

I shivered from the cool February night air, but trembled at the thought of becoming road kill. Here I was on a deserted two-lane road out in the middle of nowhere!

Since I had to get Mona there for eight, it was already dark and I didn't feel good about being out here all alone. I wasn't sure if I should try to walk back toward Hempstead, where I thought I remembered a convenience store, or take my chances and walk up toward the direction of Prairie View University.

In the hour or so that I'd been trying to make up my mind only two cars had passed along on Highway 290. During that time, I tried to flag them down with no luck and I was trying to see if the car might cool off. When it didn't, I was more than pissed. I knew Brendon would be fussing by the time I finally made it home. Whenever he was home alone with all three kids, he acted like he forgot how to father.

Suddenly what looked like a familiar car came swooshing past me. I shook thoughts from my mind; no way that was who I thought it was. I had only been stranded for a little more than an hour and I was already getting delusional. Only in my dreams would someone I know be way out here just when I needed them.

I looked back at the car that was still smoking and decided to leave it. Since it hadn't exploded, I walked back over, removed the key from the ignition, and put it near the middle console.

"Oh, well, guess I'll send a wrecker for it when I make it to the university."

I flung my purse over my left shoulder and started walking toward Prairie View University. With my luck, I'd make it before sun-up the next day.

Less than twenty minutes later, the Candy Apple 1964 Chevy Impala on spinners that first zoomed by going east was now headed west and slowing as it pulled up alongside me.

"Q, that you? What you doing way out here?" I asked, feeling so happy I could kiss him. For the first time since the breakdown, my night didn't seem as bleak.

"Whassup, Ma?" Quenton said.

Quenton Tolland and I went to Yates High School together. He had been up to no good since he could walk and talk, but at this very moment I was so glad to see him and his sidekick Trey, I didn't know what to do. It's not like I was about to marry the guy; I needed a ride, and he had wheels.

"Looks like you need a lift," Q said.

"Do I! Mona's car broke down on me a few miles back. Did you know it was me when you passed the first time?" I asked.

Trey looked uneasy, but I never liked him anyway, and I suspected he didn't care for me too much either. Knowing him, he probably tried to talk Quenton out of turning around and coming back for me.

"Girl, I'd know you anywhere," Q joked.

I really didn't care whether he knew it was me or some chick he was about to try and pick up. But, I was glad he turned around.

"Believe me playboy…this ain't the business," Trey said with his creepy-looking self.

"Aw, dawg, chill. Hope is the homegirl from the neighborhood," Q said. He turned back to me. "C'mon, hop in, we kinda in a hurry."

"Well, I'm real glad you stopped then. What's the hurry, and what y'all doing way out here anyway?" I asked.

"Whassup with all these damn questions; you working with the Feds or what?" Trey asked. He looked at me like I had stolen something from him.

Trey, whose last name I didn't care to know, had big dark eyes that made him look like he was always surprised. Other than that, his face never had any expression. He was chubby with fat cheeks and had a massive scar that ran from his left ear to the edge of his mouth. It looked like he was on the losing end of one too many knife fights.

I ignored Trey and quickly shuffled into the back seat of Q's car. I was glad they'd come along when they did.

"So Q, how's your mom and your sister?"

Quenton was cute. He was small, but growing up he was known for his quick temper and being short on patience; most times if he had trouble, it was because he started it.

"The fam's good," he said. Right when he was about to turn the radio back up, three police cruisers whizzed by with their strobe lights flashing and sirens blaring.

"Dang, where's the fire?" I said as I looked at the cars through the back window. "I'm glad we're going away from the drama, whatever's going on."

I turned my head just in time to see Trey exchange an odd look with Quenton, but that was none of my business. I figured Trey was probably still salty about them turning back for me.

"Yo, Hope, what's up with your girl Stacy; why she act like she all too good and shit?" Trey said.

I started to ignore him, but didn't want to start anything after they'd just helped me out with a ride. I wanted to say, *really* Trey are you serious?

"Stacy's married," I said instead.

Two more cruisers swooshed past us. I noticed Q's eyes glance up to the rearview mirror and it looked like he watched until the cruisers were only tail lights and strobe lights in the dark night.

At that moment, my purse toppled over and most of my stuff spilled onto the floor.

"Dammit," I said.

"What?" That was Q.

"No biggie. My stuff spilled out of my purse," I said. I quickly started feeling around on the floor of the car. I found my compact, my tube of lip balm, and the dead cell phone. I tossed them back into my purse, then felt around for the rest of my stuff.

"Oouch! What the hell is that?" I pulled my fingers to my mouth.

"Whassup?" Q asked.

"I don't know. What's under your seat, Trey? Something burned the heck out of my fingers." I tried to examine my fingers, then sucked them again for relief.

Trey looked at Q and Q looked at me in the rearview mirror, but neither one said anything.

I went back to examining my fingers when suddenly Trey's next words snapped my eyes onto the road ahead.

"Damn, dawg, what the fuck!"

My body jerked forward violently when Q unexpectedly stepped on the brakess. The tires screeched and it felt like we skidded to an abrupt stop. I didn't know what was going on, but it didn't look good.

Suddenly, my heart felt like it was about to stop, too. I struggled to catch my breath while staring ahead with wide, worried eyes. There were at least three police cruisers blocking the road with their strobe lights on. If that wasn't enough, officers stood behind open doors with their guns drawn and pointed directly at Q's car.

The very car, I was riding in!

"Q, wh-what in the world is going on?"

"Shut the fuck up!" Trey turned and hollered at me. He had a menacing expression on his face when he looked at me. All of a sudden he bent down and started to reach under his seat.

Q held his arm out and stopped him. "Nah, big homie, just chill!"

"I told yo' ass we ain't had no business turning around, for this chickenhead; now what?" He was fired up and I was confused.

"Who you calling a chickenhead…"

Now sirens were blaring from behind. One quick turn and the strobe lights were so bright it no longer looked like night outside. That's when I realized how crucial the situation was, and I was petrified.

I swallowed the massive lump in my dry throat. My heart felt like it was about to give out on me, and my body went from dry to drenching wet with sweat in no time.

Suddenly, I got the eerie feeling that maybe I should've taken my chances alone on the side of the dark rural road. There was no way for me to know then just how much of a grave mistake accepting that ride would turn out to be.